CONCRETE FOREST

THE NEW FICTION OF URBAN CANADA

EDITED BY HAL NIEDZVIECKI

Copyright © 1998 McClelland & Stewart
Introduction copyright © 1998 Hal Niedzviecki

All rights reserved. The use of any part of this publication reproduced, transmitted in any form or by any means, electronic, mechanical, photocopying, recording, or otherwise, or stored in a retrieval system without the prior written consent of the publisher – or, in case of photocopying or other reprographic copying, a licence from the Canadian Copyright Licensing Agency – is an infringement of the copyright law.

Canadian Cataloguing in Publication Data

Main entry under title:

Concrete forest

ISBN 0-7710-6815-8

1. Canadian fiction (English) – 20th century.* 2. Canadian fiction (French) – 20th century – Translations into English.*
I. Niedzviecki, Hal, 1970-

PS8329.C66 1998 C813.5408 C98-930121-4
PR9197.3.C66 1998

Design by Sari Ginsberg
Typeset in Minion by M&S, Toronto
Printed and bound in Canada

We acknowledge the financial support of the Government of Canada through the Book Publishing Industry Development Program for our publishing activities. We further acknowledge the support of the Canada Council for the Arts and the Ontario Arts Council for our publishing program.

The Credits page that follows contains information relating to individual authors' copyrights and permissions.

McClelland & Stewart Inc.
The Canadian Publishers
481 University Avenue
Toronto, Ontario
M5G 2E9

1 2 3 4 5 02 01 00 99 98

This book is dedicated to my parents, Nina and Sam Niedzviecki, for their patience, respect, and support; and for the bounty of their suburban enclave, last exit before the concrete forest.

Credits

"Altered Statements" © 1995 M.A.C. Farrant, taken from *Altered Statements* (Arsenal Pulp Press, Vancouver, 1995), reprinted by permission of the publisher. "Bash" © 1996 Richard Van Camp, taken from *The Lesser Blessed* (Douglas & McIntyre, Vancouver, 1996), reprinted by permission of the publisher. "Boxing Not Bingo" © Elise Levine, reprinted by permission of the author. "Crates of Stars" © Golda Fried, reprinted by permission of the author. "Falling Down" © Matthew Firth, reprinted by permission of the author. "Girl on the Subway" © 1990 Crad Kilodney, taken from *Girl on the Subway: And Other Stories* (Black Moss, Windsor, 1990), reprinted by permission. "The Great Hangover (Montreal, 1976)" © 1991 Daniel Richler, titled for this publication, taken from *Kicking Tomorrow* (McClelland & Stewart, Toronto, 1991), reprinted by permission of the publisher. "The Great Salmon Hunt" © 1996 Vern Smith, taken from *Glue for Breakfast . . . and other stories* (Rush Hour Revisions, Toronto, 1996), reprinted by permission. "Hello, Saskatoon!" © 1996 Michael Turner, titled for this publication, appears as a chapter entitled "A New Tune to Practice" taken from *Hard Core Logo* (Arsenal Pulp Press, Vancouver, 1996), reprinted by permission of the publisher. "Horst and Werner" © 1995 Grant Buday, titled for this publication, appears as stories entitled "Saw Blade Sky" and "A Welcome Plague" taken from *Monday Night Man* (Anvil Press, Vancouver, 1995), reprinted by permission. "I Apply" © Mark Anthony Jarman, reprinted by permission of the author. "In Various Restaurants" © 1994 The Estate of Daniel Jones, taken from *The People One Knows: Toronto Stories* (Mercury Press, Stratford, 1994), reprinted by permission. "Letters (On a Book Lately Circulating in the Offices of Transport Canada)" © André Alexis, reprinted by permission of the author. "Mandate" © Ken Sparling, reprinted by permission of the author. "Missing" © 1995 Julie Doucet, taken from *My Most Secret Desire* (Drawn & Quarterly, Montreal, 1995), reprinted by permission. "The Name Everybody Calls Me" © 1995 Leo McKay Jr., taken from *Like This* (Anansi, Toronto, 1995), reprinted by permission of the publisher. "Pigeon in Lemon Sauce" by Dany Laferrière © 1997 Douglas & McIntyre, English translation © David Homel, titled for this publication, is taken from *A Drifting Year* (Douglas & McIntyre, Vancouver, 1997), reprinted by permission of the publisher. "Purgatory's Wild Kingdom" © 1995 Lisa Moore, taken from *Degrees of Nakedness* (Mercury Press, Stratford, 1995), reprinted by permission. "The Real Story" © 1995 France Daigle, English translation by Sally Ross, titled for this publication, taken from *Real Life* (Anansi, Toronto, 1995), reprinted by permission of the publisher. "Rescue" © 1995 Cordelia Strube, titled for this collection, taken from *Milton's Elements* (HarperCollins, Toronto, 1995), reprinted by permission of the publisher. "Souvlaki" © Jonathan Goldstein, reprinted by permission of the author. "Stargaze" © 1995 Derek McCormack, taken from *Dark Rides: A Novel in Stories* (Gutter Press, Toronto, 1995), reprinted by permission. "Taxi" © Peter Stinson, reprinted by permission of the author. "Topographies" © Natasha Waxman, reprinted by permission of the author. "Under the Wings of a Big Old Bird" © 1997 Stuart Ross, taken from *Henry Kafka and other stories* (Mercury Press, Stratford, 1997), reprinted by permission. "The Wednesday Flower Man" © 1987 Dianne Warren, taken from *The Wednesday Flower Man* (Coteau Books, Regina, 1987), reprinted by permission of the publisher.

CONTENTS

WELCOME TO THE CONCRETE FOREST POPULATION 30 MILLION

Introduction by Hal Niedzviecki

> *"For the members of a country or a culture, shared knowledge of their place, their here, is not a luxury but a necessity. Without that knowledge we will not survive."*
>
> Margaret Atwood, *Survival*

The stories that make up this book evoke, in remarkably different ways, what I call "the concrete forest." But what is the concrete forest? Is it real? Can it be found on the map, or just in some imaginary mental space? For me, the concrete forest, like a border delineating one country from another, is a metaphor. It's a symbolic way to understand the perspectives that the writers in this collection all share. The concrete forest, then, is a fiction forest overgrown with the joys and terrors of the urban, a land where the events of the everyday are depicted as real to us in lasting ways that transcend the ephemera of our fleeting lives. Some of what you'll see in the concrete forest will astonish you. Other things will seem as familiar to you as the view from your bedroom window.

In the view through my apartment window, the light is always dim, as if diffused by the glow of the Kentucky Fried Chicken logo and the orange taunt of the Beer Store sign. The sidewalks and streets are littered with take-out garbage and dog shit. Strangers shuffle past, and streetcars rumble by on their never-ending way. On my corner, scuffles break out late at night, old friends hug in front of the twenty-four-hour bakery, drunks lurch past, teenagers hold hands and giggle, cops disappear down the alley across the street with their flashlights shining and their hands on their holsters. It is this same chaotic energy, this disordered routine, this pageant of life in all its grimy reality that is harnessed in the stories before you.

In choosing what represents Canada's new urban fiction, I looked for stories that not only conjured up a wholly other, distinctly original place, but also invoked landscapes recognizable to those of us whose lives are interlocked with the conflicts and crises that we share as Canadians, whether we live in large cities or small towns or remote rural cottages. So, while not every story in this book is set in the city, all the stories share a distinctly urban sensibility. Not only do these stories demonstrate the perspectives that point to a new Canadian urban literature, they are also, in and of themselves, inviting works of prose – daring, transcendent tributes to boredom, sexuality, energy, obsession, and juvenile delight. This new urban literature is anything but complacent. It challenges structure and form not just for the sake of doing so, but because, in the concrete forest, nothing can be sacrosanct – no behaviour is too outrageous or unlikely if it brings the reader into a place they are at once familiar with and haunted by.

In the concrete forest, you will find many such familiar and haunting places; decaying inner cities, tedious suburbs, labyrinthine subways, and straight-ahead highways all have a home here. And yet, despite this disparate scenery, these stories all suggest an emerging movement of new urban writing which reflects a Canada that is something more than a multiplicity of self-contained regions and ethnic groupings. Native writer Richard Van Camp's testosterone-infused account of a house party in a small town in the Northwest Territories suggests the same festivities I once held in my parents' suburban living room thousands of kilometres from the Arctic. The velocity of Van Camp's narrative, the speed of his sentences, his ability to turn a potentially generic set of circumstances into a dramatic and personable account of a boy's struggle toward an uncertain future evokes the angst not just of Native teens, but of all Canadian kids.

Up here in my apartment, the stories in the anthology appear as a mirror image, a prismed reflection of what this country looks like. I press my nose to the cold glass and see the new Canada, country of cities, country of whispering voices lost in the crowded distance between our self-same dreams.

Many will encounter in *Concrete Forest* a brash sensibility that embodies the attitudes of young people in Canada – the TV generations (anyone born after 1965). This sensibility, however, is not so much a matter of age as much as it is a consequence of diminishing opportunity in a changing country. Jobs are harder to get, choices are fewer and less inviting, and everywhere people are encroaching on other people's time and space. As a result, the writers in *Concrete Forest* speak less of personal travails and existential dilemmas than of lives lived in a shared metaphorical landscape. Their characters exist not in solitude, but in constant communication with each other about how they, collectively, perceive their milieu. They see in each others' perceptions their own possibilities, strengths, and weaknesses. Many of the stories in this book depict the reluctant camaraderie of these shared experiences the same way Van Camp's account of a juvenile pot-fest bears such similarities to my own memories (or what's left of them).

This same collective understanding allows writers of the TV generations to refer to shared circumstances without having to allude to them explicitly. Emerging writers like Golda Fried, Matthew Firth, Jonathan Goldstein, Derek McCormack, and Elise Levine cut in and out of the collective imaginative space of their peers. In their stories, a pop song, a movie, a seedy apartment building, and a doctor's office can all be speedily invoked by a single word or phrase. It's as if just a glimpse is enough to call upon the bank of universal images deposited in our minds, a giant video store of pre-fab moments that need only be referenced to be instantly recalled. This isn't solely a technique employed by a new generation of writers; Daniel Richler renders post-sixties pop images with similar rapid-fire language, sharing with these younger word sculptors a capacity to speak through chipped language and abbreviated assumptions.

The writers in this collection take some small comfort in reflecting their fragmented sense of community through shared terminology. Aren't we all, they seem to be asking, engaged in the same struggle, watching the same TV show, humming the same meaningless jingle? In an ironic jibe at the marketing forces that have long sought to use demographics as a tool to understand and manipulate younger generations of Canadians, the collective knowledge these writers demonstrate emerges from their own insistent individuality. This brings us back to the notion of the TV generations: Young writers (under the age of thirty-five, for the most part) who, having been taunted by the inaccessible through a remorseless assault of sit-coms and commercials, now find themselves best able to speak to what they do not have: a good job, a gorgeous mate, a perfect family, a fancy car. This creates an almost palpable sense of rejection and refusal. An example of this is Cordelia Strube's story, a work of brittle comedy so sharp it hurts. Cynical television reporters, child abuse, and AIDS all make cameo appearances in Strube's precise and compassionate catalogue of the woes of contemporary society. Strube is just one of several writers in this collection whose fiction best illustrates the jaded sensibilities of the TV epoch and its captives.

One of the factors behind my decision to put together this anthology was the recognition that younger generations, people without cars and mortgages, also read books – in fact, they wouldn't mind reading books about themselves. Until now, such books have not been widely available, largely because the literati and the publishing establishment have been reluctant to usher in this new urban writing. Obviously, there have been books by young new urban writers in Canada, but they have been published almost exclusively by small presses and, with the exception of the lucky few, left to their own devices in terms of finding an audience. That this book exists at all is a testament to the willingness of at least one major publisher to take on the challenge of bringing cutting-edge, risky Canadian writing to a larger public. I think of it as risky not just because it bends forms and challenges assumptions, but also because, to paraphrase what a small-press editor recently pointed out to me, publishing books specifically geared toward younger generations of Canadians can be financially dangerous: "They aren't the boomers. They don't have any money."

So it's no surprise that this movement to articulate the experiences of younger generations has emerged from the tremendous efforts of writers and publishers working without benefit of grants or editorial budgets. A number of the writers in this anthology have come up through a system of mini-presses, photocopied journals, websites, and 'zines that have served, for at least the last five years, to present a literature counter to that which has traditionally emerged from the large publishers. With few resources, the underground press in Canada has given us work as vibrant and meaningful as any published in the mainstream.

Many of the contributors to this book – Daniel Jones, Michael Turner, Dianne Warren, Crad Kilodney, M.A.C. Farrant – are owed a debt of gratitude by younger writers such as myself who came of age with the impression that ugly, subreal, urban fiction could neither be written nor published in this country. Such an impression can only be corrected by example – for instance, by the marginalized and altogether remarkable efforts of a writer like Kilodney (who, not incidentally, has given up writing in favour of the more lucrative art of market speculation). Like one of those coin-operated rooftop binoculars, these writers have shown us youngsters the possibilities for new writing in this country. We paid our quarter and were exposed to a close-up view, the looming literature of Canada, writing at once visceral, angry, satiric, ironic, funny, unflinching, strange, and disturbing.

The urban life we experience is fragmented and anonymous, and yet, somehow, deeply personal. This shared sense exists not just in cities but in all parts of Canada. Again, we return to the notion of the concrete forest as a place of urban sensibility. Leo McKay Jr. sets his story in an unidentified rural area. But the aspects of his tale – uncaring bureaucrats, unacknowledged violence along a wooded highway, events unfolding in a generic hospital parking lot – reveal a sensibility that is entirely urban. McKay takes us into the anonymous rural landscape of his imagination and shows us that the concrete forest doesn't end at the city limits.

Not only can the urban sensibility be reflected in diverse locales, but also in the forms the stories take. *Concrete Forest* marks the first time a McClelland & Stewart literary anthology (perhaps any Canadian literary anthology) has admitted a cartoon onto its hallowed pages. The piece by Montreal's Julie Doucet, icon for would-be cartoonists the world over, explores the way that the new urban literature transcends the conventions that many consider to constitute Canadian fiction. Doucet joins Calgary's Peter Stinson and others in evoking the real through a remarkably surreal montage of happenings. Because what is real and actual in Canada today is so often disconcerting, these stylists need not rely on shock tactics or elaborate plots. Doucet and Stinson, both practitioners of the visual arts by trade, tell hauntingly personal stories that offer no hope of redemption, and they do so by simply showing what is all around us every day. (And for those still sceptical of the literary merit of Doucet's comic fiction, I leave you in a dank dark metro to contemplate her mastery of jarring imagery and haunting narrative.)

Another example of new and challenging forms in this anthology is the excerpt from Michael Turner's *Hard Core Logo*, a work that creeps up on the essence of punk rock in Canada through a series of lyrics, journal entries, snapshots, and sound bites. Many know *Hard Core Logo* as a movie, a comic book, and a soundtrack, not realizing that the source of this pop-culture effusion is an enduring classic of new urban literature.

The inclusion of these writers, and others who will offend and scare and delight you, might be provocative to some readers. But this collection does not strive to shock and provoke for mere effect. Rather, I hope the book will be provocative for its depiction of a dark and unpleasant place that most of us would hesitate to call home. But where does this preoccupation come from?

There is an otherness to these stories, a desperate sense that many of the characters are struggling to survive in hostile territory. This is an ironic twist on Margaret Atwood's seminal 1972 essay that proposed survival as the dominant theme of Canadian literature. These days, survival isn't just a metaphor. It is the bleak reality of working, eating, sleeping, all without ever revealing the terrifying fact that one is not necessarily who one feels forced to appear to be. André Alexis paints a vivid picture of an office worker under siege by his co-workers' odd behaviour that strikes me as the perfect parable for this situation. This impostor sensibility can be found not just in place and story, but in the terse language and taut assumptions that the writers in this anthology all share.

Many of these stories are disturbing, and yet there is very little violence in this book. The works here are as lucidly reserved as they are psychically brutal; Leo McKay's tale of perplexed authority and hidden destruction is just one excellent example of the way these writers eschew the grotesque violence found, for instance, in the work of their urban counterparts in the United States.

Like most people, I figure meaning in any literary enterprise to be as concrete as a politician's promises, as slippery as the vengeful creature the bloated fishermen in Vern Smith's "The Great Salmon Hunt" pull out of Lake Ontario. Frustratingly, these stories won't tell us how people act, or even how they think; they'll just tell us how they are.

Natasha Waxman's contribution to this book ends with a character imprinting the embodiment of his love on his flesh. The story is an apt metaphor for the kind of aching desire for absolutes that so often appears in this new urban writing. Many of the characters who inhabit this anthology search for truths so tangible, so vivid, that they can actually imprint them on their skin. It's as if they are asking for the kinds of assurances that can't ever be taken away. Instead, they are given the urban tattoo, the cynical thumbprint that brands criminals and the needy and everyone else with identity: who you are, what you do, where you live, where you wish you lived. Are our lives really so determined, so futile? These writers don't shy away from trying to answer that question. The understated suburban maestro Ken Sparling gives us a character whose speciality is photocopying memos he can never quite believe, as if nothing is really to be believed anymore. Sparling implies that the world we live in is all faxes and e-mails and voice-mails about this and that and yet all this information adds up to nothing. That daily encounter of meaningless activity – the big "nothing" – is the reality so many of the characters in *Concrete Forest* must reckon with. It is the absence Waxman's love-struck figure can only convey through his tattooed flesh.

Similarly, in "The Real Story" by Moncton's France Daigle, the most overtly postmodern of the stories in this book, we see the illusory connections between people, and the way those connections compel us to understand the sameness of our predicament. Daigle brilliantly recognizes the stubborn, fragile radiance found in the individual's struggle against the anonymity of the urban. Her work transcends facts and statistics, as does Grant Buday's rather disturbing contribution to this anthology, "Horst and Werner." What makes his story work isn't what happens; it's not even what might happen. The story's force resides in its vision of humanity, the crowded stubbornness of a friendship born of mutual derision. Other writers shimmy up the sides of an old-growth skyscraper somewhere in the concrete forest to give us stories that loom above the morass. Social satirists like M.A.C. Farrant and Mark Jarman force us to look down at a place that we know to exist, but have never been able (or really wanted) to see. They strip away the apparatus of society and reveal the machinery of misery, the bureaucracy of belittlement, that all too often directs our lives.

"This is a great country," proclaims Stuart Ross's character in "Under the Wings of a Big Old Bird." Not incidentally, Ross's character, a Mr. Cage, is under arrest for dreaming about a chain-smoking pterodactyl. His handcuffed good cheer points to the way many of us young writers feel about Canada. This country is great because of the cops who pull me over at 2 a.m. for blowing a red light on my bike ("You been drinking, son?"). It is a great country because of its polite urbanity, its insistence on getting along, its imprint of a national myth – a lake to myself, a country road with no other cars on it, survival. Elise Levine names her character Tanis and sets her up in a cottage on a lake lined with biker bars. Tanis goes to the city for boxing lessons, has random sexual encounters with a rich high-school boy, and dreams of a still farther escape than her own dingy faux-retreat. Dreams of it, but, as the last image of the story suggests, can't quite reach the bottom depths of her own fantasy.

These urban fictions are the flip side of population analysis. Statistics of the soul, they tell us about our communities and our lives. Imagine Dany Laferrière wandering through the streets in search of a single person to join him for a meal of roasted park pigeon (his loneliness not just the solitary essence of being a new arrival in a strange land, but of coming to a city inhabited by millions of similarly disenfranchised strangers). Laferrière confronts the new Canada, a place where the challenge is no longer to explore the discovered wild, but to examine the fallacies and dangers of exploration turned inward to the cloistered confines of consciousness.

The writing in *Concrete Forest*, still wet in the poured pavement of society's interlocking perplexities, is as distinctive and compelling a reflection of post-industrial reality as any in the confining sprawl that defines the developed world. It is in our ability to explore our own imagined spaces that we find that we can understand ourselves. Start by taking a look out the window.

CONCRETE FOREST

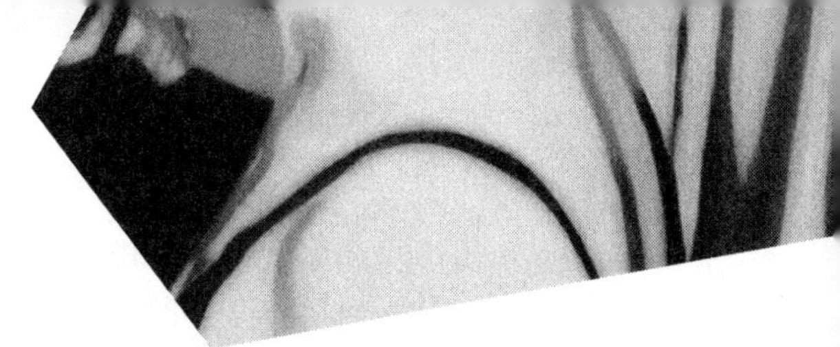

TOPOGRAPHIES

NATASHA WAXMAN

The Genius of the Nolli Map
– *An Introduction* by J. Phillip Cameron

The map which you have before you, completed in 1748 by Giambattista Nolli, is perhaps the greatest and most complete city plan of Rome ever produced. This new edition of the Nolli map has faithfully reproduced all aspects of the original (of which more later), including dimensions, and when all twelve folio sheets are assembled, you will find it measures just over two metres by one and three-quarters metres, ~~a stunning mural which opens a convincing panorama on any ordinary wall~~. A masterpiece of the

NATASHA WAXMAN CURRENTLY LIVES AND WORKS IN AUSTIN, TEXAS, WHERE SHE HOLDS A JAMES MICHENER FELLOWSHIP AT THE TEXAS CENTER FOR WRITERS. SHE IS FROM TORONTO AND IS TRYING TO FIND HER WAY HOME.

surveyor's, the architect's, and the printer's crafts, it is no less a masterpiece of art, a moving and complete tale of one of the world's great cities.

At the outset, I should state that this introduction to the new edition of the Nolli map is intended as a general one, ~~aimed at the wider audience it is fervently hoped the new map will attact~~. For detailed considerations of the various scholarly questions surrounding the map, the interested reader is advised to consult the authoritative work of my esteemed colleague Armand Sharpe, as well as the comprehensive three-volume *Pianti di Roma* (1962) by Amato Frutaz, and even my own modest researches

I refuse to believe that he is that forgetful – no, I know he isn't – he's not even dressed and his appointment's in fifteen minutes! He *knows* damn well that I hassled my ass to get home early and borrow George's car so I could take him to the acupuncturist. As soon as I walked in, the cats were mewling around my leg, five-fifteen and he hasn't even fed them for God's sake! Now Dundas will be an absolute madhouse, we're smack in the middle of rush hour. And I swear I smell smoke, I think he's been sneaking cigarettes again. Pacing around in his red bathrobe, screaming into the phone – it's the printers of course, telling him it'll be another four weeks, four months, whatever – it's all the same to them. That goddamn map! I told him if he gave them all the money up front there'd be no incentive for them to finish *ever*, but he just sneered, "And where did you get *your* M.B.A., Jake?" Honestly, that man! Pacing around with the phone to his ear, all cock of the walk, sexy in a way – I'd like to sketch him like that but of course he'd never let me draw him in such an undignified pose. Oh Phillip, sometimes I swear. . . .

What is a map but, in some sense, a topography of the human imagination, made concrete and added to by innumerable

> dreams, countless human lives? While the accurate delineation of mountains and coastlines may inspire in us a certain remote awe, the maps of our cities are the stories of our own lives as they were generations and centuries before our own births, and as they will be after our own deaths, ~~yet added to by each of our individual existences~~. That, *there*, was the street where I was born, in that very building I learned my trade, in that hospital I lay sick and dying. The ~~pioneering~~ genius of the Nolli map was to have shown the city for the first time as a coherent, *living* body, one which functioned as an organic whole. It was able to do so primarily through its amazing clarity of detail, depicting every building, street, piazza and church to correct scale. Through careful shading, solid lines, and white space, the interactions between positive and negative urban spaces – in lay terms, the relationship between private buildings and public spaces such as squares, streets, and public buildings – could be seen for the first time. The metaphor of the city as body is familiar to us – we speak of arteries, the heart of the city, and so on, and this is due entirely to the genius of the Nolli map. The interplay between

Luckily Dr. Tang's running late too, and it's not so bad after all. Such a strange colour on the walls, I mean turquoise, really, no Western doctor would be caught dead, but I guess things are different if you're Chinese. Maybe it's a lucky colour, or the colour of healing or something. Nothing to read here but some tattered Chinese magazines with practically no pictures, and across from me that ancient little Chinese crone snorfling away to herself, shooting me evil looks every few minutes. I should have remembered to bring a book or something, I hate just sitting here thinking of Phillip in the very next room with all those needles sticking out of him. I saw him through the open door that one time and it scared me, he looked so helpless. Like his pale fishiness after the valve surgery, it was so awful, I never want to go through that again. But that's over now, thank God. . . . It feels like the inside of a robin's egg in here. Neat posters, though. I like the one of a piece of ginseng – it looks exactly like a person with one leg crossed over the other. But that other poster is really something, stunning – when I asked Dr. Tang, he said it shows the flow of vital energy, *chi*, through the body, all of its nodes and pathways that can get blocked and then you become sick. "Like traffic jam, eh? Hah ha ha." Acupuncturist humour. It almost looks like a map, constellations maybe, all those beautiful arcs and curves –

Oh, maybe I shouldn't have said it, of course not, but it was just a little joke for God's sake: "Get it Phillip? Can you get your *chi* up now?" I was sorry the second it came out of my mouth. He's so touchy these days. And he looked so old at that second – with the streetlamp flashing over him through the windshield, making every line in his face cast a shadow, he looked about a hundred, not fifty-seven. But when I tried to make it up, offered to take him out to La Gaffe, there was nothing at home to eat anyway, he gave me that *look* – the same look as that first time when I went to see him about the D on my Bernini paper – his eyes sliding down my cheek, my chin, and I could tell he was thinking how young I looked, what a stupid baby I am. He said he doesn't want me to take him to Dr. Tang's any more, says he'll get George to do it –

"So fine, sure, I'll take you to the doctor's," I said, "that's not the issue. . . . Well, I don't want to wade into the middle of this, but Jake said it was just a tiny little joke and surely you can see he was just trying to lighten the mood a little. Jake's so young, doesn't understand the anxiety, he's trying to help, in his own way –" Jesus, Phillip just got apoplectic at that, said *I* was missing the point and would everybody shut up about Jake's marvellous age. "Well, all right, all right, I wasn't there, and maybe it was worse than it sounds. Of course I don't mind driving you, not at all . . ." Good heavens, rather odd for *me* to be sticking up for Jake, quite a switch, really. I've never really liked him myself, never could understand how an intellectual like Phillip could be attracted to *that* for any length of time. And he's so young, such a pretty boy, I'd be worrying all the time. And at our age, who needs that? But then again it's been three – no wait, four years –

One of the more striking features of the Nolli map to the modern eye is the fact that the city plan does not cover the whole extent of the map – rather, the edges of it appear to scroll away, revealing a landscape underneath. It points graphically and artistically to the fact that beneath the obvious schema of things, there is an underlying reality, ~~just as beneath the skin there is the furious, seething existence of a body whose machinations we can only guess at.~~ Of course, this allusion to what lies below the visible is particularly apt in the case of Rome, a city which has literally built itself out of its own ruins for thousands of years. The landscape depicted at the edges of the map is a ~~scraggly and~~ slightly surreal one, spotted with a few famous Roman monuments standing in decidedly different relation to each other than they do in life. (This technique, called *capriccio*, enjoyed a vogue in eighteenth-century etchings which I have written about elsewhere.) The foreground is scattered with the tools of the surveyor's craft – rulers, compass, calipers, and so on. In the lower middle plate, a charming, naked *putto* occupies himself with chipping away the ~~finishing touches on~~ a stone coat of arms, which is propped against an imposing incised block. It reads, in translation: *To the sanctity of our seigneurial Pope, Benedict XIV, this new topography of Rome is obsequiously dedicated by his humble servant Giambattista Nolli Comasco* ~~(Oh those mellifluous Italians! A drumroll for the elegant romantic spirit which seems so far departed from our weary rational age. . .~~)

In the end I gave up and just went ahead and ordered pizza from Massimo's. It took ages and when it finally came he said he wasn't hungry, didn't eat more than a piece, and I felt like an absolute hog, stuffing it down while he watched, but I was starving. I hate that, it makes me feel like I'm showing off my healthy young metabolism. I just burn it off, I know it drives him crazy. He didn't seem to notice this time, though. I could tell he was still upset about the news from the printers. Another month, two months, and absolutely everything he's saved sunk into it. And there's no consulting work now, even if he had the energy to go after it. He'll never see a dime from that damn map, I told him there must be a reason all those money people said no. But you can't tell him anything – nobody has any vision, *he* says. According to him the whole world is waiting breathlessly for copies of some old map that covers practically a whole *wall* for God's sake. It's all he thinks about – he'll be in the middle of talking to me and I can see him tracing the line of some stupid Italian street in his mind. Oh God, I wish he would just finish the damn thing and get some rest, he's not taking care of himself and I'm getting so worried. His skin, the way his cheeks droop. . . . Couldn't still be the valve operation. And it isn't the unspeakable, he said the tests came back all clear, and that was only a month ago. Probably nothing, just stress and tiredness, he's basically strong as an ox, a man half his age. . . . But he's so stubborn, if I bring it up, he just walks off fuming. Oh shit, that dream, yes – what was it? He was just covered in needles, like a porcupine, and I wanted to pull them out gently, kiss his face and chest, but my feet were glued in some kind of sticky stuff on the floor. Silly. And when I woke up he was there snoring beside me, hogging the covers as usual. But that panic, all day. . . . If he would just take me in his arms the way he used to, call me his *cicciolino*. Over a month, since he even *looked* at me. I don't know how much longer – I mean, I feel like reminding him I could have my pick – Well, that's not the point, I don't want anyone else, but I just can't stand this much longer, it's like everything I do is the wrong thing.

Further to the right, we see a sturdy, meditative *putto* standing at his surveying table, directing the operations of his helpers ~~(are we to think it is Giambattista himself? Hopeful boy!)~~

He acted as though I were his employee, for God's sake! George do this, George do that, pick up that please, as if I hadn't had an exhausting day at work already. And then practically *ordering* me to take him out to the printers so he could yell at the manager in the flesh. As if I have nothing else to do! Ranting all the while about not having access to the plates for reference while he's doing the introduction. He's just dominated by it, utterly inaccessible. . . . I couldn't get a word in edgewise – the Legislature Restoration project's way behind, they might not vote the additional funds for the statuary restorations, he'd know who to call if he'd just shut up long enough to hear me out. . . . Obsessive. But more than that, it's just missing his friendship, that lemony wit of his. He ought to have the sense to realize – It's been four months since I had *any*one around – Avery was no great loss, granted, but it's so quiet around the place. After all I do for him. Sure, he's been a help to me, too, I wouldn't deny it, gave me all the right names for the Legislature Restoration bid – he's always been generous with his contacts, and not many are, architectural historians are such a tight-assed bunch. But I've done my fair share, and driving him all over town to his flaky healers isn't the half of it –

I can't handle it – I mean, of all things! When I get home from work I'm still fuming because that little bitch Carolyn gave me another lecture – she's not even my actual supervisor – and Phillip's lying there talking to Hyacinth after his massage. And you can bet she was still charging, too, sometimes I feel like I might as well just sign my paycheque over to her. Not that she isn't an absolute brick, leaving those little tinfoil packages all neatly labelled – we live on them most of the week – and the place always smells so fresh after she's been, carpet vacuumed and everything straightened. Another of Phillip's indispensable luxuries, but it's worth it, I'll give him that. She's been a real help. Of course, it helps her too, getting paid for practising on top of the housekeeping money we give her, she's still got another year to go of massage school. But I was just standing there at the bedroom door, starting to tell him what happened at the office, when he yells at me for letting the cats in and asks me to leave. *Me!* To leave *our* bedroom while he talked to Hyacinth. A huge acid lump just blocked my throat and I stood there, he was lying on his stomach, not even looking at me. His back. Those red marks, like bruises, where'd they come from? And so pale. He's been dressing and undressing in the dark, won't even let me see his body any more, even when his belly was so much bigger he used to love to parade around in front of me, let me jiggle it and joke about him being pregnant.

"Well, yes it's awful, I'll agree with you there, Jake. But you have to understand, I don't need to tell *you* about all the stress all this is putting on him. He's still not up to par, looks worse if anything to me – he hates those goddamned doctors and doesn't listen to them, not that I blame him. The printers, the map, it's all at such a critical stage, you'd be cranky too. And he wants his introduction to be a real whizbanger, it's his baby. . . . Now, see, that's what gets to him, it's exactly that dismissive attitude you have about it. I don't expect you to be able to understand it in his terms, you'll see how important it's going to be, that map is going to make his name in architectural history. . . . No, I didn't mean you're too stupid to understand, I meant you wouldn't understand it the way we do – after all, this is what we've devoted our lives to."

> hard not to feel a certain nostalgia for the past. Sadly, we live in an age of debased architecture, ~~in which artistry is inevitably sacrificed to convenience and the almighty dollar~~. We lack great monuments because we do not have the pa-

tience to construct them. The great cathedrals of Europe were begun by men who knew that they would not live to see their completed creations. Such ~~touching~~ faith has much to tell our hurried age, if we would but listen. . . . It is hard, then, for us to conceive of the magnitude of the labour Nolli carried out so exactingly, using only the most primitive tools. It took Nolli eight years to complete his project, and he wandered the entire city dragging his equipment, ~~much as I myself once wandered those same streets as a young architecture student, sketchbook in hand, my only companion a thermos of that inimitable Italian fizzy lemonade in my rucksack~~

"He was hurt, Phillip, that's what I'm trying to tell you, Jake doesn't understand why you're shutting him out. Fine, fine, I'm not one to meddle but just let me tell you, you're sounding like a cranky old man. And you know I'm only saying so as an old friend, so don't get all bristly on me. Well, I'm *here*, aren't I, waiting to slay the dragon of rush-hour traffic on your behalf. . . . How was it today anyway? Doesn't it hurt when he sticks those needles in? I've been having the most horrendous back pain when I get up in the morning, God, the indignity of old age, I've been thinking I might – *JESUS!* These people drive like absolute cretins, every last one of them! Take *that* you little shit. . . . Oh calm *down*, Phillip, peel yourself off the ceiling, please. If you're not going to drive then keep your commentary to yourself. It's absolutely ridiculous that you haven't learned to drive all these years. Learned helplessness if you ask me – you've always managed to find someone to cater to your eccentricities –"

Indeed, the preparation of this new edition was an exacting task in itself. I was determined to produce as ~~perfect~~ correct a facsimile as modern printing techniques would allow. This required shooting several sets of negatives, each for different tonal values. I then superimposed the negatives, eliminating all undesired values by hand. It is my hope that the results ~~will~~ have justified the laborious means. As the Vatican owns the original plates, copyright laws were observed by making the minute change of etching my own initials in an unobtrusive spot on each plate. ~~It gives me no small amount of satisfaction to know that I have attained some tiny measure of immortality in this respe~~

At first it seemed better than it has in weeks, he actually listened to me when I told him about work and how all the shit had come right back in Carolyn's face, God it was beautiful to see. . . . He was wearing the jeans I got him last year, they fit him now, even looked loose. But then he started in again in his professor voice – what have I been drawing lately, when he knows perfectly well I haven't drawn in months. And then he asked why I've abandoned it, told me how I should be sketching every day or my skills will decay away to nothing. I told him I have plenty of time, I'll get back to it when I'm ready, and he just sneered, which really pissed me off. So I said I'd just love to know what we'd do if I wasn't bringing home the bacon, he hasn't had a consulting job in three months. I even threw up his resigning from the college – I shouldn't have done that, but I was so mad. Times like that I feel like he's trying to play my father, and I don't need another one of those, thanks. The first one nearly killed me. Finally he says, "You don't understand how quickly the time will go, Jake. So much to describe. Not half enough life to do it in," and his eyes filled with tears and he wouldn't say any more.

To an extent all cities are a study in perpetual renewal and expansion, and Rome is perhaps the greatest example of this. Since the days of Augustus, who declared that he had added a skin of marble to the city, Rome has continually shed and renewed its skins. Indeed the very stones of past buildings

> have often been used to construct new ones ~~(well may we mortals admire, even a little, this capacity for eternal renewal!)~~. From the architectural historian's standpoint, one of the real triumphs of the Nolli is the way in which it graphically represented this process. Far from being a snapshot taken at a particular point in time, the map showed the dramatic changes to the city's anatomy which had occurred over preceding centuries. In certain respects, Nolli built on the cartographic advances of such predecessors as Buffalini's sixteenth-century city plan, which showed the outlines of some famous ruins. However, he advanced these techniques significantly in order to show quite brilliantly the process of decay and renewal ~~which has always been the hallmark of Rome~~. Examine, for instance, the clear outline of the Circus Maximus on folio 7, with the delicately sketched orchards growing over the ruins

I'm fixing omelettes, wearing my black jeans with the tight red tank top, washing lettuce for salad. The kitchen is freezing and there are goose bumps all over my arms but who cares, he's always said I look like a model in this outfit. Twenty minutes in front of the closet mirror, deciding – it's like the last refuge of the desperate. Like Mom before she'd go on those dates of hers. And while I'm standing at the sink, he passes right by, stops and turns around, looks, and my heart jumps. Then all tired sounding, he says, "Hasn't *any*thing happened to you in your life? Not a mark on you anywhere. No wonder . . ." I stay cool, hold it in, and just say gently, "You happened. You happened," and he shrugs and goes into the bedroom. Mutters something like "I'll roll off that skin like everything else." And twenty minutes later I'm cracking the eggs when he just leaves, says he's going to the opera with George. Well fuck *that!* He didn't even ask me if I wanted to go to the stupid opera, just went ahead and got the tickets. Sometimes I swear, I want to tell him to take all that culture and learning and just shove it up his ass. So I haven't been to goddamn Rome, so I don't like opera, sounds like a bunch of cats being tortured as far as I'm concerned. Some of us didn't have his advantages, and meanwhile I'm stuck here giving Peanut and Djinn their flea bath and getting scratched to shit –

> The Nolli was indeed completed at a fortuitous moment in Roman history, after the flush of urban expansion during the Counter–Reformation, which gave a second youth to the city ~~much as a young lover~~. Working in a time of urban stability, Nolli was thus able to depict the cumulative results of Renaissance and Baroque changes in the city.

Only two months ago he's telling me opera's over for him, complaining about the treacly melodrama of *Madame Butterfly*, nineteenth-century overkill, colonial nonsense, et cetera and so on. Whereas tonight he was gripping his program so hard he practically shredded it, gave me the nastiest look when I pointed out the mess he'd made. God, and that noisy breathing, you could probably hear it on stage. Clicking his tongue like some old biddy at Pinkerton's desertion, as if he hadn't seen *Butterfly* twenty times. And the soprano wasn't even that good. He actually hissed "*Bastard!*" when Pinkerton left the stage – blue-hairs were craning around from three rows away, I could have died. And instead of coffee and cake like civilized human beings afterwards, he insists I take him right home – well certainly, after all, I'm just the chauffeur around here. Threatened to call a cab when I tried to talk him into dessert! Unbelievable! Although I think some of the nastiness might have been bravado, he didn't want to let on how tired he was – his skin is positively grey –

> Take a few minutes to examine the map minutely, to enter it, if you will. Look at the delicate stippling indicating the elevations of the seven hills rising ~~supple as shoulder muscles~~

above the plain. Regard the parallel lines indicating the flow of the Tiber, the tiny boats being captained by even tinier fishermen. Even twenty years ago their descendants still plied the river, shouting to one another and even at times to interested watchers along the shore

It was decidedly strained at first, I mean I'd never even seen Jake without Phillip, and we've never exactly hit it off as friends. Still, he'd chosen a nice place for lunch, terracotta stucco walls and moulded plaster, little sconces with garish Virgin Mary candles set into them, very PoMo-chic. We must have spent two hours there, he really surprised me, I didn't think he had that much conversation in him, frankly. Rather touching humility when he asked about my Legislature Restoration project – intelligent questions too, apparently Phillip missed the boat when he said all his lectures were lost on him. And to my great amazement he said Phillip had told him I'd worked *miracles* on that old Victorian monstrosity! In retrospect, I think he may have made that up just to be nice, given old whatshisname's current self-, no, his map-involvement lately –

I had no idea what I'd get, but I didn't want to look like a total clod by asking the waiter what it meant, George already thinks I'm an airhead. But it turned out for the best, gorgeous saffron rice with spicy chicken on top. I asked his advice about Phillip and he said, "If it were me, which thankfully it's not, I might try a Grand Gesture, something wild, something to grab his attention back." And then, pointing his fork at me, "That's what you young turks are good at, isn't it? I heard about those performance art pieces you used to do. . . . Oh yes, Phillip told me about the pudding-and-whips display. Not that he liked it of course, rather brazen for Phillip's refined tastes. . . . I thought it sounded rather wonderful, myself," and he gave me the weirdest look. Phillip told *me* he loved it –

for what visitor to Rome has not found himself wandering down some tiny alley which dates perhaps to centuries before Christ, with the ubiquitous Roman laundry fluttering ~~soundlessly~~ above on the shadowed balconies? One has the sense of cutting a swath through the city's very fabric, of moving toward a secret, a revelation. And, continuing, to suddenly emerge into the ~~sweet stony~~ light of a tiny piazza, where perhaps a dozen old men sit placidly at their espressos? ~~At such times one feels one has been swallowed, has entered joyously into the eternal~~

So unexpectedly sensuous. The pain, I hadn't considered it, hadn't prepared for it. Phillip's always said he hardly feels his needles. Everything narrowed down to that one point, that little red point of pain, I saw it as red anyway, a pure carmine, maybe shading out toward purple at the edges. I stared at that vinyl table the whole time, letting thoughts float by. Thinking of Phillip and his map, then trying not to. It is beautiful, I'll give him that, I'd almost forgotten – I finally found the little eighth-size copy he gave me. All those gifts he used to give me. Staring at that table, remembering how gently he showed me the way past moments of pain. How it could be like biting through something dense and rubbery, that gives right at the end. Snapping through into pleasure so deep it was like another colour. The bench I was lying on had tissue paper on it, just like a doctor's office, which I didn't expect at all. I could just see the edge of this mangy poster he's got tacked up, but mostly I looked at the vinyl, how it was engraved to look like leather, and thought about what Phillip said that day about my skin being too smooth. And I know it's the right thing I'm doing.

How rightly did Daniel-Rops observe "No city among those that have been great in human annals demonstrates so surely, and with such complexity, the fact that a human being is great only through the works in which he strives toward eternity." (*Couleurs Du Monde Editions*: Rome, Paris: J.E. Imbert, 1953, p.3)

I think I might have fallen asleep at one point, only it wasn't really like sleep. Remembering how it was at the very beginning with Phillip, before anything had even started. How I'd arrive early to his class so I could get the seat by the slide projector and watch his profile in the dark while he lectured. The softness and stubble that trembled under the chin. Fatty, the way necks get right before they collapse completely into old man's chicken neck. That little bit of gruesomeness about him, right from the start. It sharpened everything, so much more exciting than anything I'd ever felt up to then. And when I finally got up the courage to ask, he got up from his desk and took my hand, squeezed it right there in his office, I practically fainted from desire. And then he walked me out, holding my hand – he could have gotten fired if anyone had seen. Funny, I'm lying here in this grey room, and I'm doing that same walk again, all the way down to Harbourfront with him commenting on every house and building on the way. Those houses in the Annex – what was it he said? "Sensible as good shoes. Square, fat, graceless, so expressive of the WASP mentality, don't you think?" All the while grinning and waving at that matron watching us through a window, I nearly peed laughing. And then – what did he call it? The *jolly creampuffery* of the Portuguese gardens, all that wrought iron and pink. And when I said I was embarrassed that I didn't have anything to say, he kissed me, said artists didn't need to talk –

has noted this curious phenomenon of apparent yet unidentifiable modification. Even I, who have stared at this map so many times, and know it as well as the back of my own hand, have been amazed at times to find the map subtly changed. As though some minute alleys had moved, or the outline of a lesser chapel had contracted slightly. ~~Indeed there are days when the back of my hand too is altered, as today I find a rather troubling softness has deepened into a definite bruise, curiously lined with reddish venules~~

I offered to start driving him home, why not save him the subway – after all, it's not even out of my way, he waits at the corner of Bay and College, outside the Ministry building. But people always presume, take it too far, why should I have thought Jake was any different? Today he asked me to stop at the Kitchen Table and got out without even asking if I needed anything – I had to yell after him to get me some fresh pasta, and when he came out he was carrying an immense bouquet of calla lilies. So much for his poor little bureaucrat's salary! Lilies. So transparent. For Phillip, as if he'd look up long enough from his idiot writing desk to notice. "They look like thin penises, don't you think?" Jake said, all cutesy-naughty, as though it wasn't obvious to anyone with eyes, I could've slapped him. So young, so unsophisticated. To remind Phillip of Mapplethorpe's flower pictures, no doubt, and his more X-rated ones too. Imitative magic, I could have told him it was hardly anything original, but I just drove and held my tongue, the whole thing was quite annoying. And he got me tomato pasta, of all the stupid things.

It was so intense this afternoon I almost passed out. Luckily I'd taken the whole afternoon off. Lay in the little grey room, just breathing and watching that couch in the corner frothing with old foam rubber, dry and crackly at the edges, I knew exactly what it would feel like even before I touched it. After I was done I barely made it back, wobbling along the street, feeling sick and high at the same time. Then the ride home with George – Jesus, the way he drives – usually I'm white-knuckled, but today I just watched all his swerving calmly, feeling all floaty and detached. And then I got the brain wave about the flowers, like I had X-ray vision or something,

I just knew they'd be there in the store, in a red bucket. I didn't tell George what it was all about, he seemed to be in a real snit anyway. When I got in, I tiptoed into the bedroom with the flowers. Hyacinth was there tidying up. Phillip was lying flat on his back, in his red robe, napping, and I could see his belly, slack and kind of pooled out to the side underneath the robe. A triangle of grey hairs bushing out where the robe opened. God, it was just sickening. An old man. Slack and snoring. Hyacinth must have seen the look on my face because she scuttled right out of there. . . . And I just stood over him, totally repelled, thinking *I fell in love with this?* And I couldn't think of my answer, so I put the flowers in a vase and put them on the nightstand beside him. My little copy of the map was there beside him on the floor – he must have found where I'd hidden it. Somehow that made me just furious, knowing he'd been poking around my stuff, on top of how revolting he looked. . . . I was thinking, Lord, the way he used to treat me, like a god, and now look at us. I'm young, attractive, and *begging* for this old shit's attention. It's like he wants me to leave, wants everything to fall to shit. . . . It was terrible, I felt like I was betraying him right there in our own house. . . . And I was starving, I always have to eat when I'm miserable, so I made three cans of ravioli and started wolfing them down right from the pan. The taste of it brought back last summer – he didn't let me cook a thing the whole time we were at that cabin – he finally ended up resorting to canned food. I remembered how he'd arrange shells and little things he'd found in the woods around my plate. How we'd be sunning together on the dock and then he'd jump into the water and splash me until I came in too – and then all the disgust was gone, completely, and I just ached so hard for him I couldn't move. The ravioli tasted so fantastic. When I was about halfway through, he came into the kitchen and put his hand on my shoulder, said, "Thanks for the flowers." Not very gratefully, but it was a start, I thought. I told him how the ravioli had reminded me about the cottage, and last summer and stuff. And he just sighed and said "Always hungry aren't you? Can't blame you for that, I guess. I wonder how long you'd wait to find someone new –"

God, I'm just exhausted, the contractors have made an absolute mess of the cloakroom mouldings at the Legislature, thirty minutes trying to explain it to some young snip of a foreman, total waste of breath of course, and then he just walks off – the union gives a four-thirty break come hell or high water – and I'm left standing there, about to burst a vein I'm so angry. So of course I forget all about picking up Jake, have to circle back through the traffic.

Well it isn't *my* fault he forgot to pick me up, what a foul mood, on and on about the moron contractors and I want to tell him to just shut up, my dad was a construction worker and they're not all the lazy retards he makes them out to be. Listening to him jabber on, I'm thinking about a quiet evening, I'll go to the store and get a video, maybe I can interest Phillip in it if I can find some foreign thing that doesn't look too boring, and now George says he's so wound up he'll just pop in at our place and have a scotch with Phillip, see how the introduction is coming. Goddamn it –

> when I alluded earlier to the representation of positive and negative space. Even a cursory examination of the Nolli map shows the interplay of public and private, which makes Rome at once an open and a secretive city. Around the Campidoglio, for instance, note the dark clusters shot with small white veins. The dark areas are, of course, the densely crowded buildings, the white lines alleys leading inward, opening into small plazas which are invisible until one reaches them. From the map, then, it is easy to see that the architecture of the city conceals as much as it reveals. ~~Of course, architecture thrives on the tension between the hidden and the revealed. The deception of facades, for instance. . . . Creamy marble filigrees often give a modern~~

~~face to much older buildings, buildins which themselves may contain all sorts of secrets~~

We're hardly in the door when Phillip comes at us, screeching like a harpy. Screaming how he knows all about it, about Jake and me, clawing at Jake's face and saying he's known all along he'd do something like this, if Jake thinks he's just a decrepit dying old fool he's got another thing coming, on and on and on. Ranting about young men, all of them, the cats are cowering and hissing under the table. And Phillip's waving his arms around, knocking things all over the carpet. Awful, awful, like a bird flying in my face, I hardly know what's happening, and then I'm yelling at him: "What the *hell* are you talking about?" – and maybe it had crossed my mind, once or twice, not in any serious way – after all Jake's a very good-looking guy and the way Phillip's been treating him – and Jake just stands there paralysed, crestfallen, taking it like a child that's done something wrong, until finally I can see his boiling point has been passed, and he bunches up those strong twiny arms of his – for a second I think he's going to haul off and deck Phillip, but then he takes off his shirt, wincing in pain –

I'm so mad I don't even know what I'm doing, it's not ready yet, but Phillip's screaming that I'm having an affair with George. I'm so furious I want to kill him but it's so ridiculous I also want to laugh, and he's there in front of me, shaking his jowls, *looking* at me for the first time in God knows how long. But he's looking at me with hate. And I'm shaking, feeling hot and nauseous at that misery and sickness in his face. I can't even talk, I've never been able to talk when he's upset and so I just do it. Show him. That I'm marked. My whole body aches, my shirt sticks and tears the scabs where it's oozed a little. Hot darts of pain rising in patches. It's still so red, not healed yet, and he just stares. I'm dizzy and hot, it wasn't supposed to be like this. George somewhere beside me starts babbling *Oh my dear Lord. My dear Lord* over and over. And

then he finally sees what it is. His map. Tattooed on my skin. And I finally find my voice.
– "I'm not going anywhere."
– "What have you done –?"
– "So it could be both of ours."

– "My dear Lord, my Lord, oh my Lord –" I can't stop babbling. Phillip reaches out, runs his hand over the redness, that smooth chest. And takes Jake in his arms – well, more like Jake taking him, he's taller after all, and it's more than I can bear to see. My dear Lord, who could ever have conceived? . . . Nobody's ever done anything like that for *me*. Only patches, tasteful, small little details, dark and geometric against Jake's lovely dark skin – the outline of a palazzo on the shoulder, one bit going down into the waistband. . . . Patches making a whole design over the torso. Marked. And me the lonely one. As per usual.

Every move for him is painful, he groans a little as he twists to show me. *Forgive me.* That redness over black, skin cracking and inflamed. I feel it on my own back, turn around, there, and back to me. That hard stomach, jut of hip. Nothing forgotten. The day you came to me and leaned forward over my desk, your neck rising so solid off your shoulders, oh, that was terror and I was lost, marked until you would do what you chose to a helpless old fool. That shoulder, my trembling hand above it.
– "What, what's that one, here?"
– "Villa Madama. Where you told me about their parties."
– "Oh my dear Lord – Well Phillip, he never misses a trick, this one –"

Over the hard hill of his shoulder, of course! *Villa Madama*, built into the hill's round, peering back at the city. The terrace on the hill where they danced and played until the fire came and when it did Guiliano de Medici cried from the next hill as he watched it burn, still only half-built. . . . Oh your poor skin, all my doing –

There, under the nipple, *Tampieti di Bramante*, round as a little flower, the lines so straight beneath, dark and geometric against the living skin – the long walk down the Strada del Corfo, to the great entrance, down that long, stippled torso into the waistband. . . . Marked. As I.

It is time to enter the city.

UNDER THE WINGS OF A BIG OLD BIRD

STUART ROSS

STUART ROSS SPENT MUCH OF THE 1980S SELLING HIS SELF-PUBLISHED POETRY AND FICTION ON THE STREETS OF DOWNTOWN TORONTO, WHERE HE WAS A MAGNET FOR EVERY PSYCHOPATH WHO WALKED BY. CO-FOUNDER OF THE TORONTO SMALL PRESS BOOK FAIR, HE HAS PUBLISHED SEVERAL 'ZINES INCLUDING *MONDO HUNKAMOOGA: A JOURNAL OF SMALL PRESS STUFF* AND *WHO TORCHED RANCHO DIABLO?* HIS MOST RECENT BOOKS ARE *THE INSPIRATION CHA-CHA* AND *HENRY KAFKA AND OTHER STORIES*, FROM WHICH "UNDER THE WINGS OF A BIG OLD BIRD" IS TAKEN. HE LONGS FOR THE CRUMBLING LANDSCAPE OF MANAGUA.

At his driving examination, Mr. Cage held a saxophone to his lips and blorted out a low note. He waited a moment, then blorted out another of the same. His examiner was a chain-smoking pterodactyl who wouldn't roll down his window, despite the summer heat and the blue cloud of smoke that filled the car's cramped interior. "Don't you know another tune?" asked the pterodactyl from the passenger seat.

Mr. Cage blew hard and the same damn note came out. And then he did it again. And all the while he was thinking, My examiner is a pterodactyl. He pulled the instrument from his lips. The reed was completely dry.

His mouth was completely dry. He licked his lips with a dry tongue. The note sounded again. His lips were a good five inches from the mouthpiece. And then the note sounded again. It was like when the guy lifts his hands from the player piano and the piano keeps playing. This was when Mr. Cage first suspected that the driving exam was a dream. He looked over accusingly at the pterodactyl, and the huge winged creature stared straight ahead through the window, refusing to meet Mr. Cage's glare. The note sounded again. It was low and insistent. Mr. Cage put down the saxophone and opened his eyes. He was staring into blackness. He heard the note again. It was becoming anxious. He put his hands to his ears, and through the bones and flesh and skin of his hands, he heard the note sound once more. Mr. Cage sat up in his bed and flicked on the bedroom light. His window was wide open. It was winter and way below zero outside, but his rads were always on full blast, hissing and spluttering through the night so he could keep the window open and let in fresh air.

And sounds from the street. Like garbage cans rolling around in the wind, like children's backyard swings creaking, like drunken neighbours arguing and smashing things, like cars that someone tried to steal, thereby setting off the car horn, which would continue to howl until the owner came along and put the keys in the ignition.

Mr. Cage looked at the little travel clock that was perched atop a pile of books on the floor beside his bed. It was four-twenty in the morning and he already had his driver's licence anyway. He'd had it for about seventeen years. The examiner had been human, and aside from some trouble with parallel parking, Mr. Cage had aced the exam. From out in the street, the car horn blasted again. Eventually the battery would die and the honking would stop. Or the owner would come running from some all-night party and shove his keys into the ignition. Or the owner was dead.

The owner was dead and the car was a mourning dog howling over his master's favourite armchair long after the master was dead and buried deep in the ground. The ground had been frozen and it had taken a long time to dig the hole. The animal pawed the chair and whimpered, while the family argued about whether they should put the thing to sleep or try to get some uncle who owned a farm to take it.

Mr. Cage closed his eyes. It took so long to dig the hole that the horn just kept honking through the night. He flung off his covers and pulled on his pants. The car howled again and this time it sounded like grief. Mr. Cage picked up the phone and dialled a three-digit emergency number and gave the name of his street and reported a murder. He walked out his front door with no shirt, in his bare feet, and immediately saw the car, at the opposite side of the street, two houses down. The frosted grass crackled under Mr. Cage's feet as he walked across his lawn and his neighbour's lawn and his neighbour's neighbour's lawn. He stepped off the curb and onto the street and walked across to the car. He jumped when the car honked again. Then he regained his composure and yanked at the car door. It wouldn't give. He peered up and down the street and wondered why no one else had woken up. Why bedroom lights weren't turning on all along the block. Why no one was standing on their porch and peering out into the darkness, looking for the source of the terrible blorting.

Neighbours with flashlights, neighbours with rifles. In one of the houses the owner of this car lay dead, and somewhere else in this bitter night his murderer was fleeing on foot, vaulting over fences, darting from bush to bush. In someone's backyard lay the murder weapon, glistening, holding its guilty breath. Mr. Cage ran his fingers along the top of the car window, looking for a gap, but a split second after the next honk, he heard other noises, the cry of a siren, the screech of tires. Under the glare of flashing red lights, shirtless in the cold winter night, he was dragged into the back of a police car.

Familiarity whipped by him like so many slaps in the face. His neighbours' homes, the corner grocery store, the post office, the laundromat, the library whose copy of Dostoevsky's *The Idiot* he still had, the high school where he had taught for a few years before the crash, the wooden bridge, the ravine, the field. Slap slap slap. In the back seat next to him, a police officer was reading aloud from a small book. The siren had been turned off, and Mr. Cage could no longer hear the car horn's futile bellowing, and the police car sped silently through the night. A movie where this happens. Where the policeman's mouth is moving and a man in cuffs beside him, head bowed, is thinking about other things. The man looks up again, hoping to see a pterodactyl, but it's a human policeman, staring straight ahead, lips tight, jaw tensed. A thick plastic partition separated Mr. Cage from the policeman in front who was driving. A deer stood at the side of the road unblinking, slashed by orange headlights. Mr. Cage gasped. Huge faces of solid rock gradually rose on each side of the road and the police car barrelled on between them. There was no sound but that of pebbles staccatoing off the sides of the car. Now the walls of rock disappeared and there was desert ahead. Mr. Cage shivered and looked at the police officer beside him. The man was expressionless. Outside the window, the sky glowed faintly even though there was no visible source of light. The desert stretched some incalculable distance until it bumped into a barricade of mountains. The police car bumped to a stop and Mr. Cage lurched forward against the plastic partition. His head ached like the swatted muzzle of a howling dog. "Wait here," said the policeman beside him. The car doors opened and closed beside Mr. Cage and in front of him. He was alone in the car. The radio fizzed and popped and sizzled and spluttered.

He closed his eyes and hung his mouth open and breathed rapidly, emitting little noises, little whimpers. He longed for his bed, a dreamless sleep, the hiss of his blazing radiators. When he opened his eyes again, the policemen were leaning against the front of the car, talking quietly and sipping coffees. Mr. Cage became aware of a glow surrounding the car, illuminating the officers' faces and hands, and only then did he notice that they were parked in front of a truckstop café.

The café itself was empty but for the woman behind the counter, who was flipping through the pages of a newspaper far too quickly to be reading. The car shook and the policemen were back inside, and they were all sweeping silently across the desert again.

Mr. Cage rubbed his arms for warmth. He wondered if the car horn was still honking. He wondered if his neighbours were awake. "This is a great country," he said.

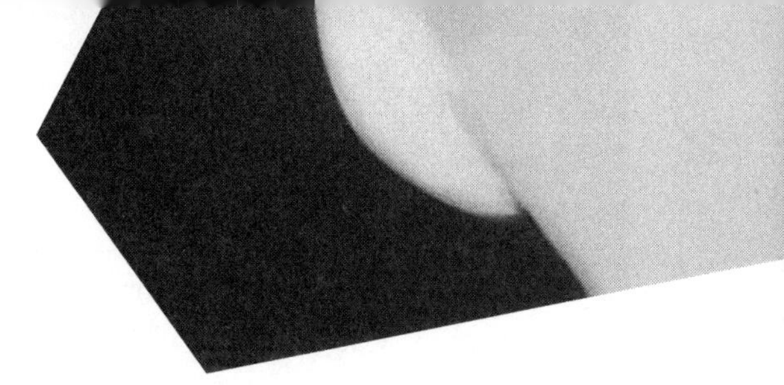

TAXI

PETER STINSON

PETER STINSON HAS BEEN DESCRIBED AS AN INTERDISCIPLINARY ARTIST (ALTHOUGH IT WAS A PROFOUND LACK OF DISCIPLINE THAT GOT HIM BOOTED OUT OF THE CALGARY TAXI INDUSTRY). AFTER A TYPICAL PHASE IN ART SCHOOL, STINSON PLUGGED AWAY AT PAINTING BUT DRIFTED INTO PERFORMANCE ART AND THEATRE. HIS WRITING HAS BEEN USED AS THE BASIS FOR COMICS AND STORIES HE PUTS IN HIS 'ZINE *LIMBO*. LATELY, PETER HAS BEEN WORKING IN CALGARY, PRINTING BOOK COVERS FOR THE CORPORATE WORLD WHILE ADMIRING THE GRAFFITI ON THE FREIGHT TRAINS SHUNTING OUTSIDE.

A very elderly couple from North Hill Safeway to Sunnyside . . . it's pouring rain and I'm annoyed. . . . They have tons of groceries. . . . The man is pretty well blind. . . . His wife is very cheerful . . .

From Sunnyside to Crowchild Inn, a guy, bar staff going to work . . . he tells me a quick way to go and he's right . . . tips good . . .

In Bowness, a native couple, going to bingo at the community centre. . . . The man's a jokester. He says, "Hey mind if I pay with a cheque?" I look at him and he and his wife laugh and laugh . . .

Stop by a used books store I'd never seen before . . . pick up some mags containing some Bill Ward art . . .

Montgomery Mac's to Montalban Crescent . . . a guy with long hair, at his house there is an amazing view and the sky's clearing in the west . . .

In Kensington, I think some guy's flagging me but he's not . . . I drive away pissed off but get flagged by a young guy with bleached white hair and piercings . . . goes downtown . . .

From a downtown hair place, a very attractive woman with strong, pleasant perfume goes to Duckey's Pub . . .

From Goliath's to Renfrew, a man named Richard, Stonewall T-shirt, so drunk he can hardly walk . . . I help him to the door . . . great garden . . .

From the Crossroads Hotel to the T and C in Forest Lawn, four British soldiers on a night out. There's a young hooker standing in the parking lot when we arrive. They approach her but she gets in another cab . . .

From the Big 4 Casino to Mission two guys, sharp dressers. . . . One complains that the gambling was not so good today. . . . I have to take a slight detour because some film production is blocking their street. . . . The one guy has seen this a lot in Toronto. "They pay you good money to use your house. Sometimes they pay the whole street . . ."

I stop and check out the film crew. It's "North of 60," the CBC show about the north. The lighting is bright and unnatural, the crew all quite robust; they tell some of us gawkers to move behind the shot. . . . I chat with an older man. "'North of 60?' Oh yeah, I watched it for ten minutes and changed the channel. . . . The whole CBC's boring. . . . And so is this spectacle . . ."

I take Ken from Duckey's Pub to Bankview. . . . He's from northern Alberta and he likes "North of 60". . . . He says it's a realistic portrayal of natives and of the north . . .

At the Westward . . . a young hooker jumps out of an Acura and complains that the guys are too drunk to ride with. . . . Besides she just made 200 bucks . . . we cruise and stop beside a cluster of young women, her friends (one of 'em I'd seen earlier at the T and C) . . . they discuss drugs, bitches, and junkies but she says she's not a user. . . . "I read the 'Prostitute's Diary' . . . it said the best nights were Sunday, really late, big bucks" . . . her busiest nights? ". . . Thursday, Friday, Saturday" . . . drop her off on Electric Ave.

A no-tip. Pints and 1/2 Pints, a bar I'm familiar with . . .

From the Airliner to the big postal depot . . . the forty-something postal worker . . . no tip but he acts apologetic anyway . . .

From Robin's donuts, to the Huntington Esso . . . it's raining again, guy, bicycle, and poor wet skinny little black dog named Ralph. . . . "Named after the Jackie Gleason character . . ." Tips me with a cherry stick donut . . . I see this guy with the little dog outside Pints a couple o' nights later . . .

A peeler from Airliner to 'Body Shoppe' . . . says she just watched a really bad horror movie in her room . . .

Juliet's Castle . . . this guy's passing out at his table . . . he wants more beer, though, and picks up a case at the Cecil . . . asks me the typical question, "So what do you really do?" "I'm an artist." "Heh, heh. . . . Well, you'll never guess what I am . . ." He looks like one of the characters from "North of 60" but says, "I'm a writer . . ."

Capri Pizza to Tuxedo, bearded guy who's very drunk . . . I can hardly understand him . . .

I stop at the bank and pay some bills.

Prince Royal Inn, a bunch of hotel staff go to Sunnyside . . . one says, "I had to go out at seven for some Parmesan cheese. . . . God, it was raining . . ."

Norm's Pub . . . Neil. . . . He's drunk but I'm polite. "Don't call me 'sir' . . . you're older than me!" he says.

From Boyztown, Danny goes home. I've picked him up quite inebriated many times. ". . . Did you used to go to the Calgarian?" referring to the ancient punk rock bar . . . "Yeah . . ."

Blackfoot Truckstop to Forest Lawn, Art has breathing problems. "Left my truck at Edna's . . . can't breathe . . . they won't give me oxygen, though . . ."

Toni, a hooker in white leather, takes Juan, a Spanish émigré . . . to the Cecil . . . his buddy follows in his car. . . . "I can't let the other girls see me take two guys . . . they'll be pissed off . . ."

HELLO, SASKATOON!

MICHAEL TURNER

JOE ON THE MIKE

Hello, Saskatooooooon!
We're Hard Core Logo.
We're gonna sing a song or two
to prepare you for tomorrow.
This one's written by Bucky Haight,
the legendary punk king
who died last year in New York City.

MICHAEL TURNER, HILLBILLY PUNK ROCKER AND DENIZEN OF DOWNTOWN VANCOUVER, CLAIMS TO HAVE DIFFICULTY DISTINGUISHING THE "RURAL" FROM THE "URBAN." THIS COULD BE BECAUSE TURNER IS AN UNCONVENTIONAL STYLIST DEDICATED TO SUBVERTING GENRE AT ALL COSTS. HIS MOST RECENT BOOK, AMERICAN WHISKEY BAR, IS A NOVEL IN THE FORM OF A SCREENPLAY. HARD CORE LOGO – THE BASIS FOR BRUCE MCDONALD'S FILM OF THE SAME NAME AND THE SOURCE FOR "HELLO, SASKATOON!" – IS A NOVEL IN VERSE, LYRIC, AND SNAPSHOT.

HARD
CORE
LOGO
RULE
SUCK
RULE
?
USA/CIA
=FASCISM

BLUE TATTOO

It hurt so bad when you got it
It went right to your head
It drove you insane
But now that's all forgotten
And you can go on
Without any pain

A blue tattoo on your shoulder
In the shape of a heart
In the middle of my name
And that's how I remember
All of the bad things
That you couldn't change

Blue Tattoo
Blue Tattoo

You had no time for corruption
You felt that the world
Was an unsafe place
You worked towards a solution
But the best you could do
Was to send me away

A blue tattoo on my shoulder
In the shape of the world
In the middle of your name
And that's how I remember
All of the good things
You took to your grave

Blue Tattoo
Blue Tattoo

JOHN'S TOUR DIARY

May 16 (a.m.)

Since there were no touring bands playing the club last night, and we had the whole day off, the promoter let us have the band rooms upstairs – for free. He asked us if we wanted to come down later, and maybe do a couple of songs on the open stage to hype tomorrow's show. At that point, Pipe charged into the conversation and said we'd do it for twenty bucks a song. We all laughed.

We ended up playing two half-hour sets. Originally we'd planned to play three or four songs, but the crowd was loving it. *Really* loving it. And by the end of the first set people were lining up at the telephone, trying to get their friends out to what was becoming a perfectly spontaneous event.

For the first time in a long time I began to realize how special this band was to people. I felt really proud. I felt part of something bigger than all of us. Standing there on the stage I got to thinking that maybe we were meant to stay together. Forever. And when Joe opened the night with Bucky's "Blue Tattoo," which caught us all off guard, I felt like crying.

When the doors closed, we invited the promoters and the owners upstairs for a poker party. Everybody took turns winning, and the beers were flowing freely. We were all having a good time, until Joe ruined it by insisting that the club should give us full payment for the extra show. And then Pipe started multiplying the number of songs by twenty. Nobody was laughing then.

PIPE UNDER HIS BREATH

Having a shitty time doin' this. Should have listened to my gut. Joe's an asshole. Billy's a jerk-off. John's a fuck-head.

I was led to believe I'd be making some okay money. Now it looks as though I won't even make my rent. Hell, what do you expect when you're doing gigs for free?

Bucky's lucky. He still gets royalty cheques. He doesn't have to worry about making ends meet. Plus he's got someone looking after him. Shit, I wish I was in his shoes.

BILLY ON HOLD AT THE NELSON HOTEL

The first time Joe and I met Bucky was backstage at the Smilin' Buddha. 1979. He was passing through town with some band from the States, and our friend, Ed Festus, was a buddy. It was our first ever backstage visit.

I never thought much of the great Bucky Haight. He was a shitty singer, an even worse guitarist. But he managed to write some pretty good songs. Songs only he could deliver. He's always been a god to Joe.

Bucky's the reason we started this band. When I taught Joe guitar I tried to get him to learn the classics – Johnson, Leadbelly, Hendrix, Van Halen. But Joe never much got into that. He only liked the music he knew. And the music he knew was Bucky.

A FREELANCE INTERVIEW AT THE WOOLWORTH'S COFFEE BAR

INTERVIEWER: I thought you guys were dead or something.

JOE DICK: We're very much alive, thank you.

I: How's the tour going?

JD: Great. All the shows have been sell-outs. We even sold out in Winnipeg, but had to cancel due to unforeseen circumstances.

I: Why did you guys decide to reunite?

JD: We decided to reunite because that's what people wanted. We've always been *the* populist band, eh? We're slaves to the people. It's what we had to do.

I: You sound like Tommy Douglas.

JD: Tommy Douglas. A great man.

I: Besides going acoustic, is there anything different about Hard Core Logo?

JD: Yes and no. (pause)

I: Can you elaborate?

JD: Well . . . what was the question again?

I: Anything *new* with Hard Core Logo?

JD: Right. Besides going acoustic we're writing again. Our song about Robert Satiacum is a smash hit.

I. Didn't he do time in Alberta for racketeering? Selling cigarettes or something?

JD: Yah, and now he's dead. He died in a Vancouver lock-up. He was charged with a crime and he died waiting for his trial. See, his heart was going and he surrendered to get medical help. He had a heart attack and the guards just watched him suffer. That's the true crime.

I: Is it true that the legendary Bucky Haight has returned to his native Saskatchewan?

JD: I don't comment on legends.

I: The last time you came through here, in '89, I had an interesting chat with your manager, Ed Festus. He was telling me that punk was gonna make a big comeback, and that he was trying to prime you guys for the nostalgia circuit.

JD: Ed Festus. That fucker!

I: Right. I understand Ed's moved on.

JD: Yah, well *we* moved him on. Fuckin' crook. We don't usually talk about Ed, but let me just say that we're suing him for stealing the rights to our name.

I: Well, how did this come about?

JD: We had some tax problems in the mid-1980s. That's when we hired Ed. He was our friend at the time, and he knew a bit about finances. Everything ended up getting transferred into his name.

I: So legally he could sue *you*? Aren't you worried about that?

JD: Are you kidding? A lawsuit would be the best thing ever to happen to us. The problem is that Ed knows that, too. If anybody else owned our name we'd be laughing.

I: So what's the problem?

JD: It's personal. It goes deeper than money.

I: I hear Ed's living in Seattle, managing grunge bands.

JD: We know exactly what he's doing. I feel sorry for the musicians signed to his company. He's probably screwing them like he did us. Look, the Ed Festus stuff is turning me off this interview.

I: Sorry.

JD: I'll allow you one more question. Better make it a good one.

I: Is there any future in what you are doing?

JD: Yes. Now fuck off.

JOE'S KEY WORDS TO A NEW SONG

Grain Tower
General store
Reduced prices
No credit

Million dollar debt
Savings and loan
Bank manager
Near the church

Poor farmer
Wheat in the donut
Feel like the chaff
Ticket punch

Bad times
Moves the family
Gives up hockey
Gives up pool

Transfer
Liar
The Reverend's opinion
Everyone's opinion

A NEW TUNE TO PRACTISE

I was having lunch
up on Broadway
and these three guys
were talking
about their fathers, farmers
up near Lloydminster.
Got most of it down
on this napkin.

THE TICKET PUNCH AT THE SAVINGS AND LOANS

I took my grain to the tower
Across the street from the general store
I almost made enough money
For a bottle of Coke and the drive back home

I owe your bank a million dollars
And every year it's a million more
I drive by there every Sunday
On my way to church, when I know you're at home

I am the poor farmer
I am the road that leads to town
I am the wheat in your donut, yes
But I feel like the chaff when you come around
The ticket punch at the savings and loans

I could tell bad times were a-comin'
When you moved your wife to Saskatoon
When you gave up Saturday hockey
When you stopped playin' pool at the hotel saloon

Now you're puttin' in for a transfer
'cause you're ready to move on to something new
But we all know you're a liar
And The Reverend Jim he thinks so, too
Yah The Reverend Jim he thinks so, too

JOHN'S TOUR DIARY

May 16 (p.m.)

Went downtown at 8 a.m., the earliest I've been up since we left. Had breakfast at the Nelson Hotel. Steak and eggs, toast and coffee.

Went to the Mennonite clothing store and bought a belt.

Practised Joe's new song – in silence.

Leaving right after the gig.

A SULKING PIPE

Everytime I look at John he's writing in his fuckin' notebook. He never used to do this before. He was just like the rest of us: drinking hard and chasing women. Mind you, nobody's chasing women any more. And Billy's the only real drinker.

Still, it picks me. But I know what he's up to. Last year I read something John wrote in Discorder: *some anonymous thing only he could have known of. It was all about the early years: Subhumans, K-Tels, gigs at the Buddha.*

I know he's writing a story on us. A tell-all thing that'll make me look stupid. There's no fucking way I'll sign a release. I'll just wait 'til it's published, then hire a lawyer.

SASKATOON MAY 16 (SET LIST)

Who The Hell
R'n'R Is Fat
Hold The Fort
Robert
The Worker's Beer
Something's Gonna
Railway
Ticket Punch
Medly #1
Blue Tattoo
Bush Party
Block. Heater
4 Nights Drunk
Medly #2
Bootlegger Song
S.O.B.
Words And Music

Proud Mary

THE BARTENDER CAUTIONS JOE

Don't get me wrong.
It's nothing personal, Joe,
but could you please tell Billy
that *our* rider agreement
specifies draught beer only?
Also, there's a six pint
limit per person,
and Billy's already
nine pints over.
And one more thing, Joe.
Could you please tell him
to lay off the waitresses?
The two on last night
have refused to come in.

JOE IGNORES THE ENCORE

The club owner wants an encore,
but there's no fuckin' way
I'm gonna go out there
and play to a crowd
of five people.

ENCORE

Thank you very much.
You've been a terrific crowd.
Joe just collapsed upstairs
from all the excitement,
so me, Pipe, and Billy
are gonna give you
our rendition
of the Safaris' classic,
"Wipeout."

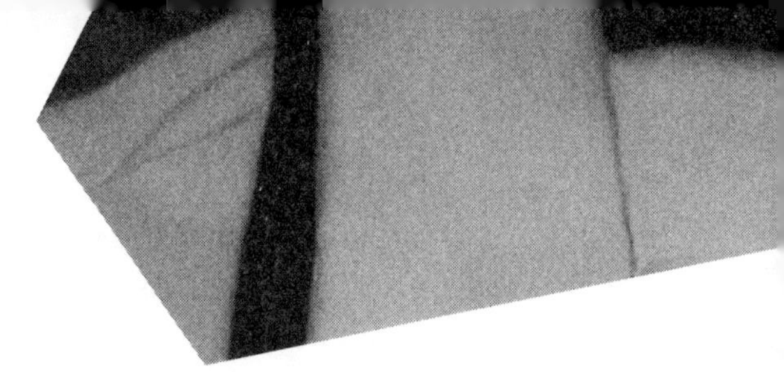

THE WEDNESDAY FLOWER MAN

DIANNE WARREN

DIANNE WARREN IS A REGINA FICTION WRITER AND PLAYWRIGHT. HER STORY COLLECTION *BAD LUCK DOG* WON THE SASKATCHEWAN BOOK OF THE YEAR AWARD IN 1993. SHE'S WON BOTH WESTERN AND NATIONAL MAGAZINE AWARDS FOR HER SHORT STORIES. HER PLAY *SERPENT IN THE NIGHT SKY* WAS SHORT-LISTED FOR A GOVERNOR GENERAL'S AWARD IN 1992. "THE WEDNESDAY FLOWER MAN" IS FROM HER COLLECTION OF STORIES OF THE SAME NAME. ALTHOUGH DIANNE HAS LIVED IN BOTH CITIES AND IN THE COUNTRY, SHE FINDS THAT CITIES HAVE BETTER RESTAURANTS.

This afternoon Dennis will be delivering, for the last time, the usual box of roses to the apartment on Ninety-first Street. I wonder if he'll be doing anything special to commemorate the occasion. Probably not. I wonder who they'll hire to take his place. Who Dennis will hire to take his own place, I should say. It burns me even to think about it.

When I got to work this morning I found out Dennis got Mrs. Boyle's job as manager of the shop. The delivery boy for Christ's sake. All this time I thought Lila was my only competition, Lila with her four-hundred-dollar suits and her phony fingernails. I didn't even think about Dennis. What does he know about helping people select the right arrangement for the right occasion? What does he know about weddings and funerals and how to let flowers do your talking for you? I'm the one who's good at that. I'm better than Lila was, too. Just as good as Mrs. Boyle. It makes me wonder who's making the damned decisions in this world. It makes me wonder if there's anybody at the wheel.

I suppose that incident with the swearing could have had something to do with it. Mrs. Boyle did have to speak to me because a customer complained. Some old biddy wanted to have lilies for her husband's funeral. He wasn't even dead yet. It just so happened I had heard about a funeral where they had lilies all over the place, tons of them, and a lot of people were allergic to them. So I told her I wouldn't recommend lilies. I told her you can't have a proper funeral with everyone sneezing their goddamned heads off. She was offended by the goddamned. Not appropriate when dealing with a grieving public, Mrs. Boyle said to me, so I watched myself from then on. It just goes to show, a mistake follows you around, even if it's a little one. The more I think about it, the more I think the swearing incident must be why Dennis got the job and not me.

It was Lila who made me want to swear, right from the day she started working at the shop. Pinching the dead leaves off plants with her clipper-like fingernails. Buying a new tailored suit every payday. Answering the phone so efficiently: "Good morning. Flowers on the Avenue. Lila speaking. May I help you?" It made me sick. She was all fake, and there's nothing that makes me sicker than a person who lacks sincerity. She didn't really want to help anybody. Take the Wednesday flower man, for instance. Lila decided he was a fruitcake and wouldn't answer the phone at all before lunch on the last Wednesday of the month.

I never used to swear, at least not much. The four and a half years I was married to Howard I'll bet I never swore more than once or twice. Of course I was young then, right out of high school. Howard and I fell in love in the high school parking lot. His grandmother left him her car when she died and he used to sit in it all by himself before the bell rang and after school. It was a big car, a four-door Chev sedan; it had room for a whole pile of kids, but no one ever sat with him. I guess everybody figured he was kind of dippy, which he was, but at the same time he had this cute lock of blond hair which kept falling over one eye. It wasn't left long intentionally. Howard wasn't that cool. Maybe the barber just kept forgetting to cut it. Maybe he'd get Howard in his chair and he'd get so bored he'd gaze out the window and forget what he was doing. Howard could do that to you. But even so, you could forgive him. He was a real nice guy, not the kind of guy to make you want to swear.

I climbed into his car with him one day and we fell in love. We decided we should get married right after graduation because we couldn't wait any longer. With that big back seat in his grandmother's Chev, there was a lot of temptation to resist.

Howard thought we should get an apartment and he would go to school for two years and get his business diploma. His grandmother had left him some money in her will. I wanted to go to California with it, see Disneyland and Universal Studios and hang out on the beach watching the surfers, but Howard said his grandmother had wanted him to go to school so that's what he did. He went to school and I stayed in the apartment and hung wallpaper and made spaghetti and meatballs for supper. After Howard got his diploma he found a job right off selling pills and stuff to doctors.

I didn't think he would do very well at a sales job, but he really tied into it and surprised the hell out of everybody. He read his textbooks so many times he practically had them memorized. And he got magazine subscriptions and read out loud to me about how some guy or other said you could increase your sales. He even dreamed about selling. Once I tried to tell him we should take a trip around the world on a freighter and he looked at me as if I were crazy.

Howard was on the road a lot so I stocked up on frozen meat pies for myself and started living for *The Edge of Night* on daytime

TV. There was a woman named April that I wanted to be like. She had soft blond hair and a curvy figure and everybody loved her. I took to dressing as much like her as I could and I spoke in a soft voice, which confused Howard at first but he got used to it.

The funny thing was, the more April became unhappy on *The Edge of Night*, the more unhappy I became in our apartment. After a while April's sadness started to get to me. I figured out I wasn't the least bit like her. "Quit moping around," I wanted to yell at her. "You're too soft. Toughen up a little." I took to writing letters to the TV station. I took to secretly writing scripts in which April got tough. But she never did and finally one day I just up and left. I took some money from our account and left. Poor Howard. He arrived home and no me, just magazine subscriptions and frozen meat pies. He needed me too. I know he did. I was a damned good woman to come home to.

Well, one thing is certain. I didn't leave Howard eleven years ago to end up a nobody in a flower shop for the rest of my life. I left Howard so I could travel around the world having affairs, maybe starring in a movie or two, meeting suspicious characters in smoky bars and being asked to smuggle heroin or diamonds across the border. I wouldn't have done anything too illegal, but just to be asked would have been something.

Actually, none of that happened. I took enough of Howard's money to go to Europe, but I chickened out at the airport and spent the money on a used Camaro instead, a real beauty. I had it painted hot pink. A year ago some young kid sideswiped it on the street, totalled it. Sometimes I really miss that car.

After I didn't go to Europe, I worked seasonal on the city parks maintenance crew. That lasted for six years. Then I saw the flower shop job ad saying *chance for advancement*, and I remembered something Howard used to say. "No sense having a job where you get stuck on the middle rung of the ladder. If you can't see your way clear to the top, look elsewhere." It had worked for Howard. When I left him he was well on his way. Twice in a row he'd been salesman of the year for his pharmaceutical company. Howard would have been proud of me, I figured, going after a job where I could move up. Not that I cared what Howard thought, but after you've lived with somebody for a few years some of their favourite sayings stick with you. I applied for the job and got it. The chance for advancement was Mrs. Boyle's age and I thought it was a sure thing.

Of course Lila thought that too. When Mrs. Boyle and the head office people decided we could use more staff, they put another ad in the paper saying *chance for advancement* and Lila made it clear her first day on the job what her intentions were.

That's another thing I hated about Lila, she tried so damned hard. She'd read books, she said, about how you should dress and act if you wanted to get ahead. That's what the suits were all about. She asked me once if I thought she should continue having her nails done, if they were maybe a little garish for her image, which was obviously conservative.

"How should I know?" I said. "You're the one who's read all the goddamned books."

"I'm trying to be friendly," Lila said to me then, getting this phoney hurt look on her face. "I like to think I can be friends with my co-workers."

Stupid, I figure. You can't be friends with the competition. Still, I feel just a little bad hating Lila now that she's dead. Not liking someone and hating them are two different things. And I hated her. Of course, I didn't tell the police that. I figured they'd be around asking Dennis and me and Mrs. Boyle what we thought of Lila and whether or not we'd like to see her dead. I was planning to lie because I was afraid they'd think I did it. Lucky for me there's been a whole rash of murders in the last six months. When the police came around, they asked if Lila had said anything about being afraid, about being followed or getting strange phone calls or anything like that. They weren't very creative in their questioning. They hardly paid any attention to us at all. If I were a cop I'd have explored a few avenues they didn't touch. Like, did any of us stand to gain from Lila's death? Did one of us have any reason for wanting her out of the way, for leaving her dead in a dark alley? Those are just standard questions, for God's sake. Anyway, we told them Lila hadn't said anything about any strange events, and they weren't surprised. They weren't expecting to hear anything that would help them, and when they left they said they figured Lila was just another woman in the wrong place at the wrong time.

"You watch yourselves," the youngest cop (he still had puberty pimples) said to me and Mrs. Boyle. "This guy is sick. He doesn't care who his victims are. Your Lila was young and pretty, but from what I've seen anybody will do."

Mrs. Boyle thought that was funny. She laughed herself silly over it. I should have been glad to hear her laugh because ever since she got the letter saying when she'd have to retire she'd been really depressed. She figured the company should have let her go on working because her eyesight and all that was still good, but when she wrote a letter about it they told her it was company policy and they couldn't make any exceptions because then everybody would want to keep working and where would that get them? It put me in a kind of awkward position. I felt sorry for Mrs. Boyle and I knew she could keep working and do a good job. But I wanted a promotion. I wanted to be a manager and I was sick of waiting. It really burned me when I heard Lila telling her she should go to the Human Rights Commission, maybe take the company to court and set a precedent. Really stupid, I thought. You're not getting any younger, I wanted to say to her. You want Mrs. Boyle to work till she's ninety-five? Where will that get us? A big waste of your expensive suits, I wanted to say.

That young cop made Mrs. Boyle laugh like she wasn't sixty-five, but I was so mad I had to go into the back room for an hour. I sat on a stool and looked at the glass vases lined up on the shelves waiting for flowers and it was all I could do to keep from swiping at the whole lot of them. Me, the one who thought she could star in a movie, in the same category as Mrs. Boyle with her white hair and polyester pantsuits. There was a mirror in the back room and I had a good look at myself in it.

The truth is, the young cop was right. Lila was pretty and I wasn't. I had never been pretty, not even when Howard fell in love with me. Mrs. Boyle had probably never been pretty either. She would have been one of those girls who have some feature that makes them stick out as being weird or unnaturally ugly. Like a really big nose. Or an especially long neck. Or hair so thin you're sure they're going to go bald before they go grey. I couldn't pick out any particular feature on Mrs. Boyle now that she was old, but I was sure she'd had one when she was younger.

Sitting on a stool in the back room, I looked at the row of vases waiting for flowers and wondered how she ever got to be Mrs. Boyle instead of staying Miss Boyle for her whole life. I wondered where Mr. Boyle came from. Mail order, I decided. Mrs. Boyle's father got worried when she turned twenty-seven or so and was still unmarried, so he started looking through magazines for a mail-order husband from the Philippines. Those magazines have mostly girls, I know, but there must be a few men who'll marry anybody to get into Canada. And that's where Mr. Boyle came from and then he probably died from some Canadian disease he had no immunity to. Thinking about that was really depressing. To be one of those girls who have such a hard time finding anybody to marry, and then finding one who up and dies. And me put in the same category as one of those girls by some stupid, pimply faced excuse for a cop. It was almost too much to bear. I wanted to scream, "I had one once, and it was me who left. Me. Not him." But I started to cry instead and Mrs. Boyle had to send me home for the afternoon. She thought I was upset about Lila.

That's the good thing about people like Mrs. Boyle. They sometimes turn into mothering types. Her sort of looking out for me is what made me think she liked me especially, led me to believe I had the job for sure.

I didn't think of it at the time, but Dennis probably saw my going home that day as a golden opportunity. Who knows what happened after I left. He probably stepped in and hustled around to help Mrs. Boyle out and make a good impression, try to get her to like him as much as she likes me. I thought Dennis was just one of those good-looking, friendly kids who don't have a whole lot going on between their ears. Then he turns around and stabs me in the back. It just goes to show, you can't trust anybody.

It's almost lunchtime and the flower man should be phoning soon. Business has been slow this morning and Dennis is hanging around in the back room with Mrs. Boyle. If he hasn't many deliveries he'll likely be hanging around out front all afternoon trying to look like a manager. Well, he's going to need a lot of practice. Dennis looks about as much like a manager as some high school kid just off the basketball court. I suppose I'll have to get used to him. If I decide to stay, that is. Maybe I'll apply for his delivery job. If I were the truck driver I'd get to take the roses to the apartment on Ninety-first Street. That would be something.

I've been thinking about that man for the whole two years he's been one of our customers. I've held off asking questions, though, because I figured you couldn't pry into a customer's personal affairs if you wanted to be manager of the shop. I do know the apartment is empty. Dennis found that out after no one answered the door three months in a row. He asked the caretaker, who said the apartment had been empty for several years, but that a man continued to pay rent on it. Dennis wanted to stop delivering the flowers after that, but Mrs. Boyle said he had to. The man made us promise.

It occurs to me I don't have anything to lose any more. I'm sure as hell not going to hang around here until Dennis retires, then have the telephone repairman become the manager instead of me. Why shouldn't I pry, poke around a bit, ask the flower man a question or two? It wouldn't hurt, of course, to exercise a little discretion. I do have an apartment to keep up, groceries to buy, payments to make on my television set. I don't get any money from Howard, never have. Not that I deserve any after deserting him in his hour of need. And his hour of need is just what it was. That old saying is true. Behind every good man is a good woman. And Howard's good woman up and walked out on him when he was getting close to the top of the ladder, just when he needed her most. Maybe he didn't show that he was suffering on the surface; Howard wouldn't. But inside, he ached for me. He probably checked the obituaries every night in the paper, maybe still does. He probably called the police and reported a missing person. He may even have hired a private investigator. Not that that would have helped him. I didn't just walk out; I really went out of my way not be found, dyed my hair and changed my name and everything. I feel kind of bad about that now. I didn't have to go to that much trouble to keep Howard from tracking me down. I should have given him at least a sporting chance.

As it was, he couldn't stand living in that apartment without me. He couldn't even stand keeping the same job. I tried to call him a month or so after I'd left, just to see how he was doing. The number was "no longer in service." I called his boss and he told me Howard didn't work there any more. I drove around in my Camaro looking for him, worried sick about what I'd done to him. Every once in a while I'd catch sight of him somewhere, but whenever I'd get close he'd disappear.

The telephone rings just before noon, right on time. I don't have to worry about Dennis rushing out to take the call. Dennis, like Lila, figures the man's a kook with enough money to throw forty bucks down the garbage chute every month. I don't think he's a kook. I think he's a man with a broken heart. He's been devastated by someone, a woman, and he's suffering, hurting where most people don't even have places. You can't dismiss that as lightly as people are inclined to.

This morning, the same cool but courteous voice places the order. A dozen long-stemmed roses to Medford Arms on Ninety-first Street. Suite 712. Afternoon delivery. Cash payment will be sent in the mail. If the flowers are accepted, phone this number. If not, throw them away. He'll take his business elsewhere if he finds out the flowers have been sold to another customer. He says goodbye.

"Wait," I say quickly. He's silent on the other end. You can have me, is what I really want to tell him. You can have me, body and soul. Instead I say, "I have something to ask you."

"No, you don't," the man says and hangs up.

Well, I don't blame him. Why should he want to talk to me? He doesn't know that I could give him more than he could ever hope to have with her. I could mend his broken heart.

The reason I know so much about broken hearts is because of Howard and what I did to him. The man's voice has blue written all over it. Grey-blue like the rain, like the hint of colour in the display windows of the shop. I wonder if they're tinted or if it's just the reflection of the bank across the street? The building has some kind of blue tiles on the outside of it. The cars passing make shadows on the surface of the building and turn it into an ocean complete with surf. A city bus shakes the pavement and creates a tidal wave.

Mrs. Boyle comes from the back room where she and Dennis have been busy looking over inventory lists. She's going to stay on for a month after Dennis takes over, but she wants to have everything in perfect order when she leaves. She asks me why I haven't gone for lunch yet.

Lunch. I look at the clock and realize I've been standing with the telephone receiver in my hand for fifteen minutes, ever since the flower man hung up. I quickly put the phone back on the hook and zip out the front door.

I didn't bring an umbrella this morning, but I like the rain. I decide to walk around for half an hour. Who cares if I look like a wet cocker spaniel. Mrs. Boyle won't say anything, not today she won't. She knows I'm upset about not getting the job. At least she thinks

I'm upset. I'm not really. I don't care. I might even quit. I might quit, track down Howard and move back in with him. That would show everyone.

It takes time to figure things out. I'm not going to quit and I'm not going back to Howard. A week of thinking about it has reminded me that I left Howard for a reason. Not a very good one, maybe, but a reason nonetheless. I'm guilty, sure, but that's not going to make things any better. I'm no salesman's wife. And Howard is never going to give up selling to sail around the world with me on a freighter. Broken heart or no broken heart, he's going to have to live without me.

I've thought about this job thing over the past week and I feel much better. Dennis starts his new job next Monday and I know what will happen. He won't be able to do it. They'll have to make him delivery boy again and they'll see that I'm the one they should have given the job to in the first place.

I must have been really upset without knowing it. Imagine me thinking I could move back in with Howard. People get crazy ideas when they're upset about something. I don't look so terrible either. That young cop must have been trying to warn me in a sort of off-hand way. He didn't want to insult Mrs. Boyle by telling me to be especially careful because I was just as pretty as Lila. You can't say things like that when there's another person who is obviously flawed standing right there.

It's a nice sunny morning and I've decided to get off the train two stops before I usually get off. That gives me about a half-hour walk to the flower shop. I left my apartment early so I'd have time to poke along, looking at things, listening to sounds. I do that a lot. I make up stories about people I see, what's happening in their lives, what's going on behind those doors and windows, who's in control. Of course you can only imagine so much, only what you know yourself. Things might be completely different from what they seem to me.

I can see a woman right now, hanging out of a third-storey apartment window. There's a clothesline in front of her and a basket of clothes on the fire escape. She's screaming. Quite a few people have stopped to stare. Someone must have stolen the clothes from her line. Yes, that's it. She set out a second basket of clothes to hang, then noticed the first had disappeared. Someone stole her clothes, for God's sake. There are people in this world with no morals, no compassion. How do you deal with people like that? It has me beat. This poor woman desperately needs something from that first basket of clothes. Her baby's christening outfit. It's been in the family for years and her baby's supposed to be christened next Sunday and now the little white dress is gone. Things will never be the same for her. And there's nothing any of us can do. No need for any of us to interfere. It won't do any good. There's nothing to be said.

I walk on, really ticked off about what happened back there. Why her? Why, today of all days, would someone steal her baby clothes? I'm so mad I don't know if I'll be able to work. The day started okay because I figured out Dennis is going to lose that job before he hardly gets going. Now I'm just another pair of shoes walking down the sidewalk. In fact, I feel like the sidewalk is pushing me along, stopping me at the red lights, giving me friendly but firm nudges when the lights change. What the subway graffiti says is true. Life sucks and then you die. Some sidewalk pushes you along for fifty or sixty years, then gives you a shove into that big hole in the ground.

A taxi cruises slowly up the street past me. The driver is wearing reflector sunglasses and a cap, has his window rolled down and his arm hanging out. I notice a pack of cigarettes tucked into the rolled-up sleeve of his T-shirt. He stares at me, almost hits a parked car because he's staring. It's a really close call. Why is he staring at me? Maybe he recognizes me from the flower shop. He bought flowers once for his girlfriend or his mother. Or maybe it's the young cop. That's it. It's the young cop in disguise. He's looking for Lila's killer. He's following me because he's worried about me.

Whoever killed Lila might be after me too. He might have come into the flower shop and seen both Lila and me. He might be watching my apartment, waiting to get me alone somewhere. Good thing I got off the train when I did. The last stop before the shop is a lonely one. Hardly anyone gets off and there's a tunnel you have to walk through to get out of the station. I should probably start getting off at a different stop every day. Randomly selected. A little shiver runs through me, but I feel better about life because it seems I did something right this morning, getting off the train when I did.

When I get to work I immediately begin filling the card trays on the counter by the till. *Best Wishes on Your Retirement. Deepest Sympathy. For a Dear Friend.* No standing around this morning. I feel strangely energetic.

An hour later, the taxi driver starts to nag me again. It's not the business about the killer, that's too far-fetched. There was something familiar about him though, more familiar than a customer would have been, more familiar than the young cop. About noon it hits me. The taxi driver looked an awful lot like Howard. Not that I'd ever seen Howard with reflector sunglasses on, or any sunglasses at all for that matter, but there are some things you can't hide. An aura, I suppose. Yes, the more I think about it, the more I think the taxi driver could have been Howard. By two o'clock, I'm convinced. The taxi driver was Howard, no doubt about it. Howard in disguise. Howard looking out for me because somehow he's heard about Lila being killed. Somehow he's made the connection between Lila and me. Maybe he's known where I was all along and he stays just a little ways behind me. Looking out for me.

Well, this is great. Just great. The first thing that goddamned Dennis does when he gets to be manager is fire me. I can't believe it. I'm sitting here in my apartment, having just been "let go," and I pick up last night's paper and see this job ad: *Sales and delivery personnel wanted for flower shop. Experience required. Apply in person.* He obviously had this planned. The ad doesn't say *chance for advancement* this time. Dennis, goddamn him, must be planning to stay for a while.

I cut the ad out of the paper and pin it to the bull's-eye of my dart board. I have it hanging on the wall directly across from the couch so I can throw darts while I'm watching TV. I'm a pretty good shot and there aren't very many holes in the wall. I'm just about to throw a few when the doorbell rings.

Damn. I don't want to talk to anyone, unless it's Dennis coming to tell me he's changed his mind. Or Howard, but I think I might have been mistaken about Howard in the taxi. I haven't seen him since. I've been watching for him and I haven't seen a thing. Not a goddamned thing.

"Who is it?" I shout, just in case.

"Lila's sister," a voice says through the door. "The Lila you used to work with."

Lila's sister? I didn't know Lila had a sister. What could she want with me? I consider going out the window and down the fire escape, but decide that wouldn't look very good. I should talk to her. I don't have to tell her I hated Lila. She probably won't ask me if I liked Lila. Why would she come here to ask me that? If she doesn't ask I won't say anything. I open the door.

A very overweight woman vaguely resembling Lila stands in the hallway. She's wearing a red poplin tent coat, the kind that's supposed to cover everything but never quite does.

"Lila would have wanted you to have these," she says, shoving a plastic clothes bag at me. "They don't fit me."

It seems like such an understatement I'm not sure what to say next. I sure as hell don't want Lila's clothes. I don't want any dead person's clothes and especially not Lila's.

"Maybe they'll fit you someday," I stammer. "You never know."

"I've been on a diet since I was eight years old," Lila's sister says. "I just keep getting fatter."

I reach out and take the clothes bag. It's too embarrassing, talking on such an intimate level with someone I've never met before. Something tells me I should invite her in, but I can't bear the thought of any further exchange.

She seems to sense this and leaves quickly. I haven't had to tell her I hated Lila. I didn't even have to say thank you for the clothes, which would have been dishonest because I don't want them.

The clothes, of course, are Lila's expensive suits. And her damned fake fingernails are in one of the pockets. Somehow, she planned this. It's like I'm the beneficiary of her will or something, and that gives me more than one motive for killing her. Everybody knows when you figure out the motive you've got the killer. Thank God for dumb cops. Still, I stick the fingernails in the sugar bowl and shove the suits down behind the couch in case they come.

It's the last Tuesday of the month again. The flower man will be calling the shop tomorrow morning. I wonder who will take his order, whether or not the man will recognize a different voice, ask about me. I wonder if the new delivery boy will follow the man's orders the way Dennis did, or if he'll simply throw the flowers into the first garbage bin he comes to. Surely he'll ring the apartment doorbell this one time at least. My plan depends on him ringing the doorbell.

I watch the clock all day, waiting for the cover of darkness. I've already checked out the balconies and climbing seven of them shouldn't be difficult as long as no one sees me. I should be able to stand on each one and shinny up to the next level. This will be fairly drastic action, I know, but I see no other way. I did try to figure out the flower man's address by going through the metropolitan area phone book entry by entry, searching for his number (which I have memorized), but I came to the conclusion it's unlisted. Break and enter, I figure, is the only way. If I get caught, I get caught.

Time passes so damned slowly when you have a plan. I don't know what to do with myself. I stare at Lila's suits. They're on the armchair where I piled them after I dug them out from behind the couch, kicking myself for that ridiculous attack of paranoia. As if the police would bother with me.

What do you wear with an expensive suit? Lila always wore light-coloured blouses, pure silk is my guess. I don't have anything like that. I do have a fancy black T-shirt with see-through lace around the neck. That would do for just trying on. Trying on is as far as this will go anyway. I'm sure as hell not planning to wear Lila's suits out in public. This is just to pass the time until tonight. When I look in the mirror it hits me that Lila's pink suit is a pretty damned good disguise.

It's Wednesday, just before noon, about the time the man phones the flower shop. The apartment is empty, just as the caretaker said. I've been here since four o'clock in the morning, having successfully picked the lock on the sliding patio doors. I'm glad my apartment doesn't have them. I've just proven any amateur can break in that way.

I limp around, favouring the knee I banged climbing over every one of the seven balconies. I look for clues. A hair on the carpet. A chip of a fingernail. A trace of perfume or hair spray in the air. Nothing. I find nothing to put together a picture of the flower man's lady friend. Until I get to the bathroom, where I find a gold mine in the medicine cabinet. She must have forgotten about it. Did I forget about the medicine cabinet when I left Howard? I wouldn't have left anything very interesting anyway. A box of Tampax and a toothbrush maybe. But this woman, she must have been a walking cosmetic counter. Makeup, cleansing creams, moisturizers, deodorant, shampoo, hair conditioner. You name it. Even hair dye. Brandy wine, whatever colour that might be. Sounds vaguely purple.

Hair dye. I look at my watch and figure there's another hour anyway before the flowers arrive.

The water's still hooked up. I bend over the sink, wet my hair and dab the gooey dye all over. I make the mistake of standing up to look in the mirror and it drips down my face and onto Lila's suit.

Shit. I want a disguise, not a Hallowe'en costume. I do my best to wring my hair out over the sink, then sit on the plush carpet by the fireplace to wait for the doorbell. I think about the time I dyed my hair to hide from Howard. I did it in the washroom at the airport, then dried it under the hand dryer. I wish I had a dryer now. The apartment is warm enough, but my wet hair makes me shiver.

The roses will be in a long box with a gold ribbon tied around it. No need to unwrap it. I already know what will be inside. Twelve long-stemmed with assorted greenery. A few of the blooms will be past their prime and I'll blame that on Dennis's mismanagement. He'll have figured they're just going to get thrown out. Little does he know. If I were manager I would never send shoddy roses. The man's a regular customer. He has a broken heart. He should get the best.

I wish I could see the look on Dennis's face when the new delivery boy tells him someone answered the door. I was originally planning to hide behind the door so Dennis couldn't figure out it was me from the kid's description. But now I don't think I'll bother. With Lila's pink wool suit and brandy wine hair I don't think I have to worry. Dennis will never in a million years think it was me. Lila come back from the dead, maybe, but not me.

I imagine that I have the box of roses in my arms.

"Ah, Howard," I say out loud. "You always were a romantic son-of-a-bitch." Then I laugh. It would have been fun to say that to Howard.

Try this. "Howie, Howie, Howie. I knew you'd find me some day. (Sigh) Where do we go from here?"

Sounds funny. Maybe it's the empty apartment. The acoustics are off.

I wonder if the Wednesday flower man will come after the roses are delivered. Yes, of course he will. Why else has he left instructions for contacting him? He will come, that's certain.

But what then? What if the goings on behind this closed door were other than what I supposed? My scenario, of course, has been that he will be disappointed that I'm not her, but glad all the same to have an understanding someone to talk to. And from there, who knows? Dinner. A movie. His place. A private yacht. Europe.

But as I sit here on the floor with the roses, other scenarios, moving pictures, begin to play on the wall across the room. The man is not a stranger after all, but someone I've seen before. A taxi driver passing slowly. A young policeman in disguise. A killer. Howard. I close my eyes to make the pictures go away, but they're inside my head. I open them again and see the red roses, red fingernails. Close. Open. Open. Close. It's hypnotizing, like someone swinging a watch on a chain in front of your eyes. Maybe it's because I was up all night, making my way up the balconies, wondering if the flowers would come. I doze off.

The doorbell. It rings and I jump to my feet and try to straighten up my hair. It's dry except for the side I was sleeping on. I hope the dye didn't leave any stains on my forehead and I pull my bangs down, using my fingers as a comb. No time to run to the bathroom and check to see how I look. However I look, it will have to do.

The ringing stops. I hurry to the door and open it in time to see a delivery boy throwing a box of flowers down the chute in the hallway. "Wait," I start to say, but he is already disappearing around a corner, disappearing so quickly I don't even see what he looks like. "Wait," I whisper, but he's gone. No flowers, no flower man.

What to do. Run after the delivery boy? Call the flower man myself and say the roses were delivered? Wait another month for another box of roses? What should I do? What would be best?

None of the above. It's a dark hour, I think, as I limp down the stairwell, a dark hour indeed. I leave the stained pink suit jacket hanging on the banister at the foot of the stairs and walk home.

Saturday morning. I've spent the last two days holed up in my apartment looking at the rest of Lila's suits. Then I woke up this morning and for some strange reason I wanted to go back to the flower shop. I don't want to go inside, but I'd kind of like to sneak a peek in the window, maybe see Dennis making a mess of everything.

It's pouring rain again, so I carry my umbrella. I take Lila's suits with me too, in a green garbage bag, and dump them into the Sally Ann drop-box just around the corner from the flower shop. After that's done I feel free. Her fingernails are still in my sugar bowl, but I might leave them there for a little remembrance.

No slow-cruising taxis today. They're all busy, going somewhere with a purpose, just like me. As I approach the shop, I see them, Dennis and Mrs. Boyle, in the big plate-glass display window, staring out at the rain. They look sad. They probably miss me. They're probably sorry about what they've done to me. Well, it's too late now. I do have a certain amount of pride.

There's a man across the street, up against the blue tile building, shaking the rain off his coat. He doesn't have an umbrella. I duck under an awning and stare at him. He begins to look familiar. If I didn't know better, I'd think it was Howard. He's fumbling in his pocket, pulling something out. Orange and green slips of paper the size of a business envelope. He looks across the street at me. He waves the papers in the air, waves them right at me, not caring if they get wet. It is Howard. Howard with two freighter tickets to Singapore. I cross the street without even a glance at the flower shop. Good old Howard. He'll be so happy to have me back.

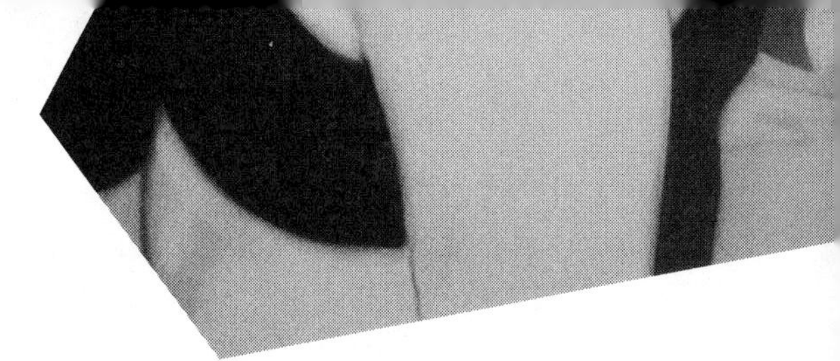

SOUVLAKI

JONATHAN GOLDSTEIN

JONATHAN GOLDSTEIN LIVES IN MONTREAL, WHERE HE MAKES BALLOON ANIMALS AT CORPORATE PARTIES AND WRITES EROTICA FOR SUCH PUBLICATIONS AS *BUTT TIME STORIES*. HE HAS SELF-PUBLISHED HIS WORK IN CHAPBOOKS SUCH AS *BLOW HARD POMES* AND *HEAD ON THE TABLE*. HE IS CURRENTLY WORKING ON HIS M.A. IN ENGLISH LITERATURE AT CONCORDIA UNIVERSITY.

The party, with its empty plastic bottles of spruce beer and the long lines for the bathroom, left me happy to be outside on the fire escape. I tried to touch a tree branch on my toes.

Inside, it was never the right time to ask for my raincoat back. I ended up writing it off entirely so I wouldn't have to think about it all night. I met her new roommate who was a school teacher. She had a face like the white lid on a toilet. She was standing around talking with two friends. They looked like neighbours running into each other on the way to the incinerator.

Her new boyfriend was pretty tall. I was talking to a cartoonist friend of mine. Tall said smilingly, “Doesn’t it smell of farts in here?” The cartoonist agreed.

At first she was this wild & drugged Pre-Raphaelite woman of china and ankle-length dresses, always coming dangerously close to tipping over. Then she became this golem of wet laundry hanging from my neck with clasped fingers, feet swinging off the ground. She found me in the kitchen looking at pictures on the fridge door. “I trashed all the photos of you,” she said. “You could have at least called to see if I wanted them,” I said. “But that was never an option,” she answered.

When we started seeing each other, she had a party that ended with everyone rushing out the door at three in the morning, looking for souvlaki. We went into her room and clamped ourselves into this very tight and serious sixty-nine that lasted until dawn when I asked her what heroin was like. “A slow trombone sliding through your veins.”

She looked like a sexy garbageman’s wife as she waved me off to work on her front porch in the morning. I would always poke my finger through the hole in her door where the lock would eventually go. I called it her psycho hole.

CRATES OF STARS

GOLDA FRIED

ORIGINALLY FROM TORONTO, HIPSTER GOLDA FRIED BECAME A FIXTURE IN THE BOOMING MONTREAL SPOKEN-WORD CIRCUIT WHILE WORKING ON HER M.A. IN CREATIVE WRITING AT CONCORDIA. SHE HAS TWO CHAPBOOKS IN PUBLICATION, *CHECK THE FLOOR* AND *HARTLEY'S STORIES*. AN UPCOMING COLLECTION OF STORIES IS ENTITLED *DARKNESS THEN A BLOWN KISS*. READING CHARLES BUKOWSKI ALLEVIATES SOME OF HER URBAN ANGST, AS DOES KNOWING THERE ARE STILL SIDEWALKS.

I catch myself bringing a broken umbrella inside. Umbrellas mean nothing to me outside. I'd rather walk the streets proving the rain does not affect me. And this umbrella is crashing crimson. I hang it on my closet door like I gave my apartment a big kiss and wished it good luck in the beauty contest. And just maybe I'd come out looking like a star to certain people far away. Forever I despised red. It clashed with my orange hair. But now I relate it to boldness and lipstick and wounds. And besides, my apartment was all white.

I was pissin' in the bathroom of the Cinema de Paris, really getting into the sound, and this girl comes in blushing, amused.

"Do you always leave the door open when you're on the can?"

I answer, "Well, never, and I just thought I'd see what it was like."

She had three different lipstick utensils out by now, and I saddled up on the counter and overtly stared. This girl must really believe she's in Paris.

"You must be on a date."

"Well, if we're getting personal," she retorted, "tell me why do you cramp over the toilet seat and not sit down?"

"I've been doing that forever. And it's faster, I guess."

"You're a real in-out, huh? Well, thank God I'm not going out with you."

Well, I think I've spent enough time in the bathroom. I head for the door and this girl goes, "Hey, I know I don't know you and all, but do you think you could walk me home? I don't live that far and the guy I'm here with is really creeping me out. He seemed real energetic and full of passion when he'd talk to me in film class, but now I just don't want him to know where I live, ya know?"

"Yeah, sure."

By the time I walked her home, we had made a drinking date for the next night. And that is how I met Christina.

Sandals through puddles. This girl's gonna think I'm weird. But we're marchin' down the street under her umbrella in linked arms. We just met yesterday. I tell her I want to meet a sailor and she drinks up her beer like a fish and all the seal-looking jackets in here are drowning. Who would've thought she was dreaming of Texas?

"Black gold."

"What do you mean he's black gold?" There was a ghost in her room, like a local call that felt all too long distance. "Is he some sort of superstar bumblebee?"

"More of a dark star."

And then we did the whole walk-through of past relationships. But if this talk was a house, we only did hallways, because the tour of Christina stopped at the tea room. Her past was shiny. And with her platinum hair and red lipstick she was a star herself.

And all Marilyn Monroe, she tells me she could never have a boyfriend that meant anything after James Dean. (Mark later told me that she was the one who used to follow him around the library for weeks until she finally said hi.) And then we get to me and who have you dated from Sunset Boulevard?

I had to be moving on.

"Can I come see your place?" she asked me.

Well, my place seemed pretty lame and I just felt like saying no all over so, of course, I did and that was that. But that night in my cosy bed there were stars in my teacup, the kind you get when you think a really cool person might just be your friend.

I was interviewing her about relationships. We were all documentary/cinema verité types that year. "So when you meet a guy, what do you find cuter: clumsiness or someone who steals ashtrays?" (Christina giggles.) This may seem like a simple question, but in my experience people who steal ashtrays usually lose them pretty fast. However, if they're clumsy, they're probably not going to be conceited. But then there's some people who selectively steal ashtrays and their bedrooms are more interesting than any museum I was dragged to as a kid. Anyway, I really felt like getting into ashtray philosophy, but who was I kidding? Christina, in this dark bar, was way behind sunglasses. The type that starts trends. Still, it was the kind of thing you wish you had thought of first because she was smiling all over the place.

"So, do you think I could come home with you on the train sometime to Halifax?" Christina asked me, still at the bar. "I've never been."

"Well, I'm not going home till the end of the year." Then, "Hey, you're done this year. What are you going to do after?"

"Well, I'm from the States, right? But I can't go back to my home town. No way."

"Where's Mark from?"

"Some small town out West. I don't know." And then Christina actually came out with, "You're going to work as a secretary for your dad, huh?"

"No, I am not. I told you, I hate when people say that. I've got to be travelling more than that."

"Well, so far you've just been crating books around, honey."

"You're a schoolgirl, too. Give me a break."

"All right, all right. I just want to make sure you're having some fun. Do you see anyone here that you find interesting?"

"I can't look like that," I told her. "I'd rather take the lets-see-what-drifts-up-on-my-shore approach and does it shine."

Last gulp. "Hey, listen, can we go back to your place and make some Kraft dinner or something? I'm starving."

"Fuck that," she says. "I have salad stuff."

As we were leaving the bar, I saw her steal an ashtray.

So I tried to make the avocado more ripe by sticking it in her microwave. It came up in every conversation she had on the phone for the next hour as I waited in the kitchen. The microwave still seemed like a perfectly natural solution to me. That night I ordered pizza for us. I asked for vegetarian and it came with everything from artichokes to zucchini. We were especially starving. Christina, opening up the cover, said, "It fuckin' looks like a box of jewels, man. Right on."

This guy salooned through her door and he was all zippo lighter and pacing the room and he had a small box or something in his black leather coat pocket which he handled like a gun.

"That's Mark," she mouthed, hand over her lips and everything. He wouldn't sit down.

"Christina, I've got to talk to you."

He dragged her towards the bathroom, the first door he could find, and she looked at me like what could she do, he was dragging her. Slam. I waited for a bit and there was a lot of noise. Laughing, I guess, and shouting and fun-shrieking.

I pictured that he was tying her to some train tracks and they think a train is coming but it's him and they get the hell out of there and laugh about how he abducted her and saved her all in one. Isn't that how the story went?

I finally left when I heard the shower go on.

The next time I saw her, she kept saying, "He's so intense, he's so intense," and that's all she could say. I thought, Right on. I was really happy for her, I swear. For the few minutes I saw him he did seem really intense.

Christina and I used to light cigarettes off the burner. Wait till it was red hot. One time it looked so innocently dark again and leaning over I scalded my whole arm. "Jesus Christ," I said. "Just when I was having a non-bumping-into-furniture day." Still, I spent half an hour that night staring at the purple bruises.

#@?! #@?!

{Stella} {Stella} I was dreaming.

(Christina!) (Christina!) Bang Kick Kabink.

Christina came out of her bedroom looking genuinely helpless. I wasn't passed out on her sofa any more.

"Christina!"

"What am I going to do," Christina said. "I can't let him in here."

"It's raining and he's only wearing a T-shirt," I said, peering out the window. "Christina, what happened? I thought you really liked Mark?"

"I do, but if I let him in this time, I'm really going to get hurt."

BANG BANG KICK.

"Listen, he's not just going to go away."

"Yes he is going away. He's going back to Calgary for sure. He told me."

"Yeah, but that's in three months. Maybe you'll go with him."

"He's not going to ask me, I know it."

"Christina, if you let him in you're going to be all over each other and everything's going to be roses."

"You open the door."

God, I felt awkward.

They came at each other with knives and gave each other new haircuts. Fun was going to the all night Pharmaprix and getting hair dye – the kind that washes out. Espionage was catching the security guard dancing to the Muzak in the aisles. Hope flashed with Christina's camera when she took a picture of Mark. Just in case.

I know that chances of this being true are infinitesimal, but according to the way I perceive the world: stars are very fast-moving molecules that rarely get to come in contact with other stars. But when the temperature gets colder and the molecules slow down, they can spend more time together and bonding can take place. Each star feels recharged and electrocuted at the same time. Bright stars tend to get brighter. Dark stars get darker. But if the temperature gets too cold, stars, being stars, will not become solid, but will break so that even their internal bonds will bust and the stars won't even know which atoms from the periodical chart they have. Sooner or later, the stars reform and orbit on, but they've acquired new parts like stolen ashtrays. And the world gets pretty cold. Hence, all the divorce announcements in *People* magazine.

"Liking snow is like liking dandruff," some girl was telling her creepazoid boyfriend. And he wasn't a skier, he was just stark raving instigating her. In the true Montreal spirit we all came out in this twenty-eight-degrees-below weather to party. I was huddled in the corner thinking something's weird with Christina.

She was floating around with glitter on her eyelids and it wasn't even a disco party. That much was her fun self. Then I realized the weird thing was not only was she avoiding me, but she wasn't with Mark.

Meanwhile, some slimebucket came and sat beside me and started whispering in my ear that he'd just strolled into town and is this what Montreal had to offer.

I heard my friend Keith's guitar somewhere and went electric. He was right by Anita, too, who was handing out ruby globs of jello made with vodka. Five jellos and two more conversations that just bounced off me later, I was feeling like there was a neon sign and flashing in my head. And realizing that this was probably as turned on as I was going to get that night, I stumbled into the bedroom to get my jacket.

There was the infamous couple-on-the-bed. Okay, they're not interested in you; you can get your jacket and they won't even notice. Then it turned out to be fucking Christina there with Slimebucket lapping up the inside. Needless to say I missed the bucket most unfortunately and puked off the balcony feeling sea-sick or something.

I should have grabbed her right then and yelled what are you doing #@?!, but at the time it was a bloody mess.

She thinks there is no blood in Texas. Only desert and white pages for her to work on a screenplay and plenty of sand to go through the hourglass while she's working on it. And she knows some guy in the industry down there, too. But she's left him before.

Some things get so familiar and then never happen again.

"He's been dicking around on me," she confided.

I guess that was my cue to step in as a friend. You know, I wanted to be the one. The best friend that was a vital phenomenon since kindergarten. We had talked often about her taking the train to see me in Halifax. She was going to send me her colourful stories from all over the galaxy where she did her film shoots, filmed shoots. Be the favourite aunt when I have kids. But I just couldn't roll out the sympathy – I would leave that to her phone mates.

"Christina, how can you complain about Mark when I saw you messing around with some slimebucket at Anita's party?"

Mouth wide open, she just couldn't say anything. Nodding her head and sighing, she scurried into her room and slammed the door.

Shit. "Christina, open the goddam door. If that was the wrong thing to say, why don't you just goddam tell me what's really going on!"

Door.

I left. And she actually rained dishes on me from the window! Cut my cheek. "You don't know me at all," she screamed. "Not at fucking all."

I kept walking.

It's too dry in Texas. I just can't see her there. I know that much. And then there's me who thinks everything will be all wet down by the waterfront docks with sailors coming in and out of my life just how I always planned it. But I started to wonder if there was a place on the map that was sticky.

Christina was gone. Texas bound. And I was going back to Halifax but to my own new apartment. Mark asked me if he could stay with me for a while until he could get a lift back to Calgary. We did our own thing and didn't talk very much. Still, I knew he was cool jazz though I am forever rock and roll. And then, on his last night in Montreal, we were both up late doing stuff and I had a craving for a vanilla milkshake way after eleven when most places were closed. He was all into walking the streets with me. We were on a *mission*. We finally found a restaurant that was open and served milkshakes.

"So is it just going to be milkshakes alone for us then?"

Well, for me, it was going to be the ol' slim milk carton as someone's sick idea of a hangover every morning for breakfast. But that's not what I really asked.

"So, what's gonna happen with you and Christina?"

And God this guy rides horses and the sunset's happening tomorrow and I'm probably never going to see him again and why aren't we friends and forget about me, what about Christina, the only cowgirl I've ever met, and I know she's singin' the blues though she won't tell me about it either.

And he just goes, "Well, I'm going back to Calgary. And that is that."

And I thought: So we're all just going to be crating stars around in milk crates then. And God, we were all impossible.

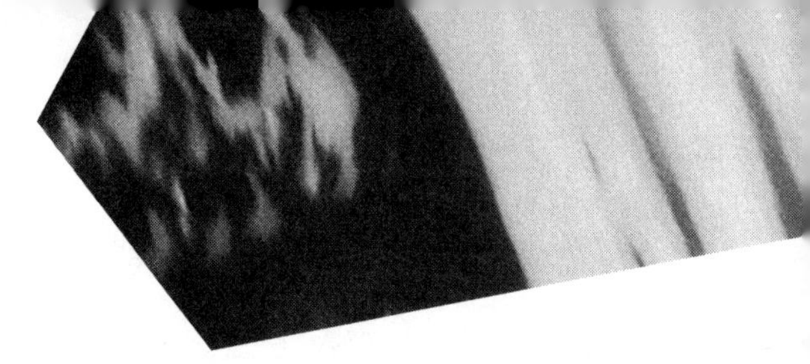

STARGAZE

DEREK MCCORMACK

ALTHOUGH THE RETICENT DEREK MCCORMACK LIVES IN TORONTO, HE CONTINUES TO FOCUS HIS LURID IMAGINATION ON THE HYPOTHETICAL HISTORY OF HIS HOMETOWN OF PETERBOROUGH, ONTARIO. BOTH HIS ACCLAIMED FIRST NOVEL, DARK RIDES, FROM WHICH "STARGAZE" APPEARS, AND HIS JUST COMPLETED SECOND NOVEL, WISH BOOK, ARE SET IN THAT MYTHICAL PAST. IN TORONTO, MCCORMACK CONTINUES TO ELUDE REALITY AND STARVATION BY WORKING AT AN INDEPENDENT BOOKSTORE.

From Peterborough I took the Greyhound. I checked into Toronto General Hospital. My room was a bed, a chair, a closet. A barred window. Streetcars sparked past in the night.

First thing in the morning I was sitting in Dr. Vine's office.

"Age?" he said.

"Eighteen," I said. "Sir."

He scribbled on my chart. "How long have you been aware of your inversion?"

I breathed deep. "Eighteen years."

In the examining room I stripped and stretched out on a gurney. He girded my shins and arms, rolled an electric generator up to me. Taped electrodes to my penis and scrotum.

He said, "I'd like you to describe your fantasies involving men."

I shut my eyes. I spoke about kissing Gary Cooper's lips and nipples and stomach and –

Dr. Vine shocked me.

Back in my room I cupped my balls in my palm. Legs cramped. After a couple of hours I signed out at the nurses' station and went down to the street.

The July sun. I shuffled north, past Queen's Park and Victoria University. At the Royal Ontario Museum I bought a ticket and wandered into an auditorium where people sat in dentists' chairs under a plaster dome. The usher seated me as the house lights died.

Over loudspeakers: "Welcome to the Milky Way."

Constellations brightened overhead – the Pleiades, Cepheus, Andromeda –

The auditorium seemed to spin. I gasped.

Come morning Dr. Vine strapped me down and hooked me up and showed me photographs of naked hulks with brush cuts flexing their biceps.

I glanced from them to him. He was drumming his fingertips against the pictures, nails yellow, uncut. My penis limp.

"You're not concentrating," he said. He lined the pictures up on an easel. He ripped the electrodes off my privates and pressed them to my temples.

I blacked out.

I walked to the planetarium. Sat near the projector. It was dumbbell shaped, fifteen feet long. Lying lengthwise it projected the night skies of the northern and southern hemispheres. Then it tilted. At a twenty-degree angle it shot out images of the planets. It tilted again and suddenly the sun filled the dome.

In the morning in Dr. Vine's office. I took off my clothes.

"You're extremely tense," he said. "Can you tell me why?"

"Because you really hurt me yesterday," I said.

"You're generalizing." He wheeled the generator closer. He wired my temples. "Your behaviour," he said. "Your behaviour is what hurts. Isn't that so?"

"Yes but I'm not sure –"

He ordered me to think men. Nude men.

"I can't, I'm too nervous."

"Close your eyes *now*!"

I came to in my room, my pillow bloody. I'd bitten my tongue.

At the Greyhound depot I bought Popsicles. My lips were grape when I pulled into Peterborough.

I tramped home to bed. Clouds blanking out the stars.

Didn't catch a wink till dawn. My alarm went off and I ignored it. Sometime after noon the telephone rang. I picked it up.

It was Dr. Vine. "Admitting told me you'd checked out," he said.

My legs cramped.

"I'm expecting you bright and early tomorrow."

"No it's okay," I stammered. "I think I'm cured."

"If you're not here in the morning I'll be forced to contact your parents. Or the police."

I threw on some clothes and dashed downstreet. The bookstore had nothing. Likewise Hampton's Novelty Shop. At Turnbull's Department Store I snatched up a celestial map and a copy of *The Amateur Astronomer's Guide.*

"You been to the Ex?" the saleslady said. She showed me a flyer for the Peterborough Exhibition. Listed among the attractions – "Science Fair and Planetarium."

I hopped the next bus to the fairgrounds. I tore into the Recreation Centre. Representing Science were an ant farm and a model of Peterborough's hydraulic liftlock. A pâpier-maché sun dangled from a ceiling fan. Nine styrofoam orbs twirled around it.

The solar system.

"That's it?" I said, punching my hip. "That's it?"

I trudged out into the midway. Wall-to-wall people. Kids swarming The Haunted House, The Caterpillar, The Chairplane. The moon a fingernail clipping.

I staggered up against a cotton candy stand and shut my eyes. When I opened them I saw a dumbbell tilting in midair. It was cherry red, studded with lights. Instead of weights it had cages full of screaming people.

I fell onto my back, hands pillowing my head, heavenly bodies whirring across the sky.

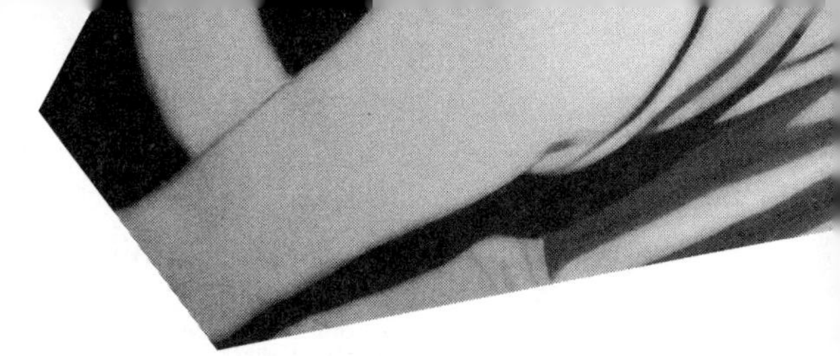

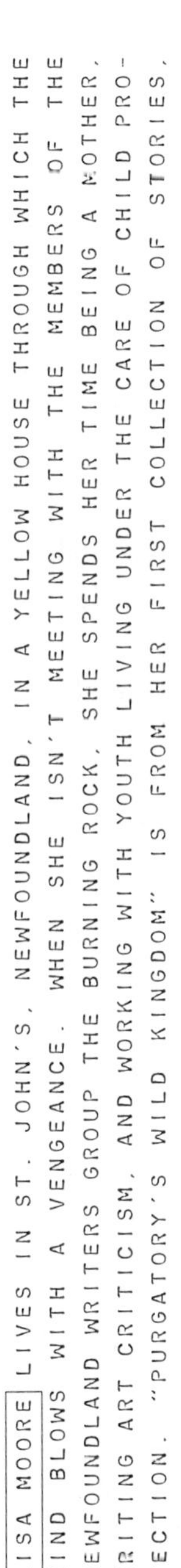

LISA MOORE LIVES IN ST. JOHN'S, NEWFOUNDLAND, IN A YELLOW HOUSE THROUGH WHICH THE
WIND BLOWS WITH A VENGEANCE. WHEN SHE ISN'T MEETING WITH THE MEMBERS OF THE
NEWFOUNDLAND WRITERS GROUP THE BURNING ROCK, SHE SPENDS HER TIME BEING A MOTHER,
WRITING ART CRITICISM, AND WORKING WITH YOUTH LIVING UNDER THE CARE OF CHILD PRO-
TECTION. "PURGATORY'S WILD KINGDOM" IS FROM HER FIRST COLLECTION OF STORIES,
DEGREES OF NAKEDNESS.

PURGATORY'S WILD KINGDOM

LISA MOORE

Julian is thinking about the woman and child he left in Newfoundland when he moved to Toronto. He's remembering Olivia preparing him a sardine sandwich, the way she laid each sardine on a paper towel and pressed the extra oil out of it. Then she cut off the heads and tails and laid the sardines out carefully on the bread. Her head was bent over the cutting board, her blond hair slid from behind her ear. He could see the sun sawing on her gold necklace. The chain stuck on her skin in a twisty path that made him realize how hot it was in the apartment. She was wearing a flannel pajama top and nothing else, a coffee-coloured birthmark on her thigh. Eight years ago.

Julian is sitting at the kitchen table with a pot of coffee. His bare feet are drawn up on the chair, his knees pressed into the edge of the table. It's a wooden table top that has been rubbed with linseed oil. There are scars from the burning cigarettes his wife occasionally leaves lying around. Small black ovals. There are thousands of knife cuts that cross over each other like the lines on a palm. He runs his finger over the table, tracing the grain of the wood. He pours another cup of coffee and glances at the phone. Sometimes the university calls for Marika before ten, although they have been told not to. Marika requires only seven hours sleep, but if she's disturbed she's tired all day. She wakes up exactly at ten every morning. She's proud of the precision of her inner clock. Julian likes to pick up the phone before it rings twice. Lately the phone has been ringing and when Julian answers, nobody speaks.

Marika is fifteen years older than Julian. The people on this street are very rich. The brick houses are massive. Some of them have been divided into apartments and rented. There's almost no traffic. The trees block most of the noise. He and Marika don't know their neighbours. Once, while out taking photographs, Julian met a man three houses up who was riding a sparkling black bike in circles. The man said he was Joe Murphy, of Joe Murphy's Chips, and they sold a large percentage of their chips in Newfoundland. He gave the silver bicycle bell two sharp rings.

"The bike's a birthday present from my wife. It's a real beauty, isn't it?"

The trees shivered suddenly with wind and sloshed the bike with rippling shadows. Joe Murphy was wearing a suit and tie. The balls of his feet pressed against the pavement, and there were sharp little crevices in his shined leather shoes. Julian noticed a crow leave a tree and fly straight down the centre of the street. He lifted his camera and took a picture of Joe Murphy. In the far distant corner of the frame is the crow. Julian leaves Joe Murphy out of focus, a blur in the centre of the picture, his face full of slack features. The crow is sharp and black.

"That makes me very uncomfortable," said Joe Murphy. "I think you have a nerve." He gave the bell another sharp ring, and pushed off the curb. His suit jacket flapped on either side of him.

For the past two years Julian has been sleeping a lot. It's taken him two years to fall away from any kind of sleeping pattern. This way he's always awake at different hours. This seems exotic to him, but the cost is that he can't will himself to sleep. He sleeps in the afternoon and then finds himself awake at four in the morning. At dawn he's sometimes wandering around the neighbourhood. The light at dawn allows him to see straight into the front windows of the massive houses on their street, all the way to the back windows and into the backyards. It makes the houses seem like skeletons, with nothing hanging on the bones.

Sometimes Julian is asleep when Marika gets home from work. If there's no supper cooked for her she'll eat white bread and butter with spoonfuls of granulated sugar. Julian likes to cook for her and she likes what he cooks. But she's also happy to eat bread and sugar. She makes coffee and folds the bread and sinks it into her coffee. The soaked bread topples and she catches it in her mouth. The cats slink in from all the different rooms of the apartment and curl around her feet, or on her lap. She lifts the kitten and puts it inside her jacket. If Julian stumbles down the stairs, half awake, and he sees Marika bathed in the light of a baseball game on TV with her sugared bread, he feels that he has failed her. The sense of failure makes him even sleepier. He can't keep his eyes open.

Marika is not one for dwelling on the past. Julian knows very little about her past. Not that she's secretive. It's just that conversing about the past bores her. Marika has a powerful charm. She's a physics professor, but most of her friends are artists or writers. At parties, for conversation, she offers crystallized stories about nature or the stars. If someone interrupts her to ask about her parents, or something back in France, you can see the charm moving out of her face like a receding blush. She answers in only one or two sentences, faltering.

She thinks of memory only as a muscle that must be exercised to keep the whole mind sharp. She is interested in sharpness. If asked, she could recall exactly what she did on any date two years ago, she will remember what she wore, what Julian wore, what they ate, the content of any conversation that occurred on that day. But this is just a game.

Marika thinks about infinite tracts of time, about meteorology, about hummingbirds, about measuring the erosion of coastlines, and about whether the continents could still lock together like a jigsaw puzzle or a jaw grinding in sleep. She thinks about fish that swim up the walls of fjords as if the walls were the lake bottom or the tower of Babel. What such swimming against the stream does to their skeletons. When she isn't thinking things like this, she watches baseball, or drives in her car, or cooks, or she and Julian make love.

Julian has watched Marika simulate theoretical galaxies on the computer. She has found this program mostly to amuse him. He has seen two galaxies blinking together, dragging their sluggish amorphous bodies toward each other across the black screen. Each blink represents a million years, until they pass through each other. The gravitational pull of each galaxy affects the shape of the other until some stars are clotted in the centre, and the rest spread on either side of the screen like giant butterfly wings. Marika has shown him thousands of things like this. She has described the path of the plague in the Middle Ages, drawing a map on a paper napkin at Tim Horton's. She told him that in Egypt they have found the preserved body of a louse, on the comb of Nefertiti. A drop of human blood, perhaps Nefertiti's blood, was contained in the abdomen of the louse. They have discovered many things about ancient disease from that one drop of blood.

Julian collects every story Marika tells him. They often lose their scientific edges. He can't remember how old the louse was. For some reason the only thing he remembers about the plague is a costume. It was a long robe with the head of a bird. The doctor looked out through two holes cut in the feathered hood, over a protruding beak.

When he is awake, Julian also pursues the moral of these stories, something other than what lies on the surface. Just as he can't imagine how much time it took to create the universe from a black hole, he can't get at that hidden meaning.

Recently Marika contracted a virus, a nervous disorder. If not diagnosed, this disease can spread quickly through the body and destroy the tips of all nerve endings irreparably. It started with a numbness in Marika's left cheek. She had it checked immediately. Of course, she had access to the best medical care in Toronto. The disease was arrested before any serious damage was done, but the nerves in Marika's saliva ducts grew back connected to her tear duct. Now when she eats her left eye waters.

Julian has begun to suspect that Marika doesn't talk about her past because she is afraid she will seem like an old woman. It was the eye, filling of its own accord, that started him thinking this way. The eye is the first sign of Marika's age. When her eye waters he's filled with fright. That fright causes its own involuntary response in him. He's remembering things he hasn't thought about in years. He has noticed that the skin on Marika's face looks older than before. The pores are larger. There are more wrinkles. The soft white pouches beneath her eyes are larger. That skin seems as vulnerable to him as the flesh of a pear he is about to bite.

He was going through their wedding photographs. He took them himself, so most of the pictures are of Marika. She is wearing a white silk jacket, cut like a lab coat, and the apartment is full of white blossoms. Her face looks so much younger that for a moment he has the feeling the photographs have been doctored.

They're eating a dinner of lamb and fresh mint. Marika's knife is whining back and forth on the dinner plate.

"Could you stop that noise?"

Marika's body jerks, as if she didn't realize he was sitting beside her.

"I was just lost in thought. Thinking of crabs."

A tear is running down her cheek.

"In Guatemala," she says, "there's a species of crab that burrows into the ground and brings up in its claws shards of ancient pottery."

She lays down her knife and wipes a tear off her cheek with the back of her hand.

"The crabs descend beneath layer after layer to different cities that have been piled on top of each other, over time. Each city is hundreds of years younger than the one below it. The crabs mix all the pottery shards together, all these ancient layers mixed together in the light of day. You really know very little about me. You know nothing about science."

Julian notices that both Marika's eyes are watering now and realizes she's crying.

In his dreams the stories Marika tells him are fables. He dreams about a crab that presents him with a jacket of glass shards that came from a wine bottle he once threw at Olivia. Olivia wears a cloak of stars, she opens her arms and the cloak is wrenched away from her, leaving her naked. She becomes two women, a blurred image, Marika and Olivia both.

That night Julian leaves the house at midnight and walks for hours. Outside the Royal Ontario Museum the moonlit gargoyles are covered with burlap bags, and look like robbers with nylon stockings over their faces. A group of five people dressed in cartoon costumes emerges from a church basement. They skip across the empty street and get into an idling minivan. A man in a Pink Panther costume trails behind. He has removed the head of the costume and carries it under his arm. The man's own head looks abnormally small against the giant pink neck of the costume. Julian takes a picture of him.

Lately, Julian thinks about a memory lit with a big number one candle, a wax monkey wrapped around it. Julian carried the cake. He could feel the yellow of the flame under his chin, like the shadow of a buttercup. He could see his daughter's face buried in Olivia's blouse, both their party hats sticking off the sides of their heads. There was a blizzard outside and Julian felt like they were wrapped in white tissue paper. He left a few days after that. He hasn't spoken to either of them since.

Julian remembers things he didn't notice when they happened. He remembers a party in the country. Someone had shoved a hot dog wiener through a hole in a screen door, and every time the door slammed the hot dog wagged obscenely. It was the night he met Olivia. At midnight everyone went skinny dipping, the sound of diving bodies swallowed by the dark water. He was drunk and naked. When it came time to get out he suddenly felt embarrassed. He asked Olivia to give him a hand out of the water, so he could hold a towel in front of himself. When she did haul him out he managed to drop the towel and got caught in the skittering path of a flashlight.

When Julian gets home he finds Marika asleep on the couch, a bowl of chips resting on her knee. She has fallen asleep in the middle of the night with her wrist hanging over the rim of the chrome chip bowl. The phone is ringing. Julian nearly trips over one of the cats in his rush to get it. It's ringing near Marika's ear. She doesn't stir.

Olivia's heels click down the hall through the loose pools of fluorescent light. It's Monday and the Topsail Cinemas mall is mostly deserted, except for the games arcade which shoots out synchronized pings and buzzes. Most of the stores have been undergoing various stages of renovation all winter. Someone has been going at a cement wall with a jackhammer. Chunks of cement have fallen away and rusted bars stick out.

When Olivia turns the corner she sees the exhibit by a taxidermist from British Columbia named Harold. He's standing next to a chair, one hand on his hip, his index fingers looped through his change apron. When he sees Olivia he immediately becomes animated.

"Step this way beautiful, beautiful lady. Let me take you on a whirlwind tour of purgatory's wild kingdom. Here you will see beasts miraculously wrested from the claws of decay. They have looked death in the eye. They have been consumed by death but they are not dust. Thanks to the strange alchemy of embalming fluid and my own artistic wizardry, they live. They live."

He does this with a little flourish of his hands and a slight bow. Then he sighs as if he has used up all his energy. Pinching his nose with his thumb, he says, "Two-fifty if you want to see it."

Olivia is twenty minutes early for the movie so she says, "Sure, I'll treat myself. Why not? It's my birthday."

Harold has a thick mop of black hair with silver at the sides; his body is very tall and thin. One of his eyes is lazy, straying off to the side.

The display takes the shape of a mini-labyrinth made of ordinary office dividers. At each turn the viewer comes upon another stuffed animal.

"Most of them are from endangered species. But the truly unique thing about this exhibit is that these animals have all been hit by trucks. Trucks or cars. Every one of them. Please don't think I would ever hurt these animals for the sake of the collection. I collect them only after they have been killed.

"I'm different than those taxidermists you see on the side of the road during the summer, of course. I've seen them in this province, in Quebec and Alberta as well, lined up in roadside flea markets next to tables that display dolls with skirts that cover toilet paper rolls. Those guys have a few birds maybe, a couple of squirrels mounted on sticks, a few moose heads in the back of the station wagon. I take my work seriously. I am always trying to get a lively posture."

Olivia has stopped in front of a moose. The moose is making an ungainly leap over a convincingly weathered fence, one end of which had been neatly sawed off for the purposes of the exhibit. The moose is raised on its hind legs. Its head and neck are hunched into its shoulders, as if it were being reprimanded.

"This moose looks funny."

Harold points to the neck, saying, "A less experienced man might have stretched the neck forward, and if I wished to be true to a moose in this position, that's what I would have done. I took this artistic licence with the moose because it died on the hood of a station wagon. The antenna of the car, unfortunately, entered its rectum and pierced the bowel twice, like a knitting needle. After that I felt this moose should be preserved in an attitude of shame."

"Are you serious?"

"I travel the continent with these animals, setting up in strip malls all over the United States and Canada. I have a licence. It's educational. Ottawa pays me. I am very serious. People have to know what we are doing to our wild kingdom. I try to respect the animals as individual creatures. Every sentient being deserves respect. Some of these species may never roam on the earth again. They're dead, of course, but I have preserved them. My part is small, I guess. I'm like a red traffic light. That's how I see myself. I do my thing, I make them pause for a minute, before they march off into extinction. It's a chance to say goodbye. We can't forget what we've destroyed."

The last item is a polar bear. The office dividers are set up so that you come upon it suddenly. Its head and forepaws tower over the divider, but Olivia has been looking at a stuffed mother skunk and suckling skunks on the floor. When she walks around the corner she almost bangs into the bear. Its coat is yellowed, its jaws wide open.

"She scared you," chuckles Harold, and he pats the bear's coat twice, as if it's the bear that needs reassurance.

"This polar bear is my drawing card. The only animal not hit by a truck. This bear was shot. It wandered into a small town here in Newfoundland. It had been trapped on an ice flow. Starved. Dangerous. A mother bear separated from her cub. At seven in the morning a woman was putting out her garbage. The bear chased her back into the house. There was only an aluminum screen door between them. She got her husband's shotgun and when the bear crumpled the aluminum door, just like a chip bag, she shot it in the throat."

Harold parts the fur of the bear's throat. He has to stand on tippy-toes to do so. Olivia can see the black sizzled hole, the fur singed pink.

At the end of the hall Olivia can see the woman in the ticket booth for the movie theatres. There's just one woman on tonight, although the twin booth is also lit with flashing lights that circle the outline of the booths. The ticket woman has taken a Q-tip from her purse and is cleaning her ear.

"You have a truck outside?"

"Yes, an eighteen-wheeler."

"Would you consider joining me for a beer? I can give you my address and you can pick me up later. I have a daughter but I have a babysitter lined up for the evening. I was going out anyway."

Olivia has asked the taxidermist out for a beer because she suddenly feels sad about being alone on her birthday. She has an image of this man driving across an empty Saskatchewan highway with these wild beasts frozen in attitudes of attack, stretched in still gallops in the back of his truck. He is the first person she has met in months who seems lonelier than she is. There's the chance he won't show up.

At the bar Olivia gets drunk very fast. Harold drinks the same bottle of beer most of the evening. At last call he buys himself another. He feels jumpy, excited. He's been on the road for six months now and almost always finds himself eating in empty hotel restaurants where the waitress watches a mini TV with an earphone so as not to disturb him.

Olivia is beautiful, Harold thinks. She's wearing a man's shirt, a moss-coloured material, and grey leggings. When she walks to the bar he can see all the muscles in her long legs. She reminds him of a giraffe, graceful despite her drunkenness and the fact that her legs are too long for her. Harold is adept at recognizing different kinds of drunkenness. In some people it twists free something bitter, but Olivia is blossoming. Her cheeks are flushed, her s's are lisping against her large front teeth. She has been telling him about the father of her child.

"My memories are like those animals in the back of your truck. I can take them out and look at them, all but touch them. Today is my birthday. I'm thirty, but time hasn't moved at all since he left. I don't look any older. I'm just waiting, that's all. Do you know what I think? I think he'll be back. I know he will. I know how to get in touch with him if there's an emergency with Rose, our daughter. I've got the number on my bedside table. But I haven't called him since he left. I'm waiting until he comes to his senses. You know what I think? I think he's been enchanted by an ice queen. You know, a splinter of glass in his eye, but one of these days an unexpected tear is going to get it out. He'll be back, don't you worry, Harold."

Suddenly Harold is seized with worry. He removes his glasses. He puts his hand over hers on the table.

"Be honest with me, now. Does it bother you that I have a wandering eye?"

Olivia lays down her beer glass and draws one knee up to her chest.

"At first it was strange. I didn't know which eye to look into."

"In some cultures it is thought to be auspicious. In some cultures it is a sign. I would like very much to go home with you this evening."

Olivia looks into his eyes, first one, then the other. Without his glasses they look even stranger. They are flecked with gold, the lashes, long and black, like a girl's.

They are lying side by side in bed. Harold is already asleep, his cheek nuzzles into her armpit, her arm over her head. He had insisted on bringing the polar bear into the bedroom. He said it was worth thousands of dollars. He couldn't afford to leave it in the truck. A gang of men in a Montreal parking lot had broken into the truck, which was empty at the time, but he hadn't yet gotten the lock replaced.

The steps to Olivia's apartment were coated with ice and when they got to the top, both of them straining with the bear, it had slipped and its head had thunked down the fifteen steps, denting its cheek. This almost made Harold cry with frustration.

He said, "What an indecency for that poor creature, the most noble creature in the wild kingdom."

The cold sobered Olivia considerably. They are lying in bed talking, with all their clothes on except for their shoes. She says, "Harold, do you mind if we don't make love?" and he says, "Not at all," but he is very disappointed.

She talks more about the father of her child. She has glow-in-the-dark stars pasted to the bedroom ceiling. When Harold removes his glasses, the galaxy blurs and it looks as though they are really sleeping under the milky way. While she talks he puts his hand under her shirt onto her belly. The warmth of it, the small movement as she breathes is so charged with unexpected pleasure that Harold becomes almost tearful. He can't trust his voice to speak, so he lies beside her silently. They both fall asleep.

Olivia's eight-year-old daughter, Rose, is awake in her bed, terrified. She heard the thumping of something large and dangerous on the stairs outside, and drunken laughter. She heard whispers from her mother's room. She makes herself small against the headstand of the bed. She sits there watching the door of her room, waiting for something terrible to bash it open. She watches the clock radio with the red digital numerals change, change, change. Then she gets out of bed. She creeps along the hall to her mother's room. The hall light is on. She squeezes the glass door-knob with her sweaty hand and slowly, so the hinges won't creak, pushes the door open. The light falls on the raging polar bear, frozen in the act of attacking her sleeping mother. Rose doesn't move. The bear doesn't move. Everything stays as it is for a long time until a man next to her mother raises himself up on his elbow and says, "Little girl?"

Rose slams the door and runs to the phone. She dials the number and it rings several times. She can hear her mother calling her. Then a man answers the phone. She says, "Daddy, is that you?"

Julian has been awake, although it is four in the morning. He has been sitting on the couch holding Marika's hand. He hasn't moved her or disturbed her in any way since he took the chip bowl from her, except to hold her hand. He says, "Yes, this is Daddy."

He has been awake but it feels as if the child's voice has awoken him. He knows who she is but for a moment her name slips his mind. For a moment, he can't for the life of him remember it.

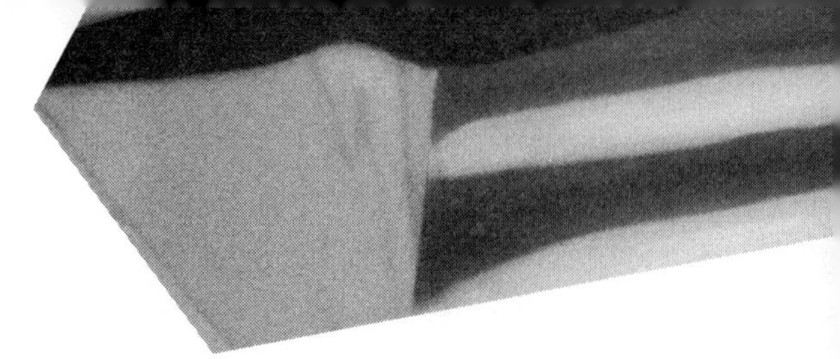

BOXING NOT BINGO

ELISE LEVINE

ELISE LEVINE: "FOR SOME TIME I HAVE WRITTEN IN APARTMENTS TO THE CONSTANT SOUND OF BUSES AND FIRE ENGINES AND TAXIS. CURRENTLY SUPPORTING MYSELF AS A WRITER, I HAVE IN THE PAST WORKED AS A NIGHT-TIME POSTAL EMPLOYEE AND A SECURITY GUARD (COMPLETE WITH GUARD DOGS). DRIVING MEN MAD IS MY COLLECTION OF SHORT FICTION, PUBLISHED IN 1995. I'M WORKING ON A NOVEL WHILE DIVIDING MY TIME BETWEEN TORONTO AND CHICAGO."

Last week she blew an Upper Canada College girlie-boy, an auburn-haired, elite private-school toy. She'd picked him up at the Bloor Street Cinema. *Go Fish* was playing. He was popping M&Ms three rows in front of her, his spindly legs splayed open, the left one jiggling furiously. Either he was queer, or he was one of those straight guys getting off on the film's lead.

She brushed against his side as they exited the theatre. Want to go for coffee? she asked when they got to the lobby. He turned to look at her and she saw his face was small and bony, with a slight hook to the nose. No expression in his eyes. Nobody home. A couple of hours later she parked in his parents' driveway. She leaned over and he pressed himself back into the seat, whimpering delicately as she slipped a hand under his shirt to finger his bird-like collarbone, his shy nipples, microphilia, the tips turned inward.

She sits up in the canoe, sees how far she's drifted. Her mother spent three months this winter in a trailer park in Florida with her new husband and got herself laid off from her summer job as a cleaning lady at the Stouffville golf and country club. Now she's down south again leaving Tanis with the run of the place. She pours another drink, shaking out the last drops as cottage sounds chime across the lake.

The cottage is actually her mother's first house. When she was finally ready to buy, at age fifty, crappy Musselman's Lake was all she could afford. Before her mother bought the cottage, they had lived with Tanis's uncle, years during which Tanis studied and stored information gleaned from visits to her friends' suburban homes and recreational properties. She winterized and remodelled the cottage herself, putting in pine wall panelling she bought cheap at an auction of a farmhouse scheduled for demolition, installing a pre-moulded bath and shower unit she found in a junkyard. She searched out discount antique-style wallpapers and nineteenth-century reproduction horsey prints from yard sales in Orangeville and Newmarket, other people's discards. She remade the cottage into her vision of a Unionville restoration, as if it were a century-old wood-framed house nestled amidst the upscale faux-English gift shops, French restaurants and high-end outdoor outfitters of a tourist town, instead of a tiny box of a place surrounded by bikers' hangouts.

She replaces the top on the thermos. Satellite dishes form a ring of moons around the blank water. The lake's small enough, she can drift as much as she likes and never get lost.

Around two in the morning she drags the canoe up the low bank. When she enters the cottage she rewinds the tape on the answering machine without listening to the messages. In the bedroom her new friend's sleeping breath gives off a faint must. This one's pretty, really pretty. Tanis met her three weeks ago at boxing class. She's taller than Tanis, has a height advantage when they spar. On the new girl's first day at class she reached out her long left hook and clopped Tanis on the side of her masked head.

Tanis loves boxing class, mostly because of Jimmy, the coach. Five-foot-two, weighing in at a hundred and ten, he's a former world welterweight champion. Wears Goofy sweat pants his wife buys for him at Wal-Mart. Good morning, good morning, and how are we this morning? Double-time skipping ladies, push ups, stomach curls, then the speed-bag, water-bag, glove work in the ring. Only you can be a better you. Girls, excuse me, ladies, some guy comes walking up to you what're you going to do? Double jab, thank you very much, get him before he gets you. How's your mother-in-law? Double jab, one-one, then one-two, hook, come back with a right uppercut. This is boxing not bingo.

After class on the new girl's first day Tanis had changed into a tank top and 501s in the tiny, skanky bathroom formerly reserved for the coaches but now used primarily by the women. When she opened the door the new girl was just starting down the stairs. Coffee?

Ten minutes later Tanis sat across from the new girl in Jet Fuel and carefully dunked almond biscotti in her skinny latte. Space, space, space, the new girl was saying. Last weekend she'd crashed a party in a new loft conversion on King Street near Dufferin. The lead singer from Crash Sheep Kills was there, turned out they went to the same high school in Winnipeg. Want to split another? the girl asked after a long half hour over froth-stained glasses. Tanis immediately thought of her ex-girlfriend Rachel; a cocktail of craziness, ran off to New Jersey with a dreadlocked white boy bike courier whose vocabulary was limited to the word *whatever*.

In the cottage Tanis watches the sleeping girl, then slips her left hand under the hollow of her right breast. There. The girl lets out the slightest exhalation. Tanis sits on the edge of the bed and thinks the usual thoughts. Love's dull abstractions inside her like acrobats, all form over function. There. Feel better?

Chris, the girlfriend of Tanis's old friend Suzanne, explains formalism, doles out her superior vocabulary. The new girl starts at the Sutherland Chan school for massage therapy in January. She looks on, nodding her head solicitously as Suzanne and Chris try to include her in the conversation.

Suzanne's parents are away for a month. She's pissed at having to leave her apartment on Sumach Street to come back to the suburbs and walk her parents' Viszla and feed their prize-winning Birmans. To Tanis, though, Suzanne and Chris look at home – so used to sitting on the leather sectional sofa in this fake Tudor house with five bedrooms, three baths, sunken living room, black marble foyer, and green marble counter top in the kitchen where the Gaggia nestles amidst the Calphalon cookware – she can almost believe Suzanne and Chris live here, in this, the newest of a series of Markham subdivisions all built to look exactly alike.

Drink? Chris asks. She brings the Glenlivets on a tray. Also, roasted red pepper spread and tapenade in matching Nambe serving dishes that sit like oversized doorknobs on the steel and glass coffee table.

Chris is quite a creature. Her hair is backcombed and piled on top of her head, stuck together with bobby pins. Escaping wisps fall around her neck. Absently, she twines them around a slim finger. Her brown velvet a-line mini skirt has ridden up high on her skimpy tight-clad thighs. She's kicked off her platform Fluevogs. For the last half hour she's been addressing her speeches solely to the new girl.

So, Chris says, the way it works is, my next film has to be smart, smart, smart. She snaps her fingers in time to the words. Her father is a neurosurgeon. She grew up in Forest Hill. Went to film school at NYU. In America, she says, it's all about where you went to school. Later, she offers the view that Americans are quixotic, and peers at the new girl to see if she understands. They go, go, go, she says. Up to their eyeballs in credit.

When Chris chops her hands through the air – Smart and snappy, she says, is how it all works – everyone in the room nods in agreement. Suzanne follows every word, Tanis expects to see her mouth moving in time.

Smoke break, behind the house. Tanis watches her new friend light up, Ubervixen in punch-coloured capri pants. Bite me, Tanis thinks. Please. Ash brown hair arcs across her face, pale slip of a thing wisping across her mouth. About tonight she'll try to remember the wind or the fence, or the night-cold rattle as she and the girl hold each other.

Back inside the house Chris asks the new girl to help her in the kitchen. As they walk away, Chris puts her arm around the new girl's waist. I like this, she says, rubbing her hand over an aubergine bubble top. Too retro.

It's midnight by the time they leave Suzanne's parents' place. Tanis is tired. You drive.

But the new girl doesn't know how. Tanis finds this a little shocking, although it does seem like a logical progression to her romantic history. She's always taken care of her girlfriends. She knows how to put a new washer in a leaky tap, do an oil change on a car, stupid, basic things that her girlfriends can't be bothered with.

For the past couple of weeks, they've travelled the concession roads north of the city – stretched fields covered in bales of fog. The new girl sits in the driver's seat. The car slowly rolls along. Tanis sleeps. When the girl comes to the intersection at Highway 7 she engages the clutch and wakes Tanis, who leans over groggily to switch gears. The girl panics, pops the clutch. They stall across the highway, and Tanis, still half-asleep, dreamily contemplates their languid drift into the path of oncoming traffic. So far all they've been is lucky.

The phone is ringing as they enter the cottage. The machine comes on. Hi, Chris says. Tell your bunny to call me.

There are three other messages on the answering machine. Tanis rewinds the tape. Aren't you going to listen to your messages? the girl says. All a hundred million of them?

The phone rings again and the girl picks up. Just a sec, she says into the receiver before passing it to Tanis. Chris. Tanis passes the phone back to the girl, who's now lying across the couch, long legs crossed. MuchMusic is on TV. She chats quietly for a while. Yeah, sure, she mostly says. She passes the phone back to Tanis and Tanis hangs up. A Fashion Television rerun comes on, then a CityPulse newsbreak, new graphics for the weatherman. Cool, the new girl says with alarming accuracy.

Tanis surprises herself by seeing rich-boy once more. She picks him up at his parents' house near St. Clair and Avenue Road and takes him for a drive. She asks him how school is. Sucks big time, he says. She pulls off Bayview Avenue onto the Glendon College grounds. By now it's fully night. They lie on the grass, the doors to the car still open, the interior light shining. He gags little cat noises when he goes down on her. She drops him off at his parents'.

The streets here are long and empty, the tall trees rattle in the rising wind like spears. She stops at the Burger Shack at the corner of Eglinton and Oriole Parkway. She sits at one of the orange Formica booths with a coffee and donut and makes plans. Rich Americans come to Salt Spring Island and some years from now Tanis will take them around, sea kayaking, fishing. She'll cook, she'll clean. What else can she do? Her partner will be a potter, keep an extensive garden and have two grown-up children. Tanis's biggest challenge will be to remain strong enough to never succumb to healing crystals and lengthy meditation rituals leading to full-blown Wiccan festivals. Instead, she'll take the ferry to the mainland. In Vancouver she'll hang out at the Lotus, with a mostly older crowd. Coffee the next morning at Delaney's on Denman

Street. Then back to Salt Spring. From here to there. She pictures the blue-green of the Pacific Rim. She spikes her empty coffee cup in the garbage.

Speed-baby, junkie-heart, sugar donut gilding her chin. She takes her shirt off while she drives. Once she drove down the 401 while her almost ex-girlfriend Rachel punched her in the head. She felt as if her skin had cracked open, something thin and white twirling away from her, sound like a didjeridu keening across the sixteen-lane exchange. She flips her dirty T-shirt into the back seat, holds the steering wheel in her left hand while she slips her right arm into the sleeve of her white button-down. She's glad she remembered to bring a change of clothes, as she often does when she comes into the city.

She parks near the Gladstone Hotel. Chris and the new girl at a small round table in the back. Double drafts and a salt shaker in front of them. Neither moves their legs off the two chairs beside them. Tanis stands uncertainly. Her hands dangle, fat boxing gloves. Groovy, she thinks stupidly. Smart, smart, smart.

Once when she and her mother were still living with her uncle Tanis walked in on him in bed with a woman Tanis had never seen before. The woman was naked, zipping over her uncle's bulk in a brisk uh-huh. He was smiling, lifting her skinny breasts.

Tanis wants to have a baby, feel it lodged inside her like a dark torpedo idling just below the surface. She takes the fibreglass canoe out of the shed and eases it into the water, lowers herself in along with a thermos of rye and Coke. For once the neighbouring dogs are quiet. It's Friday night. Dancehall noises from the far shore. The lake is calm, not deep.

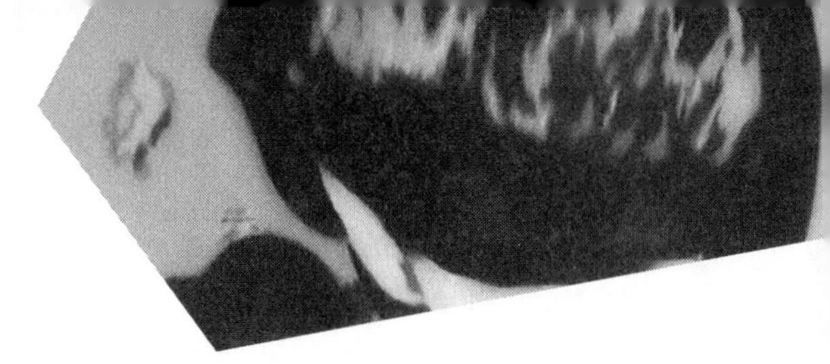

MANDATE

KEN SPARLING

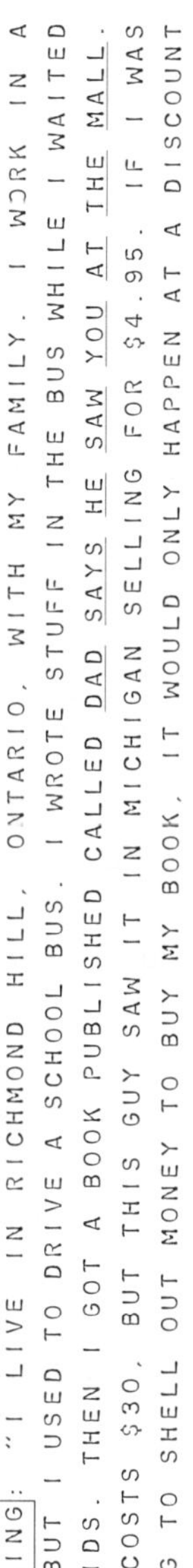

KEN SPARLING: "I LIVE IN RICHMOND HILL, ONTARIO, WITH MY FAMILY. I WORK IN A
LIBRARY, BUT I USED TO DRIVE A SCHOOL BUS. I WROTE STUFF IN THE BUS WHILE I WAITED
FOR THE KIDS. THEN I GOT A BOOK PUBLISHED CALLED DAD SAYS HE SAW YOU AT THE MALL.
THE BOOK COSTS $30, BUT THIS GUY SAW IT IN MICHIGAN SELLING FOR $4.95. IF I WAS
EVER GOING TO SHELL OUT MONEY TO BUY MY BOOK, IT WOULD ONLY HAPPEN AT A DISCOUNT
STORE WHERE EVERYTHING IS 50-75% OFF."

We were supposed to hire a bunch of people from other countries. People from other countries, and women. They had to look like people from other countries. They didn't actually have to be from other countries. As long as they looked like they were from other countries. You had to be able to tell that their ancestors were from another country just by looking at them. The best were women who looked like their ancestors were from other countries. If a woman who looked like her ancestors were from another country came in and applied, we hired her right away. We didn't even interview her. We just asked how much she expected to be paid and then told her when to start.

At first it was sort of fun. It was like a big party. All these foreign-looking women wandering around the office. No one had a clue what they were supposed to do. It was sort of funny. Everyone was having a good time. A couple of the women didn't speak English very well and anytime anyone said anything to them they would laugh. There was a lot of laughter and happiness.

After a few weeks, though, the party atmosphere disappeared and things began to get tedious. No one smiled any more. Every now and then an argument broke out.

Then the boss started dropping by. He called me over one day and said he wanted to talk to me. "Let's get a coffee," he said. He took me around the corner to the coffee shop. "I want to see everyone smiling when I come in. I want everyone to be happy. If the employees are happy, the customers will be happy."

I didn't tell him that we didn't have any customers. We'd lost all our customers a few weeks after we hired all the foreign-looking women. No one was terribly worried about having customers, though. We were an equal opportunity employer. We had fulfilled our mandate.

The boss didn't come back to the office. After we left the coffee shop, he stood out on the sidewalk with me for a moment. It was just starting to feel like spring. The sun was out, and it was warm. It was a day like the day my father was born. I knew this because my father had told me a few months before he died. "I was born," he told me, "on a day when spring was starting to seem like a serious threat." He was lying on his bed in his pyjamas, cancer cells migrating through his bloodstream like puppies broken out of the pound.

I told the boss, "This is the same weather as the day my father was born." The sun reflected off the parking meters.

"I'm glad to hear that," he said. He slapped me on the back and gave me a fatherly smile. He got into his car and drove away.

In the elevator, on the way back up to the office, I decided a memo would be the best thing.

Me and a girl named Jane were the Human Resources Department. I told Jane what the boss wanted.

"Memo?" Jane asked.

"I think so," I said.

Jane did the memo. Memos were her speciality.

My specialty was photocopying. I had that right on my résumé, about the photocopying. It's what got me the job.

I photocopied the memo and put it in everybody's tray, and then Jane and I sat down at our desks and waited.

We received a directive from Head Office telling us not to call our customers customers any more. Customers should now be referred to as patrons, the directive said.

The boss dropped by. "I'm not actually your boss," he told me in a whisper. He looked at me and smiled. "I work for Head Office, just like you. There really isn't any boss." He laughed.

"Is this some sort of new directive?" I asked.

Candy had perfect skin and came to us from southern Georgia. She sat back in chairs, her long fiery hair falling down her back in curls that she painstakingly recreated each morning. She looked relaxed wherever you found her, like she'd never been anywhere else, had always been right there in her present form forever. I couldn't look at her.

One afternoon Candy failed to lock the door on the staff washroom, which we all used – the men and the women – and I came upon Candy with her pants down around her ankles and her big orange-coloured legs fanned out over the toilet seat, and she looked at me with a face that made me think she must have been born on the toilet.

Candy's lips moved when she read things she saw on her computer screen. Her lips were red and glossy, like maraschino cherries.

They looked like they belonged in Coke, and her body in a white bathing suit. The motion she carved as she moved to gather up the phone. Finally, we got her a headset, but she had difficulty managing her hair.

Jane came into the staff kitchen. I was buttering bread.

"I want to show you something," Jane said, unbuttoning her blouse. Her face looked for the surface of the window, reflected back at her, cross-dressed in light, like some ancient prediction of photography.

I spent my evenings doing things on the little computer we kept in a room in the basement. My wife spent her evenings in the kitchen, eating things.

"What's the name of the joint between the tip of your finger and the rest of your finger?" I yelled from the basement. I was looking at my pointer finger, trying to bend the first joint without letting the middle joint move. It was impossible to do without holding the middle joint firmly in place.

"What?" my wife shouted back.

"That first joint on each of your fingers. It has a name. What is it?"

"Pardon?" She couldn't hear anything I said when I was down in the basement.

"There's a dead man on our back porch," I yelled.

"What?"

"I'm fucking a gorgeous woman down here," I yelled.

"What?"

"I'm fucking Candy!" I yelled.

"I can't hear you!"

"I'm fucking Jane!"

A winged grasshopper going in circles, round and round on the pavement, must obviously have something wrong with it. This particular grasshopper that I was looking at on this particular day early in September was going in circles on the concrete patio of a café I was sitting in on my lunch hour. The grasshopper, I determined, was most likely dying of some illness, perhaps a stroke. It was late in the season for grasshoppers, and I thought of Fluffy, our old cat, bumping into walls those last few days before we had to have her put down.

There seemed to be a problem with all the grasshoppers at this point in the season. With all insects, in fact. Bees and wasps lay on the sidewalk spinning around in circles, their wings buzzing frantically. Flies lay upside down on window ledges, not moving, their feet in the air, like slugs that had glutted themselves, too fat to move, the way I sometimes felt late at night sitting in front of the TV eating cake.

This particular grasshopper seemed to be having a problem with one of its hind legs. The little creature pivoted round this leg, now and again dragging the leg a little to get it back into position and continue circling.

I remembered being at my cousins' house for a week once, staying with them for some reason, my mother away somewhere maybe, or just sick of me so she sent me off to stay with the cousins. I had a slingshot with me and I got some stones from the road and fired them at a grasshopper I'd found. It took three or four stones to kill the grasshopper. The first few stones just crippled it and it hobbled around trying to get away from the next stone I was about to fire at it. I was convinced that it could see me, see the slingshot in my hand, and that it knew my intentions, and that its fate was in my hands.

The veterinary clinic was just around the corner, so when I came home with groceries one afternoon and found Fluffy walking into one of the living room walls and then backing up and walking into the same wall again, I carried her over to the vet's place in my arms. She gave me no trouble, snuggled her head into the crook of my arm, in fact.

People might have seen me. It wouldn't have mattered. It was a small event, carried out on an otherwise cool and sunny day. I brought along a blanket to carry Fluffy back to our apartment in when she was dead.

Sometimes, when I was seventeen or eighteen, there were streets I would walk along with apartments on one end and then the houses getting bigger and bigger surrounded by trees and poles of light would go up, only this wasn't light like you think, it was beams of darkness coming out of the sidewalk, and there were screams I couldn't hear, I could only feel, the screams of all the memories I'd forgotten.

One day a woman came into the office. Her name was Virginia, but she told us to call her Andy. She had an envelope in her hand.

"I'm looking for the Human Resources Department," she said.

"That's me," I said. "And Jane." I pointed back toward the office where Jane was sitting at her desk.

"I have a memo from head office," Andy said. She held the envelope out toward me.

"Jane takes care of memos," I said. I took the envelope back to the office and handed it to Jane. Jane removed the memo from the envelope and read it to herself. When she was through reading it, she looked up at me. Her hair was pushed back off her forehead. Jane had thick hair. It stood up in front like a little forest of spindly black conifers.

"It says," Jane said, pointing her little nose at the memo, "that the bearer of this memo is our new boss."

I laughed.

"But what does it really say?" I said.

Jane handed me the memo. I read it.

"I'll make photocopies," I said, and I hurried out of the office and around the corner to the photocopier.

The new boss, Andy, tried to corral the office chaos by talking. She laboured to erect fences of words around all activity; but words don't connect together the way fences do, they don't notch into each other. Fences form boundaries, and maybe there are ways of using words to contain chaos, but I don't think so.

I hesitate to deny anything, of course, particularly as a member of the Human Resources Department, but it seems to me that any language designed to designate boundaries is doomed to failure from the start; any attempt to control chaos through language will only cause more chaos.

Fortunately, Andy never really tried very hard to hold anything together. She rambled, is what she did. On and on until your head hurt from listening to her. There was no form or flow, random thoughts spilled out of her, unchecked in any way. It was a joy to watch, as long as you didn't have to pay too much attention.

There was really no need to pay attention, anyway. Every now and then something you needed to know slipped out, and somehow you grabbed onto it, enough of it to get by anyway, while the bulk of what she said drifted by you like the gentlest whisper of a warm spring breeze slipping off the lips, propelled only by the tongue.

The sense of chaos Andy brought (like wind in her skirts) is what motivated us all. You felt you could get away with anything, so an amazing period of creative activity followed the arrival of Andy's devastating blather.

Did it ever occur to you that where the paragraph breaks there is a point of artifice, and that there was a time in your life when the paragraph never broke?

You can enter the meaning of your life like a swimmer diving through the surface. Then you can save it to ASCII.

At the end of the day, Jane and I left the office. We stepped out the door, into the air, and Jane turned her back to me. I could see the reflection of her face in the glass door. The back of her head was covered in thick, cropped hair that had the consistency of carpet. I almost reached out and touched it.

It was autumn. Jane pushed the key into the lock and turned it. We got into Jane's car. We could see the new boss through the window. She was sitting in her chair at her desk with a pencil in her mouth. Jane's car shivered to a start.

The sun was setting. That peculiar moment when the quality of light robs the world of all its ugly detail. I chose that moment to look at Jane's cheek.

Our office is just minutes away from the highway. Jane got her car onto the ramp. There wasn't much traffic. I noticed a donut shop at the bottom of an exit ramp. Every now and then a car ripped past going twice our speed. Jane was in the right lane, going slow. She had her window rolled down and her elbow resting on the door frame. After a while, she signalled right and slid onto an exit ramp.

We descended to where the road dropped below the highway, circled under it, then veered off and away into the vast plane of muffler shops and failing businesses. There was hope there, but it was buried in broken glass and bits of chipped sidewalk. We kept on driving.

HORST AND WERNER

GRANT BUDAY

GRANT BUDAY: "AFTER FLUNKING OUT OF BOTH SIMON FRASER UNIVERSITY AND THE EMILY CARR COLLEGE OF ART, I SPENT EIGHT YEARS WORKING IN A MASS PRODUCTION BAKERY INHALING QUANTITIES OF BLEACHED FLOUR. EVENTUALLY, I GRADUATED FROM SFU THEN I TAUGHT ENGLISH FOR FOUR YEARS, BEFORE QUITTING TO LIVE LEAN IN VANCOUVER'S EAST END, WHERE I DELIVERED FLYERS AND WORKED IN A HOSPITAL. THE STORIES IN MONDAY NIGHT MAN, TWO OF WHICH ARE REPRINTED HERE UNDER THE TITLE "HORST AND WERNER," COME LARGELY FROM THOSE DAYS."

Horst knew he had to move on. Either that or suffocate. He thought again of getting a different apartment. One that didn't face an alley. One where the seams between the squares of lino weren't so dirt-swollen they looked like infected cuts. One with better light so he could grow a wider variety of plants. But a better place meant more money. More important, it meant breaking his link with the past, with Corinne. They'd lived here together.

He recalled her first visit. The look on her face when she stepped into his private jungle. As if she'd entered a secret grove. All evening they watched shadows elongate across the walls and commented on the elegant shapes.

Horst said it was like bird watching. And Corinne knew exactly what he meant.

But Corinne left. People did that. It happened. It happened to Horst's neighbour, Werner Rugg.

"It's like this," Werner told Horst. "You got a corpse hanging between your legs. And the deal is, you got to find the woman whose coffin's got your name on it."

Werner had snagged Horst in the hall.

"Lorraine's coffin's got my name on it. But she's trying to deny it. She left me, man, she left me. And you know what?"

Horst shook his head.

"Monday. She wants to see me Monday nights! Saturday she's out with some guy drives a Volvo, so I get stuck with Monday. Monday Night Man!" Werner's eyes were round and blunt as bottle caps and he was breathing fast.

Monday Night Man. Horst knew all about that.

Horst opens the door anyway.

Werner – drunk. He jerks his thumb back over his shoulder at his apartment down the hall. "Got tired of sitting in my box."

Horst sees Werner's on one of those drunks where Horst doesn't know if the guy's going to hug him or slug him.

"So," says Horst. "What's up?"

"My box, man." Werner's pharmaceutical focus travels up the wall. "You know what I'm saying?"

Horst nods. He knows exactly what Werner's saying.

Werner squints past Horst into his place. "Anything to drink in there?"

Horst leans into the doorframe, blocking Werner's view. "Shit no. I'm dry."

Horst's head races, thinking up excuses. It's Saturday night and he doesn't want to get stuck with Werner dumping his crap-cart of bitterness on him. Shit, thinks Horst, I should never answer my door.

"Fucking Lorraine, man. Took all that wine I made."

"All those big jugs?"

"Doesn't realize I love her."

"Where's she living?"

"Where's she living? There, man." Werner jerks his thumb to the right, which is west. "Living with the Volvos." Werner means the West Side of Vancouver, west of Main. Lorraine dumped Werner last year. It was inevitable, but the capper was him accusing her of ripping off his car and selling it on him. A rusted-out Impala that sat for a year in the alley out back next to Horst's Pacer. Lorraine and Werner argued for days over it.

Horst avoids Werner's eyes, recalling the incident.

The car disappeared all right, but it wasn't Lorraine – it was Horst. He called a scrap-metal dealer and got it hauled away. It would've sat out there forever.

Horst misses Lorraine. They had some good talks. Then she picked up Werner, like a disease. After that when Horst knocked on Lorraine's door, instead of her swinging it open and inviting him in, the door stayed shut. Werner'd be standing behind it, all paranoid, saying: "Who's there?"

"Horst."

"Who?"

"Horst. From down the hall."

"Oh. Oh yeah man. Whataya want?"

"Lorraine there?"

"She's busy."

Well, now Werner was at Horst's door.

"Kind of caught me at a bad time," says Horst.

Werner stares with his nicotine eyes. He's forty-five, has long black hair, a face shaved blue, and a little jaw, like he's been clenching it so tight so long it's shrunk. Then he's nodding, like he's got Horst's number. "Okay man. I hear you." And he's travelling back down the hall to his place, shaking his head at Horst like – What an asshole.

Horst shuts the door. "Fuck." He goes into the bathroom to listen. Werner's got his TV on and he's making sarcastic noises at it. He's lonely. Horst thinks – Maybe I should invite him in after all? And in fact he does have half a bottle of red. But shit . . . if I share it with Werner I'll never get to sleep. . . . Horst sits on the edge of the bathtub. He can't believe he's feeling guilty. Werner's never given him the time of day. Christ, thinks Horst, that bastard wouldn't piss on me if I was on fire! And Horst knows if he lets him in once he'll show up regularly. He might even want to use the toilet. Besides, if he lets Werner in he'll see the plant stand Horst pinched from the basement. It was Lorraine's. She wasn't using it. Hell, it was broken. Horst saw Werner chase Lorraine into the alley with that plant stand and break it across her back. Fortunately, Lorraine's three times Werner's size. She just turned around and flattened him. Fifty-year-old ex-junkie scam artist. She liked that. It was exciting. She told Horst so. If Werner recognizes the plant stand, who knows, he might go off the deep end and shoot him. Lorraine said Werner's got a gun. Well, a sort of gun, a flare gun. Stole it from a boat. Still, it would burn a good hole in me, thinks Horst. What a way to go, done in by Werner Rugg. Like dying of rat bite.

Horst wonders if Werner knows he slept with Lorraine. Maybe all this time he's been next door there brooding ugly revenge, thinking of ways to torture Horst for having made it with his woman. Though of course it wasn't like that. Horst and Corinne had been fighting and she was saying fuck this and walked out. Horst paced around then knocked on Lorraine's door. It was a Saturday night and Werner was doing weekends in jail on a possession charge. Lorraine kind of liked that Werner was doing time. It gave her life an edge. Made her feel inner city. She was very much into being the hip momma. So she welcomed Horst. She had a bottle of red and they got drunk. It was the hugging that got it going. Lorraine was into this New Age hugging and it went from there into some old-time fucking. Horst remembers the bed had black sheets and smelled of cigarettes and BO. Lorraine was the biggest woman he'd ever done it with. Not fat, but massive. Felt like he was humping a chesterfield, and when she got on top of him – Christ! – it was like he was trapped under a mattress. He spent the night though, and they did it again in the morning. Corinne was sitting at the kitchen table when he stepped in stinking of sex and cigarettes. Six months later they were divorced.

The morning after Werner knocked, Horst peeks through the blinds and watches him peg sheets on the clothesline.

Horst nearly drops his coffee. And not just because he's never seen Werner do laundry before, but because Horst recognizes the sheets. Two sheets and two pillow cases, a set. When Werner's gone, Horst steps outside. Fuck. . . . These are mine, thinks Horst. They are. . . . They belonged to me and Connie. The sheets are a deep blue with moons and clouds and a kind of night-on-the-desert look. Werner's got my sheets, thinks Horst. And if that's not ugly enough, he's slept on them. Werner's probably jerked off or fucked some slut on them. . . . Horst steps back, appalled. Horst and Corinne got the sheets as a wedding present. And now Werner's got them. Werner, who's probably infested with lice.

Horst is halfway around the house to Werner's suite when he halts.

Number one: Werner's got that gun.

Number two: maybe he's simply got sheets with the same pattern. Is it possible?

Horst dials Moose Jaw. Sunday morning the rates are reduced. He's got to talk to Corinne and get this straight.

Gary answers. Horst tightens the cloth over the mouthpiece.

"Is Corinne there?"

"Who's calling?"

Horst stammers.

"That you Horst?"

He pulls the cloth away. "Yeah."

"Well fuck you."

"I gotta talk to her."

"Talk to yourself."

"Gary."

"She's busy."

"What kind of sheets you got?"

"Why are you such an asshole? She's eight months pregnant. What the fuck you mean, sheets?"

Horst's voice falls. ". . . Eight months?"

"Eight. You got a message I'll pass it along. That's as close as you're getting."

"The pattern. Just tell me the pattern."

"White sheets, Horst, we got white flannel sheets. Now go back to bed and sleep it off."

Horst heads down to the beer and wine store at the Waldorf.

If Corinne didn't take the sheets, thinks Horst, then she must have left them down here in the basement, which is where Werner found them. Werner's always prowling through the boxes left by people no one, not even Leo Buljan, the landlord, remembers. People from the sixties and even the fifties. Maybe further. Horst sets his wine bottle on a trunk and looks around. It's musty and dank and the rough cedar planks supporting the main floor are only inches from Horst's head. In a corner lies a gutted mattress, paint cans, a roll of carpet that stinks like a sack. Horst spots Corinne's wicker picnic basket. . . . A couple of rolls of wrapping paper stick out. Images of Christmases past pump tears to his eyes. He reaches for the bottle, realizing he should've got two.

The bells ring for five o'clock mass up the street. Drunk, Horst recalls how a couple of weeks ago, he was walking over to the track in the evening, and as he was passing the church he saw an old lady slowly climbing the steps with a cane. She was wearing her best clothes. Horst smelled her face powder from the sidewalk. He didn't know whether to laugh or cry. He nearly turned around and went into the church himself. But he knows what it looks like inside – he and Corinne got married there. He kept going. He bet heavy that night.

Horst watches those sheets float on the October breeze. Hell, he thinks, I'm taking them back. If Werner comes knocking, say – I don't know. Why would I take your sheets, man? What the fuck can Werner say to that? Horst finishes the last inch of wine, listens for sounds from Werner's suite, then steps onto the porch and takes them. He strips his bed then remakes it. Then he sits, and slides his palm slowly over the surface. . . . He remembers that time in Alberta, near Red Deer, way out in the middle of nowhere, all rock and dirt and flat land. The car broke down and he and Corinne were arguing. As usual, Horst was losing. Even when he was right he managed to lose arguments. They argued until they were exhausted. Horst remembers thinking how bleak Alberta was. Tumbleweeds snagged in barbed wire, coulees full of baked red dirt. What a fucking hole. They used up all the windshield cleaning fluid in one day. The car was crusted. They sat out there under a sky the colour of a rusty saw-blade, the pebbly prairie wind nicking the windows and the gusts rocking the car. That's where it ended. That's where Corinne said she'd had it.

She'd stared straight ahead: "I hate Vancouver. I hate the rain. The mountains make me claustrophobic. The sea stinks like a sewer." She'd turned to him.

"So what's it going to be?"

Horst had avoided her eyes and said nothing, which pissed her off even more. As usual, by doing nothing, he was forcing her to make all the moves.

"Well?"

Horst had shrugged. He was relieved and crushed at the same time.

Horst pulls the sheets up and pins them back onto the line. He stares out at the blue-black sky. The sun's gone, leaving blood-red clouds above the rooftops. He hears the popping of firecrackers. In two weeks it'll be Hallowe'en. Then everyone'll be knocking at his door, expecting something.

Werner Rugg painted houses for a living. Maybe it was the paint fumes, but lately Werner was getting stranger. Saturday night was the worst. First of all, he barked like a dog at his TV. Then he went in and out of his apartment. He stepped outside, stepped back in, a minute later went out again. Back and forth, in and out. He went in and out twenty times in an hour. Horst counted. Werner knocked on doors. He knocked on Leo's door. Leo was usually drunk and passed out so didn't answer. Then Werner tried Horst's door. Werner knocked, listened, knocked again. Horst sat inside as quiet as possible. Werner went into the basement, rooted through the boxes, and talked to himself. Some Saturday nights Werner had visitors. Werner welcomed them in his lithium-smooth voice. Yet an hour later he'd drive everyone out the door, screaming what mutt-fuckers they all were.

Horst hears feet stumbling about in Werner's place next door, then the sound of slapping. A woman's voice shouts: "MAKE IT HURT!"

Horst groans. He hears another slap. Two bodies bump so hard the picture on his TV screen jumps.

Horst goes naked into his bathroom and stands listening. Water suddenly gushes on next door in Werner's tub.

"Get him in! All the way!"

Horst leans closer to the wall. Fuck. . . . They're drowning someone. . . . Maybe they're drowning Werner. . . . Horst feels a flicker of hope at the thought. He doesn't hate Werner, but he'd like to get rid of him and have some quiet elderly couple move in. Horst wonders what to do. It really would be great to get a better neighbour. A kick against the wall bangs open Horst's medicine cabinet door. He leaps back.

Horst hauls on his jeans. He doesn't feel safe naked. And he doesn't know whether to run down the alley and hide, or go over and knock. He peeks into the hall. Then he tiptoes down and taps Werner's door.

That woman's voice barks: "Yeah?"

"What's goin' on?"

"Who're you?"

"Neighbour."

"The fuck you want?"

"Where's Werner?"

"Takin' a bath."

"He all right?"

"Call him tomorrow."

"What was all that noise?"

"Nothin'."

"I'm calling the cops." He listens. He hears whispering.

The chain drops off and the door opens. A small blond woman stands there. She's slender and pretty. Horst hadn't expected that.

"So you live here, eh?"

Horst points down the hall.

She leans out and checks both directions.

"Hey, sorry 'bout the noise. We got a situation here. Don't got a smoke do ya?"

Horst pats his pockets even though he doesn't smoke. He steps into the room's dog-blanket stink and sees a puddle of vomit. He follows her past a kicked-in TV, and on into a tiny bathroom with a bare bulb.

"Hit himself up with a boot-full," says the blonde.

Horst sees Werner slumped in the tub. Cold water sloshes around him. He's fully dressed in his work clothes, paint-scabbed shirt, white pants, General Paint hat. A biker-type in a ripped jean jacket, goatee, and long greasy hair flung straight back, splashes water on Werner's death-white face.

Horst is fascinated. In fact, he wishes he was here earlier to see Werner shoot up. Horst's never seen anyone shoot up. He leans in close, studying the blue-black bruises inside Werner's elbow. Maybe

Werner'll die. Horst hasn't seen anyone die in years. It'd certainly salvage a dull Saturday night. The bruises remind Horst of a picture he saw in a magazine of a torture victim from Argentina. The police had beaten the guy's arms with axe handles. The picture had terrified Horst. It had made him weep. But this doesn't make him weep. It occurs to Horst he should suggest they call an ambulance. That'd liven things up even more. There might even be a TV crew. But, at that very moment, the biker suggests exactly that:

"Like, maybe we should call him an ambulance?"

"No fucking ambulance!" The blonde shoves by Horst and leans over Werner. "Baby, you don't want a dirty old ambulance, do you?"

Werner stares at his knees.

The blonde makes a fist and punches Werner in the cheek.

Horst cringes.

Werner doesn't blink.

The blonde grips Werner by the jaw, turns his face one way, then the other, then lets go. His head flops forward. She looks at Horst and the biker. "Get him up. He goes under now that's it. He's dead. I've seen it." Then she glares at the guy in the jean jacket. "Ambulance! You piece'a shit. Ambulance means cops!" She raises her arm as if to give him a backhand. Defiant, the guy stands up tall and flexes his chest. Then the blonde sees Horst just standing there by the sink. "The fuck you waitin' for? Get him up!"

The biker gets Werner under the armpit then looks at Horst. "Get in here!"

Horst wishes he wasn't such a good neighbour.

They drag Werner up, along with half the water in the tub, soaking their feet. They step high and curse. As they haul Werner into the front room his feet start moving, as if they've been kick-started.

"That's it, baby. Come back to us." The blonde's voice comes from the kitchen, where she's got her head in the fridge. "Fuck! We use all the ice?" She pours vodka into a glass, gulps, then pours more.

For the next half hour, Horst and the biker walk Werner back and forth past the kicked-in TV, avoiding the puddle of vomit. Werner's arm is slung across Horst's shoulder, and Horst can feel Werner's clammy armpit and smell his hair, his BO, and the rancid blanket they've wrapped around him. The blonde, meanwhile, drinks vodka, and bitches.

"Fuck this. I'm gonna be a stewardess. I mean come on! I've been a waitress. I know what they do. Sure there's that safety shit – life-vest, oxygen mask. But fuck. Hey, you got any ice?" She stares at Horst.

Horst looks at her crotch-taut jeans. He thinks you'd have to have a cock like a hammer to fuck her.

"I'll check." He knows he doesn't have any ice. He never has ice. His ice trays are in the drawer by the kitchen sink. But he figures this is his excuse to get out from under Werner's armpit. He leaves Werner slumped on the biker and heads out. Back in his place, Horst scrubs his hands and face and neck, getting Werner's stink off. He wonders if he should run down to the 7-11 and buy a bag of ice. She might get pissed off if he comes back empty-handed.

When Horst returns, he finds Werner face down on the floor and the others gone.

It takes Horst half an hour to wrestle Werner into a coat and shoes. A half hour of touching and holding the guy. When he finally gets Werner outside, the winter air hardens Horst's lungs to sacks of ice. His ears turn to tin and his clothes hang as stiff as aluminum. The air smells sharp with impending snow. Horst whimpers in frustration at what he's got himself into. He struggles just to hold Werner up. "You junkie shit motherfucker!" Horst stops cursing only when he has to shift sides, at which point Werner collapses to the frozen sidewalk, "Fuck!" Horst is already exhausted. He stares at Werner, then glances round, thinking of just leaving him. But it hits him – they have to keep going.

Horst hauls him up. They head toward the waterfront because it's easier walking downhill. They're halfway there when Horst thinks – Shit! Why didn't I just call that ambulance? They arrest Werner for smack it's fine with me. He stops, and, propping Werner up like a mattress, looks for a phone booth. Nothing. So Horst tries hurrying on, suddenly frantic to find a telephone. He slips on ice and goes down, forehead hitting cement.

Horst isn't sure if he passed out, but when he's thinking again he knows he's freezing to death. He crawls out from beneath Werner. Blood, like red glue, has sealed Horst's left eye shut. He wipes it away. His forehead is hot, and delicate as a soft-boiled egg. It's the one warm place on Horst's body. He touches his forehead with numb fingers. Werner is face down, half on the sidewalk and half off. Horst nudges him with his foot. "Hey." Nothing. Horst hauls at Werner's arm (and flashes on a scene from the evening news of a fireman pulling at a man's arm and the arm coming clean off, and the fireman falling backward still holding it). Horst tries heading them back uphill toward the house, but no way, it's too steep. And so, having to move or freeze, they go downhill, across the railroad tracks where Horst hears the gunshot shunt of coupling railcars and sees, every fifty yards, patches of glass glittering beneath cones of light. In a moment that hits Horst like an hallucination, they pass a bag lady standing with her shopping cart in the narrow alley between shipping containers stacked four high. Her face is turned upward, basking in the light of a tower lamp.

When the containers end, Horst sees the black water of Burrard Inlet. Long scarves of red and yellow ripple on its surface. From up ahead comes the crack and roar of the Alberta Wheat Pool. Beyond, the Second Narrows Bridge spans the inlet. They cross the frozen grass of New Brighton Park, and by the time they reach the pissy stink of pigeons and fermenting grain at the wheat pool, Werner is finally walking on his own. Horst is relieved, but has to admit it was warmer with Werner's arm over his shoulder.

Like a zombie come to life, Werner says: "Paid her fifty bucks and she got away."

Horst stares. Not a word of thanks. Not a word about the blood all over Horst's face. Horst realizes he has as much chance of a thank you from Werner as he does from a lizard for throwing it meat.

Still, Horst keeps moving along with Werner, past the wheat pool, whose massive pipes and silos are lit up like some 1930s science-fiction city. Horst is beaten. He's done in. His frustration has burned itself out and exhausted him. He wants only to sleep. His feet are bricks, his pant legs stiff as pipes, the fronts of his thighs frozen, and his forehead throbs.

Horst and Werner are heading back to the house when the snow finally begins. The first flakes settle slowly. Then they speed up. And suddenly Horst is engulfed in a swarm of white, a welcome plague of snow-white locusts that will scour the city. Horst's glad it's snowing. When it snows the city becomes clean and quiet. Raising his face, he feels the flakes touch his bruised forehead.

"Bitch was standing in this alley right here," says Werner, pointing.

Horst looks into the alley. The dumpsters, the cars, and the ground are white and still and innocent.

"I'll be looking for her," says Werner. "You thought I was fucked up. But I saw her." He hunches his shoulders and leans harder into the spinning snow.

PIGEON IN LEMON SAUCE

DANY LAFERRIÈRE

TRANSLATED BY DAVID HOMEL

DANY LAFERRIÈRE WAS BORN IN HAITI, WHERE HE PRACTISED JOURNALISM UNDER DUVALIER. WHEN A COLLEAGUE WAS FOUND MURDERED, HE WENT INTO EXILE IN CANADA IN 1978. HIS FIRST NOVEL PUBLISHED IN THIS COUNTRY WAS *HOW TO MAKE LOVE TO A NEGRO* (1987). IT BECAME AN INTERNATIONAL BESTSELLER AND WAS ADAPTED FOR FILM. "PIGEON IN LEMON SAUCE" IS FROM *A DRIFTING YEAR*, A NOVEL IN VERSE EXPLORING THE AUTHOR'S FIRST YEAR LIVING IN MONTREAL AS AN EXILE. DANY NOW DIVIDES HIS TIME BETWEEN MONTREAL AND MIAMI.

The worst thing that
can happen to you when
you move into a new
apartment is to find
an unplugged fridge
with a beer in it.

I met a girl in the park
and asked her back to my place.
She insisted I come
to her apartment on Rue Saint-Dominique.
That doesn't happen to me every day.

The difference between Port-au-Prince and
Montreal is space. In Port-au-Prince, when

a girl meets a guy, the problem is finding shelter from the millions of pairs of eyes that never blink. In Montreal, both partners have their own key.

The room was tiny
with dolls everywhere.
She pushed the table
against the wall to dance
to a Gainsbourg song.
Her body was well proportioned,
but she was so small
I was afraid to touch her.
On the stairs I got the feeling
I'd done something really stupid.

I walked more than two hours
south
without meeting a single black.
That's a northern city for you, man.

I can choose between having
one good meal with wine
and fasting the rest of the week,
or eating pigeon and rice for seven
days.

I can't wait to get home
to that filthy room
with a pile of dirty dishes in the sink,
cockroaches everywhere
and the heavy smell of beer.
I can't wait to lie down on that bare
mattress
my arms crossed

thinking that
this is the spot I occupy
in the galaxy.

"You got here too late, man,"
the African told me.
"Five years ago
you could have rented
a room for twenty dollars a month
and still complained that the fridge
wasn't working the way you'd hoped."

The pigeons in Parc Lafontaine
cast quick, worried glances in my direction.
They know I have an excellent recipe
for pigeon in lemon sauce.

It fell on my shoulder.
I watched the awkward flight of the fat pigeon
that had just shat on me.
Heavy, greasy, ugly, it could hardly
get off the ground.
It'll end up in my stew-pot.

After pigeons, cats will be next, naturally. Their meat is soft but somewhat elastic. Boil it with papaya leaves to tenderize it. It tastes like skinny goat. Cat-hunting is difficult because the cat is the most protected animal in North America. Check out the neighbourhood around the SPCA. There's always one or two hanging out there.

I like the girls
other people think are ugly.
Unfortunately, they're
more difficult than pretty ones.

A pretty girl will take your word for it
if you tell her she's magic.
An ugly girl wants proof.
For the time being, I don't have
either kind.

Most people say,
"If I were rich . . ."
I say,
"If I had twenty dollars . . ."

On Wednesdays, everything
is cheaper
at the grocery store,
but you have to get up
before the superintendents,
the housewives, the old folks
and the coupon-clippers.

I thrust it feathers and all into boiling water, removed it twenty minutes later and placed it delicately on a white plate to pluck it, one feather at a time, before slitting open its belly. Then I marinated it a good hour in lemon juice. I got this pigeon recipe from an old rubby in the park, a great connoisseur of free meat.

"For a starving man," said the old bum,
"a pigeon is steak
on the wing."

Simple fare: rice, pigeon, carrots, and onions. I roasted it all together in the little oven. The slow-cook method. The smell filled the room. I couldn't bring myself to eat alone. I went out to look for someone in the park. Nobody was there. Sometimes, solitude is worse than hunger.

When I rented the room, I found a photograph pinned to the wall. It came from a department-store catalogue. It showed a couple from behind. The man must have been three times as old as the woman: fat, short, wearing a bowler hat and a grey overcoat. The svelte young woman was dressed in a fur coat. The caption read, "The gentleman paid for the lady's coat."

Everything is new to me.
This little room with
a refrigerator, an oven,
a bathroom, electricity
twenty-four hours a day
and the opportunity to invite a girl
into my bed or drink myself into a stupor.

I lay down on the filthy mattress beneath the window but I couldn't sleep with all that racket: police-car sirens, taxi horns, bums fighting it out, all kinds of sounds. A little breeze set the leaves dancing in the tree, just within the square of my window. The music tree. All sounds faded. I fell asleep.

The guy lives on welfare. He spends all day in front of the TV, in his undershirt, a case of beer at his feet. Every time I go by his room, he tries to get my attention.

"Get a load of this."

Carefully, I entered his room. It smelled like Vicks VapoRub.

"You know her?"

"That's Diana Ross," I answered.

"That's some broad, man!"

"She is beautiful."

"I've humped her, man."

"I see," I said, moving towards the door.

"You think she's too good for me.... She's just a nigger bitch.... *I hump her whenever I want to!*"

I took a quick look back as I went out the door and saw he was masturbating to Diana Ross on the TV screen.

Hold on to your anger, man, it's precious.
One day it will serve you.
In the meantime, keep your
nose clean.

Yesterday, I got home dog-tired, around midnight. I couldn't sleep a wink. The guy next door was fucking and the girl, a new one, kept whimpering in this plaintive voice, "Talk to me, talk to me, honey." The guy's the kind who fucks in silence. It went on all night. "Talk to me, please, just say something to me." Around five o'clock in the morning, I couldn't take it any more; I went and knocked on the guy's door. He opened up. I told him, "Tell her something, anything, so I can sleep, or I'm going to burn this building down." He closed the door without a word, but ten minutes later I was in the middle of a complex erotic dream.

There's always noise here at night
and the police have practically set up shop
in the stairway of my building.
Normally, silence returns
around five in the morning and it's quiet
till two in the afternoon.

Sometimes,
a gunshot
will split the night
and one of my neighbours
will make the headlines
in tomorrow's
paper.

In my building, guys are always going in and out of jail like a revolving door. One of them accosted me on the stairs.

"You don't steal, you don't push, you don't have no girls working for you – how do you live, man?"

As if he were my older brother, concerned about my welfare.

Johanne, the nude dancer,
found in a pool of blood
on the floor of her room.
A note on the table, requesting
that her things be sent back to her mother.

I peer out the window
that overlooks the courtyard.
The night is ink-black.
I can just barely make out the shadows
slipping into the building that burned
last year.
They say the price of a blow job has
gone up again and it's
out of reach for the ordinary working man.

The police knocked on the door.
A dozen of us blacks
were drinking beer
and watching the game on TV.
The cop stayed
till it was over.
His team lost,
but he was a good enough sport
to warn us
to watch out for the guy in 16.

I woke up in the middle of the night
with my stomach growling.
I rummaged through the fridge
and found an old bone.
It wasn't the first time
that bone helped me out.

Someone came into my room
while I was in the bathtub
and took the rent money
I'd left on the table.

I don't know why
I couldn't stop laughing,
I laughed for half an hour,
until my neighbour on
the left started pounding
on the wall.

I told the super I
was taking out the garbage.
Two green bags.
He looked at me suspiciously.
I went out.
I turned right at the first corner.
I hoped I hadn't left anything
in the room.
My fourth move
and it's only August.

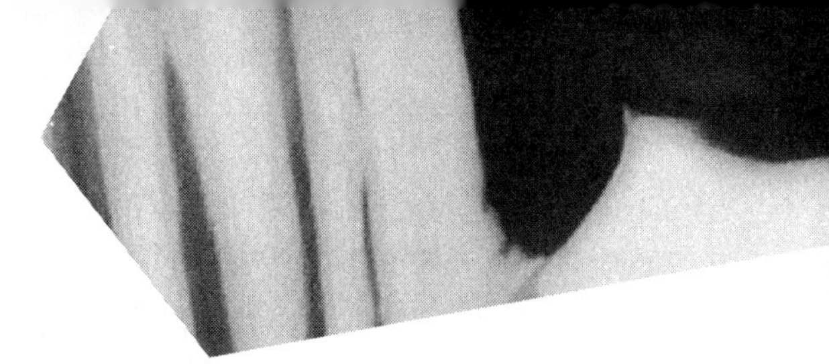

AT THE TIME OF HIS DEATH BY SUICIDE IN TORONTO IN 1994, THIRTY-FIVE-YEAR-OLD DANIEL JONES WAS BEST KNOWN FOR HIS 1985 POETRY COLLECTION *THE BRAVE NEVER WRITE POETRY*. THE HAMILTON-BORN JONES TURNED AWAY FROM POETRY AT THAT TIME AND DEVOTED HIMSELF TO WRITING PROSE, PUBLISHING FIVE CHAPBOOKS AND *OBSESSIONS: A NOVEL IN PARTS*. *THE PEOPLE ONE KNOWS*, FROM WHICH "IN VARIOUS RESTAURANTS" IS TAKEN, WAS PUBLISHED POSTHUMOUSLY IN 1994. JONES'S LAST COMPLETED WORK, *1978*, A NOVEL ABOUT THE FADING PUNK SCENE IN TORONTO, WILL BE PUBLISHED IN 1998.

IN VARIOUS RESTAURANTS

DANIEL JONES

I dial Nicola's number, and Nicola's husband, David, answers the telephone. I have met him only once, on the street, briefly.

"Is Nicki there?"

"She'll just be a minute," David says.

"How are you, David?"

"I'm fine. And you?"

"I'm fine, thank you."

There is a pause, and then a click, as the receiver is lifted from the cradle of another telephone in a different room. David says goodbye, and he hangs up.

"Hello," Nicola says.

Her voice is tentative, brittle. There is an edge of terror in her voice, as if she suspects that the caller intends to harm her, that the breath she has just expelled is her last. She will be suffocated.

I am twenty minutes early for my appointment with Nicola. The Unity, a small café on the corner of College Street and Clinton, is empty. I take a seat by the window. It is snowing outside. Thin, wet snow. It is early afternoon but nearly dark.

The owner, Amedeo, appears out of the shadows of the kitchen.

"There is no food today," he says.

"Not even a salad?" I say.

"I have no food," Amedeo says.

"A coffee, then, while I'm waiting. *Uno caffè latte.*"

Amedeo disappears behind the espresso machine. I take out my cigarettes but there is no ashtray. A man walks into the café and speaks to Amedeo, in Italian, over the top of the espresso machine. Both men leave the café, and I watch as they cross College Street and then continue to walk up Clinton, until their bodies are obscured by the snow.

Ten minutes later Amedeo has not returned. Nicola is chaining her bicycle to a post outside the window. I walk outside to meet her and we cross the street to the Bar Italia. We do not speak.

Inside the Bar Italia it is dark and crowded. There is the sound of many people talking all at once and of billiard balls striking other billiard balls. Two writers I know stand leaning against the bar drinking espresso. I manage to pass without them seeing me.

We find a small table in the back. Nicola folds her raincoat neatly over the back of her chair. She is wearing a pale green dress cut high around the neck and with large buttons down the middle. The dress accentuates the whiteness of her skin and the flecks of green in her blue eyes. The dress makes Nicola look terribly thin, which in fact she is.

I have not seen Nicola for several months, not since she married David. Her hair, then, was cut short above the ears and neck, and she had dyed it a reddish shade of orange. She has let her hair grow down to her shoulders, and it is blond once again. She is not wearing earrings or make-up. I notice the wedding ring on her finger, and then I am conscious of my own wedding band, a plain, sterling-silver ring, which I am twisting around and around my finger.

I ask Nicola if she minds if I smoke. She says she does not mind. I always ask and this is always what she says. The waiter comes and places two menus on the table. I order a *latte macchiato*. Nicola asks for a glass of water and pushes her menu to the side of the table. I order the salmon salad – *insalata di salmone, patate nuove, cicoria*. Nicola asks for the same. The way she pronounces the words, in her precise English accent, makes it sound like something different, something I wish I had ordered as well.

I have not yet lighted my cigarette. I tap the unfiltered tip against the surface of the table.

"How is your writing?" Nicola asks.

I shrug and my lip forces the corner of my mouth upwards, as if I am sneering. It is what I always do.

I ask Nicola about her novel.

"Actually, it is going very well," she says.

I want to tell her that I liked her hair better when it was shorter and dyed orange. But it is not the sort of thing that I would tell Nicola. Instead, I ask her about David.

Today is Friday, the sixth day of November, 1992. It is almost nine years since Nicola and I met. That was a Friday also, late in October.

I know this because I save my appointment books. They are placed chronologically on a shelf in my study. Yesterday I flipped through the pages of the book for that year, 1983. I also read Nicola's letters. I keep them in a file folder in a cabinet reserved for personal papers. There are eleven letters, spanning a period of eight months, though the first of the eleven letters is not dated.

The first letter is also the shortest. It is written by hand in black ink on heavy, cream-coloured paper. "I shall be at the International

Festival of Authors on Friday as I am very fond of Ted Hughes. Perhaps we could meet there." There is no salutation. Her name and phone number appear at the bottom of the page.

I had placed a classified advertisement in *The Globe and Mail.* I did not know what or whom I was looking for, only that I felt terribly alone. I was also an alcoholic. I was about to hit bottom, as my therapist puts it, though I did not know that then. In the spring, Paige had left me because of my drinking. I was living in a rooming house on Adelaide Street.

I placed the advertisement early in October. "Single, white male, 24, alcoholic, heavy smoker, dabbles in poetry . . ."

Only Nicola responded.

I remember almost nothing of our first meeting. I met Nicola at Harbourfront where Ted Hughes was reading. In my appointment book, I have noted six other meetings over a space of three months. There were others planned, but Nicola did not show up, or I called to cancel because I was too drunk and I did not want Nicola to see me like that. When we did meet, it was in restaurants, always in the late afternoon. Nicola did not want to be seen anywhere else. Nicola never came to my room.

After our meal, I would walk with Nicola to her residence. She was in her first year of university, studying English, and lived in a women's residence on campus. Nicola's parents lived in Calgary, but Nicola rarely visited them. They had emigrated from England when she was a child.

I had dropped out of university several years earlier. I was twenty-four. Nicola was then seventeen. I had had a job as a dishwasher and then as a security guard, but I had quit that as well. I was about to publish a small book of my poetry with money that Paige had lent me.

Nicola and I talked about writing. We had both published poems in the literary journals at the university. We were both attempting to write fiction. We had dismissed poetry as unimportant. I was going to write short stories. Nicola was writing a novel. We talked about books we had read, but very little else. Nicola was reluctant to say anything about herself. There were things that I wanted to tell her about myself, but I knew that they were better left unsaid. If I was confused by her reticence to speak of personal things, I later found out that she was equally frightened by me and the life that I was leading.

We never kissed or touched hands. I would stand on the sidewalk outside the women's residence and watch Nicola enter through the glass doors. She did not look back as she stood waiting for the elevator. I would then walk to the nearest bar.

My book of poetry was published in December. A launch for it was held at the Main Street library, but Nicola did not come. I had been drinking heavily for several days, and someone had given me a quart of vodka. I called Nicola late at night, after the launch. She had been sleeping. I told her that I could not go on with things the way they were. We did not have a relationship. I told her she had to make a commitment to me one way or another. She had to tell me where she stood. And then I hung up.

I received a letter from Nicola in the new year. "Perhaps you would like to write to me. I am afraid that is the only worthwhile kind of contact I can offer. I can't form any sort of relationship at the moment," Nicola wrote, "I am not quite sure why."

I did not answer her letter.

Nicola wrote, "My novel is the only thing that matters."

She enclosed a poem she had written about me. The last stanza read:

Your eyes watery,
something black.
It is awful
what will happen.

At the end of March I was hospitalized after attempting suicide. According to my appointment book, Nicola visited me in the hospital three times. I was heavily sedated, and I remember only the last of these visits. It was a Sunday near the end of April, and I was soon to be released. I had been given a three-hour pass. Nicola and I walked to the art gallery. It was raining, and we shared her umbrella, but said little.

In the foyer of the gallery, I stared at a bronzed torso by Rodin. One arm seemed to have been hacked off with a knife. The body was contorted in such a way as to suggest extreme, inhuman pain, the vulva pushed out for all to gaze at and touch. I thought of the tragic life of Camille Claudel, whose own work was plagiarized by her lover and obscured by his fame. What was it that I had wanted from Nicola and that she had refused me? She was young, but her body was like a child's. She was nothing but a skeleton covered in pale skin and long wisps of blond hair. Was it her fragility that attracted me? Or was this only the way that I had sculpted her in my mind? She was an object upon which I wanted to throw myself. Because I suffered, I wanted to break off her arms.

I told Nicola that I was not well and that I had to leave. We had tea in a Chinese restaurant on Spadina Avenue. I watched the street fill with rain.

In the summer I received a letter from Nicola written from England. It is the last of the eleven letters I have in my file folder. She had gone to England to visit a man whom she had loved since she was a child. "He is very immersed in his work," she wrote. "We discovered that although we have this obsession with our respective work in common we have little to talk about." She planned to return to Canada soon afterwards and to live with her parents in Calgary.

"A pony bit me once when I was a child," Nicola said. And there was a horse who only turned in circles and would not stop.

We were sitting in the back corner of the Express Café on Queen Street West. It was cold outside, snowing. Nicola wrapped her hands around a white porcelain bowl of café au lait. Her nails were torn where she had bitten them.

"Horses have never liked me," Nicola said.

Alex and I were married late in 1985. I had quit drinking and was in therapy. The poems I had written up until then were to be published by the Coach House Press. They were the last poems I ever wrote. After the book was published, I received a large grant to write a collection of short stories. I was trying very hard to put my past behind me.

When I ran into Nicola on College Street, I did not recognize her at first. If anything she seemed thinner, her skin more pale.

"I was not sure that you would want to see me," Nicola said.

I told her that nothing had really changed. We were sitting in a booth in the window of The Squeeze Club on Queen Street West.

Nicola picked at her salad with a fork. "For a while, I did not want to see you. Your depression and your self-obsession were overwhelming me."

I took a sip of my ginger ale. My therapist had suggested that I avoid coffee. I was taking tranquillizers for my anxiety, and antidepressants as well. Nicola speared a wedge of tomato with her fork, then placed the fork down upon the plate.

"Before I left for England, there was a student at the university whom I was peculiarly attracted to," Nicola said. "Perhaps, *perversely attracted to* is the expression I want. He was a Divinity student. At first I wrote him poems on the backs of postcards. He did not know who sent them, of course. I didn't sign the postcards. It was a wonderful relationship. I had an intimacy with him because of the postcards, but without actually having to be involved. I imagined his responses to the poems, and this gave me pleasure.

"But then we became involved. He was also a writer. I showed him my writing. Then he showed me his writing, and he had stolen my words and ideas. He was plagiarizing my writing. He would not admit to it. I asked him to stop plagiarizing my writing, but he would not. He wanted to have a relationship. But I could not have a relationship with him. Not with anyone."

The waiter removed Nicola's salad from the table and replaced it with another dish. Nicola had ordered the chicken in a watermelon sauce. I was having the Cajun meat loaf with roasted potatoes. I began to eat, but then I pushed my plate to the side of the table and lit a cigarette.

"I never told you this," Nicola said. "I did not tell you because you were in the hospital. I had dropped out of university. I was failing all my courses. I had stopped attending lectures. I could not concentrate on anything. The Divinity student was destroying me.

"I was having a breakdown. I went to England and then I came back and lived with my parents in Calgary. But I could not live with my parents. I had no money and nowhere to go. I had no more friends. My parents could not understand anything. They could not understand I was having a breakdown. They would not take me seriously as a writer. My mother thought I needed to get married. She thought that I should marry the Divinity student.

"But all this time I was having a breakdown. My parents put me in the hospital. It was horrible. There was nothing the doctors could do for me. They gave me drugs, but the drugs only made me worse. No one would listen to me. I had to get away."

Nicola had returned to Toronto to finish her degree at the university. She was working part time in the gift shop at the art gallery and was trying to write her novel.

"I am supposed to see this therapist," Nicola said. "My parents are paying him to see me. But I don't go. He doesn't understand my writing. He gave me anti-depressants, but I flushed them down the toilet. They were making me worse. I need to work at my writing. The therapist doesn't understand this. He doesn't understand my writing."

The waiter took our plates away. We had barely touched the food.

I had ordered a slice of double-chocolate cake, but now I did not want it. This was the most Nicola had ever told me about herself. I did not know what to say. I felt her pain, but I could not respond to it. I was absorbed by my own suffering. I thought that now perhaps I could be closer to Nicola. Instead, I felt even more distant. There was nothing she was asking from me. There was nothing she wanted from me. And I had nothing to offer.

My arms lay across the bare table, the tips of my fingers a few inches from Nicola's hands. Across my wrists several thin, white lines were visible where I had cut myself with an X-acto knife. That had been nearly two years ago. I would always have these scars. I often wondered if they were visible to anyone but myself. Did people see the scars on my wrists? Did they know? No one ever mentioned them. That was what frightened me.

I paid the bill with Alex's credit card. Nicola and I walked outside onto the street. This was in the spring, but everything was filthy grey. It was raining or it was not raining. We stood a few feet apart, looking at each other, but not really looking.

Nicola unlocked her bicycle and rode away along Queen Street. There was a great deal of traffic and soon I could no longer see her.

Nicola says that it is strange with David. She is not used to being married.

"Sometimes I don't know what to think," Nicola says.

The Bar Italia is almost quiet now. The lunch crowd has dispersed, leaving behind writers and artists, actors, the unemployed. They are mostly men in their early thirties, much like myself.

The waiter brings our meal. The large, china plates have been sprayed at the edges with thinly diced parsley. Steamed new potatoes rest on dandelion leaves. In the centre is a mound of warm flakes of Atlantic salmon, crossed with fried strips of the salmon skin. Virgin olive oil drips from the potatoes. The waiter stands grinding pepper above our plates.

Eating is what I enjoy most. That and drinking coffee and smoking cigarettes. Nicola eats slowly. We finish our meal, and I order another coffee and light a cigarette.

Nicola is happy with the way her novel is going at the moment. It is the same novel she has been writing for several years. A young woman becomes involved with her writing instructor at the university. He is married, and much older than she is. The woman becomes obsessed with the man, and with his wife, to the detriment of her own sanity.

"I do not know how the novel ends," Nicola says.

I have read various drafts of the first chapters. Nicola writes and rewrites, and then tears up what she has written and begins again.

I have been working on a collection of short stories for several years now. But I have not written anything for the past few months. I try to explain to Nicola why I can no longer write. The stories are about people I know and have known. I reveal much about their personal lives. Other parts I make up, but only as it suits me. There is a cruelty involved. In truth, I am a cruel person. *Self-obsessed*, Nicola said.

Nicola says, "I don't quite see the problem."

I say, "Suppose I were to write a story about you, about your relationship to me, and about your marriage to David. The names would be changed, and much of the story would be fictional. But the story would reveal personal things about you that only I know. You would clearly recognize yourself in the story, as would other people who are close to you."

"But that's nonsense," Nicola says. "I do that in my novel. All writers do."

"Suppose, then, that I were to write into the story that you had an affair with someone." I look directly at Nicola.

"I still don't see the problem," she says.

"What if David were to read the story?"

"That would be David's problem," Nicola says.

The waiter replaces my ashtray with a clean one. Nicola asks for more water and is silent while the waiter pours it from a jug into her glass. Nicola sips from the glass and then places it on the table. She dips the tip of her index finger into the water and leaves her finger resting on the edge of the glass.

"I am not certain I am ready for monogamy," Nicola says.

I tell I her I feel the same way. That I miss the excitement that each new relationship brings with it at first.

"No, it's not that," Nicola says. "I want the security I get from being married to David. Relationships always made me miserable. But still I wonder if I might have an affair. I don't know how David would feel."

"Marriage is a frightening thing," I say.

"No, it isn't that," Nicola says. "I think it is only that I need to have an affair."

Outside the Bar Italia, it is no longer snowing. The sun has come out, though only barely. Nicola wants to take my photograph. She has begun a class in photography at the Ontario College of Art.

Nicola stands on the edge of the sidewalk and focuses the lens of her camera. I am standing on the damp sidewalk in front of the Bar Italia in my polished, black Dr Martens shoes. I am wearing my black leather jacket, dyed black jeans, and my black beret. My hair is tied back in a ponytail. I am thirty-three years old. Nicola's finger presses down on the button and the click echoes against the storefronts along College Street.

I have no photographs of Nicola. She would never give me one.

I watch as Nicola pedals her bicycle away from me and disappears into the traffic.

What I had wanted to say was: What if I wrote in my story that you had an affair *with me*? But I did not say that. It is not what I want. Perhaps I think it is what I want. What I want I do not know. It is possible that what I want has nothing to do with Nicola.

Clint Burnham comes past the next evening, and I take him to the College Street Bar for dinner. Clint has recently separated from his wife, and he has no money. The waiter brings a plate of sautéed black olives to our table. Clint takes an olive in his fingers and rips the flesh from the pit with his teeth. Then he tells me that he is gay. He drops the pit back onto the plate and takes another olive.

I do not know what to say. I am surprised, but hardly shocked. Rather, I am jealous that he knows what it is he wants, and that it is something different.

"I am happy for you," I say. Then we discuss Clint's new manuscript, a collection of poetry that he has recently finished.

Later, Clint and I walk along College Street to the Bar Italia to play pool. But it is crowded and we cross the street to play at the Oriental Recreation Centre instead.

As we pass the Unity, the windows are dark. There is a piece of paper taped to the door. It is a bailiff's notice.

Toronto is like that. I find a place I like to eat and then it closes. Last week the windows of Viva, the new restaurant on Bloor Street, were covered over in newspapers.

There will be new restaurants, other cafés. I will sit in them in the afternoons and evenings, drinking coffee and smoking cigarettes, testing new dishes, learning the names of the waiters. It is all that I know of Toronto. All that I can understand, all that I can grasp onto.

I do not go to movies, or to the theatre. I avoid literary events. I have not been inside a museum since I was a child. I do not travel. I have few friends, and none whom I am close to. The thought of having close friends frightens me.

Nicola and I will continue to meet every few months, always for lunch, in various restaurants. We will not talk on the telephone, except to arrange our meetings. We will never meet in the evenings or on weekends. We will always meet alone. When we part, we will not kiss or touch. I will walk with Nicola to the street. She will unlock her bicycle and ride away. I will walk somewhere else for coffee and to read the newspaper, or to my postal box to collect my mail.

It has been this way for nine years now. I am not sure that I would want it to be any other way. Nicola and I will be friends. We will never be close. It has taken us nine years to come this far.

It has taken me nine years.

Toronto is the only city in the world where people will sit outside on the patios of cafés in late autumn, when it is barely above ten degrees Celsius, or in early spring, when it is just above zero. There is always the slightest glimmer of sun. There are so many things to talk about, so many things to say.

GIRL ON THE SUBWAY

CRAD KILODNEY

CRAD KILODNEY USED TO SELL HIS BOOKS ON THE STREETS OF TORONTO BUT RETIRED IN 1995 AND INTENDS NEVER TO WRITE AGAIN. BEFORE GIVING IT ALL UP, HIS SHORT STORIES APPEARED IN SEVERAL COLLECTIONS INCLUDING LIGHTNING STRIKES MY DICK AND GIRL ON THE SUBWAY. THESE DAYS HE LIVES MODESTLY OFF THE STOCK MARKET. AS HE PUTS IT: "I NEED A WIFE VERY BADLY."

I asked Ted to meet me at Danny's Grill at eight o'clock and sit with me for a while before Laura arrived at nine. I was pretty sure that this would be the last time I'd be seeing her. I knew she was very unhappy with me, and I expected that she was going to make the break-up official tonight. I'd tried not to see it for a long time, but the warmth was no longer there. It's all those little things that set the tone – the look in the eyes, the body language, the inflection of the voice. When I compared them now to what they were at the beginning, it was hard to believe I was dealing with the same person. I've always been kind of stupid about these things. My heart prevents my mind from reading the signals until they're palpable enough to trip over. Of course, it was remotely possible that Laura was going to be gentle and conciliatory and that she'd say we should keep things going. It was a faint hope, that's all.

I wanted Ted to sit with me beforehand and help me build up my courage because facing a break-up was something I never was able to do bravely. I wouldn't have asked anyone else to do this favour for me. Ted was the only man I ever bared my soul to. In fact, I think he was the only man who'd ever seen me cry in my entire life. And I'd seen him at his worst, too.

I was in a booth toward the back, and he instinctively looked for me there. It was very cold out – well below freezing – and he had on his heavy coat, which he'd bought at Goodwill for eight dollars.

"Hi," he said, slipping into the seat opposite me. The waitress came by, and I let him order a double whisky, on me. It was the least he had coming to him for having to sit with me under these circumstances.

He let out a deep sigh and looked at me with that slightly twisted smile of his that conveyed a variety of meanings but which in this case was intended to be sympathetic. "Have you thought of what you're going to say to her?"

"Not really. I figure she'll do the talking, and whatever I have to say won't matter much. Her mind will probably be made up."

"Just don't make a scene. That's the worst thing."

"No, of course I won't."

"Well . . ." he sighed again, reaching for an inside pocket and pulling out a small envelope – the kind suited for a thank-you note or an invitation. "I got this today."

"From your brother?"

"No, my sister-in-law. Arlen is no longer speaking to me."

"Oh, Christ."

Ted unfolded the handwritten letter. It was written on stiff, rose-coloured paper that crackled. "I won't bother reading the whole thing to you, but this part sums it up: '*How could you hurt your brother in that way? We're both very, very disappointed in you . . .*' See that? The *very*'s are underlined for emphasis." The waitress brought him his drink, and he immediately took a large swallow. I decided to have another myself.

Ted had written a story about himself and his brother, and his brother had taken it in the worst possible way. I understood better than anyone else how badly this hurt Ted. His worst moments were the ones when he got drunk and talked to me about his relationship with his brother, and then so much pain would come out that I could only sit there quietly and let him talk himself out. Arlen was four years older. He was a very successful lawyer. His wife, Sarah, was an art dealer. They had a huge house in the suburbs. I'd been up there once. Sarah had seemed nice enough. Arlen I couldn't really size up. He had a polished formality that made me feel I was seeing a carefully constructed image rather than a flesh and blood human being. But Ted had assured me, "That's just the style that carries over from his work. When he loosens up he's a good egg."

Ted was, in his own words, "just one of those typical starving writers," and he usually said this with his twisted smile and a forced laugh for the benefit of others. But in his case the term "starving" was not so far from the truth. He was always broke. He refused to take any permanent or "career" job because he insisted on being a writer first and a worker second. He would do unskilled labour on a temporary basis – the sort of thing where you show up at the agency at 7 a.m. and wait around hoping to get something. He made a few dollars from his writing now and then, but that was only enough to cover his supplies and postage. I'd treated him to meals plenty of times. I was happy to do it. He couldn't bear to ask his brother for money. Not that Arlen wouldn't have given it to him. He would have. But he would've done it so condescendingly as to make Ted feel like a failure or a child. Arlen had already given Ted such an inferiority complex that he felt ill at ease among prosperous or successful people.

I considered Ted a brilliant writer, much too good to ever be commercially successful. His devotion to his writing was the thing that kept him going. He cared about it more than anything or anyone else, and he would become very angry if anyone suggested that he "write to sell." I recall one occasion when we were introduced to an editor for a big publishing house, and this fellow said to Ted, "Why don't you write something that'll make you some fast money so you can sit back and write your more literary stuff?" And Ted looked this guy in the eye and said, "Why don't you have your daughter turn a few tricks to earn money for her wedding?"

One time Ted dragged a cardboard box out of his closet and showed me some old photos of himself and his brother when they were kids. Typically, they had their arms around each other as they stood smiling for the camera. "That's me and Arlen at the beach." "That's me and Arlen with a fish we caught." "That's me and Arlen just before he went away to camp." "That's me and Arlen with our mother a few months before she died." Arlen was the stronger, the faster, the more aggressive. Arlen could wrestle him to the ground in five seconds. Arlen was the popular one in school. Arlen got a scholarship. Never did I hear a bad word about Arlen. But no matter how much Ted looked up to Arlen, there was a gap between them. And as the years went by, the gap widened. It wasn't that Arlen didn't like Ted. He just couldn't or wouldn't show it. They could sit together in a restaurant or bar and talk, but the talk never got very personal. Arlen's tone was friendly enough, but there was not much feeling in his conversation, and he preferred small talk or talk about his work or the house. When Ted told him they ought to "sit down and get to know each other again," Arlen snickered and said that was a lot of "sixties hippie bullshit." Because of distance, they saw each other only on major holidays or special occasions, and this made Ted feel the lack of communication even more keenly. Arlen also took no great interest in Ted's writing. He wasn't against it, but he never displayed any enthusiasm for it either. His standard remark to Ted was, "When're you going to write a best-seller?" And he once introduced Ted to a friend of his as "my kid brother, Ted, who's trying to be a writer." At that point, Ted had already been writing seriously for fifteen years and had published stories in nearly forty magazines.

I think inside of each person there is one fundamental problem or conflict or theme that underlies everything else and sets the tone of the whole personality, and until you realize what it is, you don't really understand that person. On one occasion when he was pretty drunk, Ted told me tearfully that he loved and admired his brother from the bottom of his heart and that all he ever wanted was to have his brother love and admire him in return, and that it hurt him more than he could express in words that his brother would not open up to him and show him any real affection.

Ted admitted to me that perhaps the main reason why he was so dedicated to his writing was so that someday he might become recognized enough to make his brother take him seriously and admire him and want to understand all that was inside him.

Which brings us back to the letter he'd just gotten from Sarah.

Six months before, Ted had written a story called "Brothers," a thinly disguised story about his relationship with Arlen. He even set it in the same restaurant where they had sat for dinner and reproduced part of their conversation. It was a very beautiful but very painful story. Its meaning was obvious to me: there was an unbridgeable gap between the narrator and his older brother, and the narrator was suffering silently because of it. The story had gotten published recently in a literary magazine, and Ted had sent a copy to Arlen.

But what he never anticipated was that Arlen would misconstrue it as a personal attack on him – all the worse for having been published "for everyone to read." And Sarah had agreed with Arlen that it was a cruel personal attack.

Ted folded the letter up and stuck it back in his pocket. He frowned and looked off vaguely into space. I just shook my head and stared into my drink. Then he gave a cynical little laugh and said, "Hell, I didn't even make any money from that story!"

I was tempted to say that Arlen was an asshole, but instead I told him, "The only guarantee a writer has is that he'll be misunderstood frequently, and sometimes by the people who ought to understand him best."

"That's for damn sure," he said, finishing his drink.

"You want another? I have plenty of dough today. We might as well, seeing as how we're both feeling so terrific." So I ordered another round for us and tried to convince myself that when nine o'clock rolled around and Laura arrived, I'd be anaesthetized enough to have my head cut off neatly and take it like a man.

"Well, now that I've cheered you up," said Ted with a twisted smile, "why don't you tell me something amusing?"

And then I thought of the girl on the subway. "Well, it's not very amusing, but. . . ."

"That's okay. I want to hear it anyway."

The waitress brought us our drinks. I waited till she left before I began.

A few nights before, I was on the subway coming home from Laura's. It was quite late, maybe one in the morning. There weren't too many people on the subway. There were two girls across the aisle from me sitting perpendicular to each other rather than on the same seat. They were in their early twenties. One was a mannish blonde with short hair, no make-up, and very plain clothes. The other girl was dark, maybe East Indian or from somewhere in the Caribbean. She was quite pretty – nice makeup, colourful clothes, a lovely smile. She seemed a bit coy. She did most of the talking, however, and the blond girl was leaning forward to hear her better above the noise of the train. I could see the blonde looking at her very intensely, her eyes travelling all over the coloured girl. The coloured girl made only occasional eye contact with her. Most of the time she smiled bashfully and looked at her hands on her lap or at the floor. I couldn't hear what they were saying, but I got the impression that they knew each other but not particularly well – maybe as co-workers or classmates. I watched them discreetly all the way up from Bloor Street to Lawrence Avenue. At Lawrence the coloured girl got off. She smiled and said goodbye to the blonde and then hurried off, walking briskly toward the exit without looking back.

After that, the blonde's expression changed radically. She just stared at the floor, her hands folded. She looked profoundly sad, and I felt great pity just seeing her sitting there lost in an apparent cloud of inner pain. In that moment, I felt I understood the whole scene intuitively: the blond girl was in love with the coloured girl but couldn't tell her so because the other girl was obviously straight. Perhaps she'd been trying to get up her courage to say something before the coloured girl got to her stop but then realized she'd missed her chance. Maybe I was completely wrong in my interpretation of the scene, but my intuitive feeling about it was very strong.

I kept watching the blond girl out of the corner of my eye. Her gaze wandered to the window, where the wall of the tunnel was rushing past, and I could see her faint reflection in the glass. What a look of sorrow! How I wanted to go over to her and try to console her in some way. But one doesn't do things like that on the subway. Like most people, I'm conditioned to mind my own business.

I had to get off at York Mills, the next stop, and I saw the blond girl get up, too. I deliberately went out by a different door and then walked toward the north end of the station, in the direction of the stairs leading to the bus platform.

When I cast a quick glance over my shoulder, I saw the girl standing at the south end at the edge of the platform. She was looking at the tracks. I became alarmed. In a few seconds we'd be the only two people on the platform. She was obviously thinking about jumping, and it was up to me to do something.

I pretended to go up the stairs and then walked out of her view behind one of the pillars. I was shaking. I walked back in her direction, using the pillars to keep out of her sight. When I finally came close to her, she saw me and stiffened. I went over to her and put my hand on her arm. "I'm sorry to intrude," I said. Wasn't that a ridiculous thing to say! *I'm sorry to intrude.* Jesus!

"Get lost," she said, pulling her arm away.

This time I held on to her arm more firmly. "Look, I'm not prepared to see something like this. Why don't you come with me?"

"It's none of your business," she said harshly.

"I know, I know, but please, why don't we just go upstairs, okay? Come on. Please. What do you say?"

She gave me a long, hard look I couldn't interpret, then she turned toward the escalator at the south end, and I followed right behind her, trying to hold gently on to one arm.

"Maybe you'd like someone to talk to? We could go somewhere or I could escort you home. Whatever you want." I was still shaking and felt unsure of what to do.

"Never mind," she said, not looking at me. "You don't have to hold my arm. I don't need that." I felt like an idiot.

We ended up at the south exit, south of the Shell station. I had no idea where to steer her. We were on the wrong side to get on a bus. We just walked south on Yonge Street.

"I sort of got the impression that something went wrong between you and that other girl," I said. She was walking at a steady pace. I don't think she was trying to get rid of me exactly, just ignoring me. It was a very cold night, but I felt flushed and uncomfortably warm. She wouldn't say a word. I kept trying to soothe her, to get her to talk. Did she want to go home? Did she want to come home with me? Did she want to sit down someplace and have a drink? (There was no place to sit down in that area anyway.) Did she want to talk about her problem? Part of me wanted to kiss her out of sympathy, and another part of me felt resentful and foolish because of her coldness.

Right in the middle of my pathetic monologue, she spied a cab coming toward us and signalled. "I think I'll just grab this cab," she said. "Thanks. I know you meant well." And without another word, she got in, and they made a U-turn and headed back south.

I walked home. It was a long walk, and I felt very mixed up inside. I felt ridiculous, but I kept telling myself that at least I had prevented a suicide.

After hearing all this, Ted sat back and replied, "Maybe, maybe not. Maybe she went and did it anyway or still plans to. You'll never know."

"Well, I haven't read anything in the papers about a suicide on the subway."

"You wouldn't in any case. The transit commission has a strict policy of never acknowledging them. They feel the publicity would only encourage it."

"I didn't know that."

"It's true. I know somebody who works for them. There's an average of one suicide or attempted suicide per week on the subway. Nobody ever reads about them in the papers." He let out a deep breath. "Anyway, you did the right thing."

The waitress came back. "Care for another?"

"No, thanks," said Ted.

"I'm still waiting for someone," I said. She left us.

Ted looked at his watch. "She ought to be here pretty soon."

"Maybe she'll make me wait. She's done that a few times." Despite all the alcohol, my courage had melted away again.

"No, she'll be on time," said Ted. "She'll want to get it over with."

I said nothing.

"I know this isn't any consolation to you, but I saw this coming a long time ago. Laura's just not right for you. I'm not putting her down, mind you, but I think she's just not a good match for you."

"We had a terrific relationship for a while."

Ted shrugged and made a face. "In a relationship you see what you want to see. You think, oh, this is the big one, this is real love, this is the one I was destined to meet, and all that crap. And then when it's over you realize how wrong you were, but you repeat the process with the next one. It's all very banal, very banal."

"I'm trying to figure out just what I did wrong."

"Look, now that I'm a little drunk, I'll tell you what I think about human relationships. All our best efforts to reach out to someone aren't necessarily enough. You think you can win the other person over or break down the barriers, or whatever, just because of what *you* feel inside *you*, but you can't transplant your feelings into another person. Every person is locked into his own reality. In fact, I think very few people really understand each other. They connect in some limited way, maybe even for the long term, and they just become habitual to each other if they're compatible. I don't know, maybe it's inevitable. Maybe it's even preferable. Maybe too much communication and openness is threatening to people. It seems to be enough for most of the human race to just muddle along unthinkingly. . . . Not that this applies to you. You're certainly more open and honest than almost anybody else I've ever known. . . . Anyway, that's Psychology 101 *à la* Ted Butler. Tuition fee, two drinks." He held up his glass for emphasis. "Cheaper than university."

I twiddled my melting ice cube with the stick and picked the lemon wedge. "Ted, this is going to hurt me like hell. And there's nothing I can do about it, absolutely nothing."

"It's only pain, my friend. It won't kill you." He sighed. "I'm sorry if I sound so hard-nosed, but you know, I've been through so many break-ups, it's positively banal. *All* break-ups are banal. Every man in your situation thinks his particular case is unique or especially tragic, or that his pain is worse than the next guy's. But all it adds up to is this: first you love her, then you have problems with her, you break up, and you go back to being a poor masturbating son of a bitch."

"You know. . . . I always had this thought whenever I had to go through it . . . that there must be some *meaning* to this kind of pain. There must be something to *understand*. And if I could just understand it, I'd be a lot wiser and maybe avoid it next time."

"You want to know the meaning? I'll tell you."

"What?"

"There *is* no meaning. You just suffer. Period." He looked at his watch again. "I'd better let you face her alone. If you feel like calling me later, I'll be up late." He put on his coat. "Thanks for the drinks."

"Sure thing."

He patted me on the shoulder and left.

I felt alone and miserable. But then I thought maybe, just maybe, we were both wrong, and it was all going to turn out okay. Then I'd be calling him up and telling him, and he'd be happy for me. Anyway, I told myself I was going to be very calm because Fate is kinder to a gentleman. And then I thought about the girl on the subway standing at the edge of the platform. I replayed the whole incident over in my mind, changing what I would've said and done, trying to figure out what the perfect thing would have been to say or do to ensure that the girl wouldn't commit suicide. I had done the only thing I could think of at that moment, but maybe it wasn't enough.

I looked at my watch. It was 9:01. Laura was at the door, dressed in her expensive black coat and looking as sleek as a fashion model. As she opened the door, I saw the look of cool reserve – of *firmness* – on her face, and I knew at once that this was the end. The glass door swinging closed behind her caught the reflection of the neon sign of the night club across the street, such an icy blue crackling mercilessly through the cold winter air, and my heart fell back to the stained glass ornament that hung in her bedroom window – a white bird poised between a rainbow and a garden of flowers – which I'd gazed at so many times as it caught the warm rays of the early morning sun and cast a soft patch of coloured light on the edge of the white blanket under which we had slept.

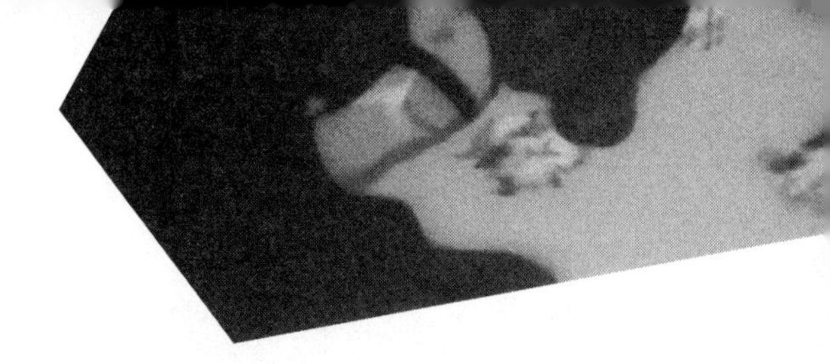

MISSING

JULIE DOUCET

MONTREAL COMIC ARTIST JULIE DOUCET'S WORK IS CHARACTERIZED BY ITS DETAILED DRAWING STYLE AND UNSETTLING SUBJECT MATTER. HER WORK HAS ALWAYS BEEN CONTROVERSIAL: SEVERAL OF HER COMICS WERE SEIZED BY CUSTOMS OFFICIALS IN CANADA AND ENGLAND AT A TIME WHEN *THE NEW YORK TIMES* CALLED HER "A WIDELY ADMIRED YOUNG CARTOONIST." DOUCET'S MOST RECENT WORK IS *MY MOST SECRET DESIRE*, FROM WHICH THE STORY "MISSING" IS TAKEN. TRANSLATED EDITIONS OF HER COMICS HAVE APPEARED IN FRANCE, SPAIN, GERMANY, AND FINLAND.

A C →
L →
MiSSiNG
AN OTHER BAD DREAM
BY→JULIE DOUCET 1992

?

BRIGITTE?

HEY! BRIGITTE?
L

EXIT
B...BRIGITTE?
SHE MUST HAVE TAKEN THIS TUNNEL!..

EXIT
....

WHY did SHE DO THAT??

UH OH!

WHAT NOW!??

B G
OH WELL...

AH?

←EXiT

B DOWN TOWN
NO BRIGITTE AROUND...!

JULIE! NICOLAS IS DEAD!!!
?!?
NICOLAS!?
IT'S TERRIBLE SOB SOB!!
UH YES...

SOB!.. YESSS
IT... IT'S HIM!?

OOOH
NICOLAS!..

?!
RRRING!!

WHAT IF..?
RRING!!

HELLO?
DDR...

HEY JOHN, Hi!!!
HOW YOU DOING?

...FINE, FINE... i...i'D LIKE TO ASK YOU... UH... iT'S ABOUT... UH
YES?
YOU KNOW THAT..... PRODJECT YOU HAD?

a PRODJECT? WHAT PRODJECT?
YOU WANTED TO..., TO.... i MEAN...

YOU KNOW, THAT PRODJECT!

THAT PRODJECT? ??? do YOU MEAN THE ONE ABOUT GETTING MARRIED FOR U.S. CITIZEN-SHIP?
YES YES THAT'S IT!
HA HA WHY, YOU WANT TO MARRY ME ?? HEH HEH HEH!
Y...Y..YES...
REALLY!? HO WOW!!!
WOW! BUT...WHY WOULD YOU DO THAT? JUST FOR HELPING ME? OR...
...FOR LOVE?
JOHN?

JOHN ARE YOU THERE?

JOHN?..
HELLO?

HELLO?
HELLO? HELLO?
END

FRANCE DAIGLE HAS LIVED ALL HER LIFE IN MONCTON, NEW BRUNSWICK, WHICH IS THE CLOSEST ONE CAN GET TO URBAN ACADIA. SHE HAS PUBLISHED NINE BOOKS IN FRENCH. HER WORKS EXPLORE THE BOUNDARIES BETWEEN IMMOBILITY AND MOVEMENT, REALITY AND FICTION, AND LIFE AND DEATH, TO NAME A FEW. *1953 CHRONICLE OF A BIRTH FORETOLD*, HER MOST RECENT BOOK IN ENGLISH TRANSLATION, IS A GOOD EXAMPLE OF HOW ALL THESE THEMES MESH TOGETHER. "THE REAL STORY" IS TAKEN FROM *REAL LIFE*, HER FIRST BOOK TO BE TRANSLATED INTO ENGLISH.

THE REAL STORY

FRANCE DAIGLE

TRANSLATED BY SALLY ROSS

PART I

61. A QUESTION OF WARMTH

The medical director of the cancer treatment centre summoned Elizabeth to his office one day. The middle-aged man began with a few general inquiries. He asked Elizabeth whether she was satisfied with the way things were going at the centre, whether she liked Moncton, whether she was content with her apartment, and whether she felt at ease with the Acadians. He also shared some of the comments he had heard about her. A number of patients had told the other members of the medical team that they found Elizabeth somewhat distant and not particularly comforting. In fact, they found her rather cold.

62. CONTINUATION OF THE INTERVIEW WITH CLAUDE

Claude explains that, after a while, his clientele was composed almost entirely of women. He had not taken exception to this state of affairs. He had realized, without having given it too much thought, that women felt at ease with him. In those days, he was devoting a fair amount of time to his other more informal job as a picker. Indeed, he quite enjoyed looking around for rare or valuable objects. Not wanting to see these objects disappear, and not interested in keeping them for himself, he told friends and collectors about them. This second job gave him a great deal of pleasure and satisfaction, and occasionally, a nice financial reward.

63. A DIFFICULT WOMAN

Even though he would have preferred a less embarrassing pretext, the medical director of the centre was pleased to have this opportunity to approach Elizabeth. He had already noticed that he felt himself a different man in her presence. So he personally relished the minor challenge of penetrating a bit of the mystery of this apparently inaccessible woman. He thinks he knows how to reach women whom one might qualify as difficult.

64. KEEPING THINGS SIMPLE

Claude understands why his practice has come to be surrounded in an aura of discretion. On the one hand, he does not advertise his services, and on the other, his clients are, for the most part, career women who feel that it should be possible to obtain intimate care without attracting attention. Located away from the busier sections of town, Claude's apartment helped keep things simple.

65. A FREE ZONE

Elizabeth was not surprised by her director's remarks. She had long since been aware that, in medicine, a lack of friendliness was more or less equivalent to abruptness. So she tried to be careful. But it was important for her to create a distance, a kind of free zone, between herself and the people who required care.

66. FREER AND FREER

Claude responds more and more freely to the questions he is being asked. Yes, perhaps in a certain way he had espoused the women's cause, as he had done in the past with regard to the suffering of the Jews and the Blacks. No, his own sexual identity has never been a problem for him. Yes, he had already felt that there was a need to catch up, to correct something. No, he no longer pretends that the breasts and the pubic region do not exist. And yes, on occasion he does bring a woman to climax.

67. THE INSECURITY BELT

Elizabeth did not want her patients to cling to her as a doctor, at least not in the early stages. The free zone, the empty space that she created, forced patients to be alone, to face themselves and not her. She felt that this insecurity belt was essential to the healing process, and she found that it was essential to establish this solitude right from the start. It also provided important clues about the patient's capacity to respond to treatment.

68. A MATTER OF CONSENT

Claude concludes by saying that he has never once doubted his own motives and that he has never taken advantage of the situation to exploit a client. He says that he relies on his personal ethics and the implicit consent of the woman. He says he is aware of the danger, of his precarious position with regard to the law. Sometimes he is concerned, but he remains confident.

69. THE RELEVANCE OF A DISPERSAL

Elizabeth had found it significant that the Acadians resisted the all-too-necessary self-analysis. She had not forgotten that the Acadians were a people who had been dispersed. The Greek word *metastasis* literally means a change of place. She thought this dispersal must be relevant from a medical point of view. She also felt it would be worth exploiting the stubbornness of the Acadians for medical purposes. Listening to her director, she wondered if there were not a way of transforming their collective refusal to die into an antidote that would be effective on an individual basis. She knew that one should also look in the opposite direction from logic since many remedies work in a totally paradoxical way.

70. INTRUSION

Real men, men who wear construction boots and walk on steel beams without losing their balance, don't spend their time thinking they are being watched. They work non-stop, moving with infinite ease towards each strategic junction, where they take hold of the next beam the crane passes them so that it can be attached permanently to the structure. To amuse themselves during their break, they whistle at women, especially the attractive ones leaving the beauty salon. Despite everything, they have great respect for the nurses at the hospital. For these men, sickness is something mysterious and concrete that can bring suffering to a member of the family.

PART 2

71. THE NOON-HOUR RUSH

Denise and Rodriguez are sitting on the terrace of a busy downtown restaurant. The sun is shining and there is a warm spring breeze. They are relaxing in silence, watching the noon-hour rush. A waiter brings them each a glass of wine which they sip peacefully. He comes back with two pizzas. Rodriguez says something that makes Denise laugh. They start eating.

72. THE ROAD SLIPS BY

Elizabeth is very cheery this morning. She has just left for Montreal. She has returned several times since she has been living in Moncton. She quite enjoys the twelve-hour drive in each direction. She likes to see the time and the road slip by. She takes the opportunity to listen to taped lectures and research reports related to her work.

73. RODRIGUEZ THINKS AS HE EATS

As he eats, Rodriguez thinks he would like to give Denise a gift to thank her for her pleasant company. He would like to give her something meaningful. He tries to imagine what type of gift would be appropriate. Normally, he doesn't have any trouble choosing a present for a woman, but this time it's different.

74. ELIZABETH JOTS SOMETHING DOWN ON A NOTEPAD

Still driving, Elizabeth turns off the tape recorder, reaches for a pen and a notepad on the seat beside her, jots down a few words, then puts down the pen and the notepad. She doesn't turn the tape back on. The sun is beaming, her face is radiant. She is thinking of Denis. She feels she's grasped the essence of the film he is about to make.

75. THE BEST SPOT

Denise and Rodriguez go back to the car amid the bustle of downtown. Rodriguez asks Denise to drop him off so he can look around the stores for an hour or so. Nodding affirmatively, Denise asks him discreetly what kind of shopping he has in mind, so she can let him off at the best spot. She confesses she plans to profit from the break to have a snooze since the second glass of wine has made her a bit drowsy.

76. TAKING THE BODY SERIOUSLY

With both hands on the steering wheel, Elizabeth remembers that she hadn't taken her friend seriously when she'd suggested that she make an appointment with the masseur. Her friend, also a doctor, had tried in vain to persuade her gently into trying out the experience. Elizabeth wonders why she was so quick to brush aside the suggestion. Since then, she has not only grown to like massages, but she also draws on them for some interesting leads with regard to the relationship between the mind and the body, between minds and bodies.

77. RODRIGUEZ GETS NOWHERE

Rodriguez has wandered around several shops, but he still hasn't found anything for Denise. He sort of thought he might find himself in this predicament. He looks at his watch. He doesn't have much time. He gives up and tries to convince himself it isn't necessary to go overboard. Could he not give Denise, rather than Alida, the illustrated edition of the Bible he bought this morning?

78. THE CIRCLE OF LOVE

Elizabeth has always found herself outside the circle of love. She doesn't know whether it happened by choice or by chance. Love has slipped between her fingers, so to speak. It has not held anything that she was able or wanted to keep. Whether this fact is trivial or momentous, she does not know. She thinks perhaps it is too early to say.

79. WRENCHED FROM THE PAST

Rodriguez finds the taxi, climbs in the back seat, and explains to Denise that he looked for a present for her, but unfortunately, he wasn't able to find anything he liked. Not being able to surprise her, he offers to give her something she would really like. Denise, who rarely deals with such class, is thrilled by the idea. Caught off guard as to what she would really like, she points to the delicately tinted scarf protruding from the pocket of her client's overcoat. Rodriguez pulls out the scarf and unfolds it carefully so that Denise can see it. Rodriguez feels the moment has come to let go of this souvenir of his father that he wears from time to time as a sort of talisman. Aware of the solemnity of the moment, Denise is just about to change her mind when Rodriguez touches her hand, indicating that the matter is settled. The taxi starts up again.

Rodriguez feels his stomach twist with fear. He falls back on the seat as if forced into the last gap in his defences.

80. INTRUSION

Seated across from her doctor, Alida announces that she has decided not to undergo the treatment he has suggested. She explains that it will not work; instead of curing her, it will crush her, and leave her more vulnerable than ever. She says the disease must resorb itself from within. She says she will continue to look around, and that she is not afraid of dying.

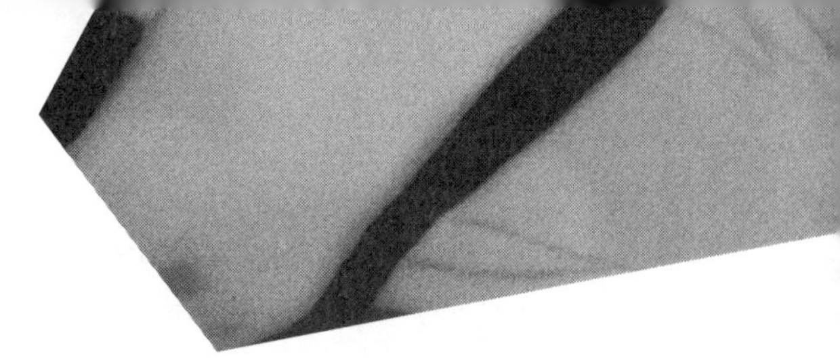

I APPLY

MARK ANTHONY JARMAN

MARK JARMAN: "CHARACTERS IN MY STORIES ARE URBAN, BUT I LIKE TO DISPLACE THEM, MOVE THEM THROUGH BOTH COUNTRY AND CITY. MY RECENTLY PUBLISHED NOVEL, *SALVAGE KING, YA!*, EXPLORES THE TENSION BETWEEN URBAN AND RURAL THROUGH THE CONTRIVANCE OF HOCKEY. SOMETIMES I WANDER AROUND DOWNTOWN VICTORIA AND WORRY ABOUT THE GENE POOL; TRAVELLING THE BACK ROADS THROUGH RANGY-TANG BOONDOCKS I HAVE THE SAME CONCERN. ANYWAY, I TEACH PART-TIME AT THE UNIVERSITY OF VICTORIA. I WRITE AT MY WINDOW DESK IN A HIGH, WELL-LIT ROOM LATE AT NIGHT WHILE THE KIDS SLEEP."

I didn't mean, "Send in a CV" as in *literally* "Send in a CV." Obviously, the more parties that apply the better – but perhaps I meant it more as a signal of sorts: up the flagpole, who salutes, sell the sizzle to the Eskimos in Head Office, snake you to the front of the line.

But have we firmed up anything? Made headway? Well yes and no. You must be patient. You must learn the language, listen for nuances, the laugh down the beige hall that means the power to requisition, to say yes.

I knew your father well. Penchant for profit. As you know. Please refrain from touching my desk.

In the interest of fair play, civility, I'll show you the lever – so you'll know. No surprises. Walk in with your eyes open. Just so. Here is the lever. Quite simple really, unassuming in appearance, dark metal. People expect too much.

I was young once like you, that person a stranger to myself now. . . . I hunted quail on the plateau, frolicked in billowing grass, kissed the girls and made them cry. In the mountain valley the high grass thrashed to and fro, grass and wind swaying against our hips, good fields and rivers right under the steep mountains, and I had a powerful roan horse that rolled on me and broke my pelvis like pulling a wishbone apart. Would you guess that? Look at me – do you see that young person? Am I inside myself here? You don't look at me and see that person. I gave up that person. Now. What I gave up you must give up. Fair is fair. Think career. Be singular in your attentions. Forget your favourite band from Manchester or that daft earring you removed before coming in here. Child is father to the man. Agree to any and all conditions. What I gave up you must give up fourfold.

You could be a find, the bees' knees, a quasar, feather in my cap.

Or not. You have an edge. We might have to take that off. Take that edge down a step. PR, direction, spin. Not a lobotomy but obviously I have to be able to work with you. A little Vaseline. Easy entries and exits are crucial, crucial. You're young.

Why refuse our input? Why? When we know what's good, what's proper, what's worked in the past. Do we not? We're in the real world, we're not up some ivory tower, we're not *sequestered*.

Your clients are *our* clients. A potential pipeline. Especially if our man does well in the election. After the election we'll all have more time. Time for nearest and dearest. Loved ones. How I can love loved ones, given the right circumstances.

You would consider plastic surgery? Check the appropriate box if so. The right eyes – you can make a fortune.

We demand loyalty. There is no remuneration on our fast-track apprentice program, which is clearly advantageous, neatly sidesteps the pitfalls of consumerism. A ground-floor opportunity for a young go-getter, for a gambler, the risk-takers. Are you one of them? Seventy hours, some weekends, say a Sunday afternoon. Get in on the ground floor. Then? Up like a shot.

You've a clear-eyed look about you, an unclouded gaze. Sky's the limit really for some of you in the younger generation. Sky. Limit. How I envy you. Taking the train at dawn. A son of the land once removed.

Each manager has a view of one incense-bearing tree. Each manager is allowed one green seat cushion. The cubicles are in the centre and the offices surround them on three sides. The fourth side is glass, the common walkway with a view of the inner courtyard and that metal sculpture atrocity two storeys down. There are no seat cushions in the cubicle offices.

In clement weather you may eat your lunch down there on the courtyard steps, glance at each other thinking vaguely about metal, statues, legs, earrings and other half-formed images just past the edge of sight, the maritime light of dreams of ships and hovering horizons, salty tears in the tea-rose gazebo, no baldness or vanity, no Abba revivals or scrofula. You may daydream about one man or woman in white whose dedication and affection is without condition or testimony, a person who truly knows you with love like relentless light, light that seems sadly absent on your shrunken lunch hour on the cracked cement steps. Or you may think about seat cushions. In our staff lounge someone senior is not paying for their coffee. I may be on the verge of a huge compromise.

Do you have your own first-aid kit? Last fiscal quarter Watson banged his hand terribly in the desk drawer: every single bone quite smashed. And a fortnight later the contractor's nail-gun incident; took down several blond temps. All the first-aid kits were used up before year end. Accounting was livid, hence the change in policy.

In the event of a position that could be your desk over there; just watch the smallish drawer. We cleaned it up. Invisible hand. A joke. You may laugh though not loudly.

No desk you say? That's a bad sign. Desk not there – yet my department. Perhaps the janitor. Or else something is up, some adjustment, some fluctuation. Then again it may be evidence for the lawsuit. Now you've got me wondering. Fluid situation. My boss is but a shadow. If I'm not here next time you're in you'll understand, surmise something of it. Perhaps you'll have my job. A little levity. Ha-ha. You could be in my chair, with this fabled lever. You'll need more expensive clothes. I recommend my half-brother at The Clothes Horse. His card.

You must, sir, be sartorial, savvy. At the sound of the beep – promises to keep.

The desk (which seems not to be here this moment) is ergonomic, the latest model, friendly shock if the workstation computer not used for work. A small shock, legal levels of course. We've spared no expense for machinery, for capital expenditures. We keep abreast.

If anything we're too generous, too large. An acquisition has to be exceptional to interest us. But we do have to acquire – no choice in a global economy. Bigger and bigger or kaput. It never stops, unless it stops.

If you do get the job we can't tell you anything. You'll just have to know when and what we demand, what the department finds valuable, and you'll have to work fast and cheap. As I said, there is actually no budget as we speak – at this point in time – but there may be a retroactive dispersal – at a later point in time – if funding frees up. The wheels turn slowly. Cut some deadwood in the middle meanwhile. Growth through cuts. Perhaps my own head on the chopping block.

But do I complain? Not a word of it. A word of advice. That resentment you feel? The bile? Get rid of it, get it squared away. It's a matter of efficacy. What is our bottom line? The bottom line is our bottom line. No percentage in angst. Nihilism and mealy-mouthed moping may get you a B in college, and such philosophies may be fashionable with beatniks and bunhead ballerinas, but ultimately it's all sterile, counterproductive.

You could perhaps work on spec until things are ratified, ergo the merger with Drombo Western? There's a happy ending to this. Funds were frozen for this purpose, this work – a respectable amount.

And of course the interest. Yes, there is always so much interest in any position. One of the many tiny benefits of market forces, the invisible hand, so beautifully silent and sure. The invisible hand touches us all like an unswerving God, like mountain wind on greening wheat, like wind crossing a pewter river.

That river – we needed that river, despite the protests and propaganda. Someone will always bellyache. The salmon enhancement programs didn't take. Unfortunate. No more government contracts. The salmon stocks were bad. Some of the loggers: their hearts not in it. Mistakes were made. But that's all in the past, all in the past. Our hearts are in the right place. And you can't go back to the caves. We represent what is respectable, civilized.

If only you believe, know how to *see* correctly, you can create. Create forests, create fish, create opportunities, create wealth, stimulate, manipulate, propagate the wealth of nations. It's not pillar to post; it's not willy-nilly. You must have a vision, a leap of faith. Profit and clout are delivered to those worthies who have that vision, profit and clout come to those who sacrifice, those with a calling. There are no barriers. Perhaps another boom. We'll wear red suspenders again, put the pension fund up our finely flared nostrils.

Money. Clout. You may wonder, what exactly is clout? Clout is not bone structure or a box seat, an English country garden, a German motorcar, a trip to Spain. Clout is not a naff restaurant knowing your name and how do you like your passé greasy lobster. No. These are smokescreens, by-products, red herrings.

Clout is much more tangible and immediate. Clout can be quite tiny and precise.

Take today. I was extremely busy, understandably so in this profession, thus an instance of delayed urination. Reverse headhunting, coordinating, marshalling, unpleasant nose-to-nose meetings (I enjoy meetings), firming up poison pills, a lucrative Saudi-Asian conference call, then finally a pause at the porcelain, the issue at hand, and that palpable release and pleasure, pure pleasure, from the wellspring so to speak. Spend a penny and the penny drops. The greatest pleasures can be simple, invisible, inexplicable.

Clout, likewise can be invisible, inexplicable, hidden. Clout can be mental or clout can be metal – cold and hard; can mean I can, with impunity, pull this lever, say in mid –

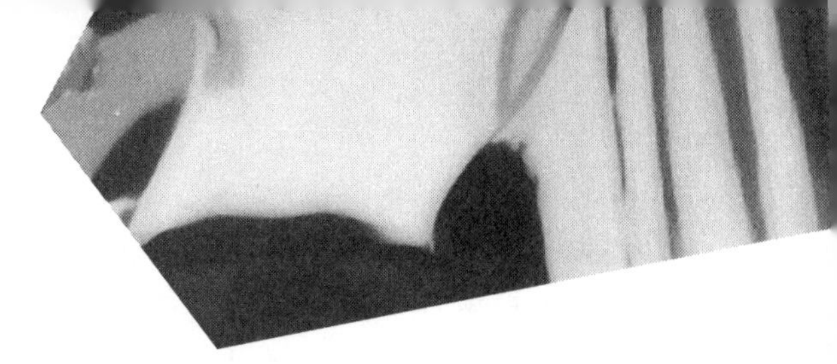

LETTERS
(ON A BOOK LATELY CIRCULATING IN THE OFFICES OF TRANSPORT CANADA)

ANDRÉ ALEXIS

ANDRÉ ALEXIS IS AN OTTAWA WRITER LIVING IN TORONTO. IT ISN'T SO MUCH THAT HE MISSES OTTAWA, BUT THAT OTTAWA LIVES IN HIS IMAGINATION LIKE A PARASITE. IT INFLUENCES THE WAY HE SEES THE WORLD, THE WORLD BEING SO MANY PERMUTATIONS OF OTTAWA (HIS NOVEL, CHILDHOOD, IS ABOUT GROWING UP IN, YOU GUESSED IT, OTTAWA). WHEN HE DIES AND WALKS INTO THE LIGHT, THAT LIGHT IS SURE TO BE THE SUN OVER THE PARLIAMENT BUILDINGS. IT WILL BE SPRING; THE VOICE OF GOD WILL SOUND SOMETHING LIKE THAT OF PIERRE ELLIOTT TRUDEAU, CIRCA 1970. PURGATORY.

After being inadvertently unfaithful to her husband, Mrs. Martha Williams of 123 Baffin threw most of her possessions away in disgust. Among these were seven letters from her cousin, Geoffrey Morehouse, a clerk in the Ministry of Transportation.

1. January 11, 198-

Dear Cousin,

How are you? I am using my lunch hour in the spotted cafeteria to write to you.

I hope Aunt Lisa is well. Has she recovered the feeling in her hands? And Uncle

Arthur? Are his nasturtiums brighter than they were last year? I know how much his greenhouse means to him. Since moving to Carleton Place, I see so little of my family. I am almost tempted to buy a car.

Things are more or less well with me. Today I ate macaroni and cheese. There was nothing green in it, not even parsley. I was relieved. And it was a beautiful day. From the cafeteria windows I can see the snow-covered buildings and the blue sky. And there are skaters on the canal. They look like ashes.

Transport is the same as ever. They rearranged our floor again this year, for efficiency. Our cubicles are a little wider than they were last year, but not as wide as two years ago. Our partitions are a little more orange than they were and a little taller. The fluorescent bulbs are softer, and some of us have new typewriters. (Not me.)

My own cubicle is still in a corner. I do not have a window, of course, and I have only one neighbour. I do not miss company while I am at work, and the sound of other voices would be a distraction. And yet, despite my seclusion, I have lately caught a whiff of something peculiar here on the fifth floor.

You know, Martha, it would not surprise me if everyone in Transport Canada needed clinical attention. I am not certain I could tell the difference. The gossip here is already so disturbed. I know more about Mrs. Weem's colon than I do about her. I have heard that Mr. Burton's wife left him for a woman, that Mr. Allard refuses to bathe regularly, that Mrs. Pirgic cannot control her bowels. (And yet, their hands are warm and their breaths smell of mint.) I feel so lonely knowing these things.

Anyway . . . these last few days I have noticed that five or six of my co-workers have taken to reading. They are not reading their True Romances or Jacqueline Robbins. They are reading a leather-bound red book. Most of my co-workers are still reading the usual stories of carnage and carnality, but as I said, a handful of secretaries are poring over what looks like the Bible.

I suppose this means we are going to have another religious revival. The last one was led by Mr. Dixon, a born-again Hindu (believe it or not), and people on this floor kept things from India on their desks and quoted from the Bhagavad Gita at the slightest provocation. It is difficult to credit, but that revival lasted until Mr. Dalpy sent out his memo about incense at work.

How tiresome.

Yours,

Geoffrey

2. January 22, 198-

Dear Cousin,

How are you? I am using my lunch hour in the spotted cafeteria to write to you. I hope all is well with Aunt Lisa and Uncle Arthur.

I am doing quite well despite today's special: spaghetti. I do not like it when the noodles are overcooked and the meat sauce is watery and tastes of thyme. I suppose this is why it costs so little, but even $4.50 is dear for a poisoning. I should not complain, though. I eat spaghetti at least once a week here, and it is never good.

Transport is the same as ever, really. I have grown used to the restructuring in our office. Of course, my cubicle is still in its corner, and I am still comfortably windowless. The days pass quickly.

I was pleased to receive your letter last week. It sounds as if you and Frederick are as happy as ever. And I am pleased you have decided to do something about the ants. You should not allow them to mar the comfort of your new home. (Still, how awful to discover an infestation. I would be wary of baths too, after that!)

I have recently begun *Our Mutual Friend* and, so far, I am not enjoying the Dickensian run-around. I know it is your favourite, so

I will persevere with the Podsnaps and Headstones, but I must tell you I feel uncomfortable carrying the book around with me. I think I mentioned, in a previous letter, that some of my co-workers had taken to reading a thick, red book. Well, even more of them have been reading it these days and, when they see me with *Our Mutual*, they assume I am reading their book. A few of them have been vigorously disappointed to discover I am only reading Dickens, and one or two have gone so far as to push the red book at me, all in the spirit of goodwill, of course . . .

And then, yesterday, I had a peculiar encounter with Mr. White from Accounting. I do not see him often, but Mr. White is one of the most pleasant men in Transport Canada: cordial, articulate, never an unkind word. But yesterday, by the water fountain on the sixth floor (where I had gone to make photocopies, our copier not working again), he came at me like a loon. Seeing my copy of *Our Mutual*, which I had brought with me, he said something very like:

"– Oh . . . yes, very. . . . Love the way it. . . . Oh. It's not. . . . Well, you should. . . . Geoffrey, it'll change . . . yes . . ."

I could not make head or tail of it. It was as if sand had gone through the springs of a Swiss watch. It was the same Edward White. He was cordial and kindly, but he was completely inarticulate.

I did not make much of it at the time, but in the past weeks, Mr. White's has been a typical response. Everyone with whom I have tried to speak of the book has been just as inarticulate. Still, now that I think of it, he was the first whom I knew to be articulate who lost his bearings after reading the book, and I find it odd that he, Edward White, should be inarticulate in exactly the same way as the others. Do you see what I mean?

All of this has actually roused my interest in the book. Is it a sacred text? Is it a course in grammar? A novel? No one has been even remotely able to tell me. They simply push the book at me, and, up to now, I have just as politely pushed it away. As of today, though, I will begin to trace the book's effect on the office. I will make a list of any notable changes in my co-workers. That should be interesting. (It will be difficult at this time of year, with the new budgets and all, but I am not a little intrigued by all of this.)

Anyway, please write. Let me know how things go with the ants, and give my best to Frederick.

Yours,

Geoffrey

3. February 2nd, 198-

Dear Cousin,

I am in the spotted cafeteria. My head is down, and I am writing you surreptitiously. I am not frightened, but I was lately reminded that discretion is a useful quality. I have been discreet in the past. I think it is wise to be discreet. I have had an unpleasant surprise.

I believe I have written you about the red book. It has spread through Transport Canada like a pox. It really has, and it really is like an illness. To begin with, there were Mrs. Adams, Mrs. O'Brien, and Mr. Flanagan. They are the first I remember seeing with their arms around the book. Then, there were Mr. Leonard, Mr. MacGibbon, and Mrs. Bonaventure. And, after that, if memory serves, Mr. White, Mr. Alleyn, and Frieda Morganstern. Since then there have been others (two of the janitors, for instance, and I must admit I was confused to see the janitorial staff reading), but it is no longer possible to keep track.

Still, the main thing is not their number, though their number is constantly growing; it is their behaviour. It is not the usual thing. Not the usual thing with literature, I mean. In my experience, and you know how much I read, a book is, at very best, a way to moderate intellectual modification. One reads a book and, if it leaves a strong impression, one approaches the world in a slightly different way. (I myself was much kinder to animals after *Born Free.*) But, in my experience, it has never been a physical matter, a physically manifest change. I mean, you would not expect someone to limp after reading a book, no matter how good the book. And, what is more, you would not expect all of the book's readers to limp, even if it were possible for this book to give one of them a gammy leg. Each of us reacts to books differently. We react to the same book differently, in my experience.

And so, you can imagine how odd it was to discover that my co-workers, those who had read the book, have changed in small but observable ways; ways that have nothing to do with my imagination. For instance:

1. They speak in fragments. (As though they were constantly overwrought. Overwrought buying cigarettes and coffee; overwrought peeling oranges, typing letters or drinking from the cooler on the 6th floor.)

2. The tips of their tongues protrude, whatever they are doing. (Up to now, the rest of us have been too polite to mention this, but I believe I am not alone in finding it unpleasant).

3. They will say neither "I" nor "eye" (nor "aye" for that matter). (This is the affectation I most dislike. I first heard it from Mr. White, and then I realized the janitors were doing it too. And, sure enough, I began to hear it from all of the book's readers. Last week I heard Mrs. Bonaventure talking about an operation on her "oose." Since then I've heard "oosight," "ooball," and "ooglasses." You can imagine my disgust. There is nothing I hate more than a verbal tick.)

I am not certain what these habits mean. They are more annoying than threatening. They may even be humorous in their own way, though it is distracting to look a man in the face when his tongue has not quite found its way back to the burrow, like a mole, snout out (Mr. Alleyn), like a squirrel from the knothole of an elm (Frieda Morganstern), like a rat from under a heap of leaves (Mr. Flanagan). Anyway, you see what I mean. It is downright peculiar.

Unfortunately, the pressure to read the book is becoming just a little aggressive. From their sentence fragments, I gather the book is percutant, "fascinating," "brilliant." All I can see is that it looks well bound, and that is exactly what I tell them before I push the thing away. I have mountains to read, from the letters of complaint coming in to the official apologies going out. I do not have time to read the book at work, and at home I am reading *The Waning of the Middle Ages*. Still, it has become inopportune to turn them down, now that Mr. Freedman, my immediate superior, has come in with his tongue protuberant, a copy of the book under his left arm. If he asks me to read it, what will I say?

Anyway, I am eating macaroni and cheese.

What has happened to your ants?

Yours,

Geoffrey

4. February 13, 198-

Dear Cousin,

Today, I am eating in the spotted cafeteria. I have taken a late lunch. I am alone. The city is as beautiful as I have ever seen it. The snow has fallen for three days now, and it falls as I write you. From where I sit, I can see the Laurier Bridge. It is as white as your woollen sweaters. Even the cars are white. It is a day of falling snow and silence. I have rarely felt so sad.

I am eating macaroni and cheese, which I have not had for some time. Perhaps it is responsible for my mood, though I can not imagine the cuisine here as otherwise than dull. That is part of the cafeteria's charm, after all, that and the view of the city which, on days like this, is like a view of my own soul, if you see what I mean.

Anyway, how is life? I was pleased to read, in your last letter, that Aunt Lisa has recovered partial feeling in her right hand. It must be a relief for her to feel some of the things she touches. And I was equally pleased to hear about Uncle Arthur's African violets. I can imagine his "restrained and enigmatic" smiling.

On the subject of the wingless hymenoptera, who shall otherwise be nameless, your basement must indeed be unusual. I can not remember ever having seen the little pests this deep into winter. I hope the stinking powder works.

Finally, thank you for your kind words about my "situation" here at work. Frederick's idea that the book is a sex manual is funny but, for all I know, he is right. No one has yet told me the book's title, and they are incapable of discussing its matter. The sex angle would certainly explain their loss of coherence, and maybe even the protruding tongues, but very little of the sex I have had has changed my accent. Perhaps I should have more of it with other people . . .

In any case, this morning Mr. Freedman insisted, in his inimitable way, that I "take this . . . take home, please . . ." There was no way to push the book away without offending him . . . and so, I am writing you with a copy of the red book at my elbow.

At least now I know that it is not physically dangerous. I haven't changed after mere contact with it. Still, it is just as well I recently began a long, white book by René Belletto. It gives me an excuse to put off reading the red one, to carry something else around with me. If I read slowly, it may take as long as a week before I have to pick up the other one.

I hope I am able to read slowly.

Yours,

Geoffrey

5. February 24, 198-

Dear Cousin,

I am at home. From my bedroom window I see the moon over my neighbour's roof. I am not well, and I have not been well for a week. I know what is going on, though. A week ago, Mr. Freedman gave me a book to take home. You know the book I mean. It was not a work-related document, so I have had nothing to do with it. I have had nothing to do with it because I suspect it of being something other than a book. You know what I mean. It has clearly changed those in the office who have read it, and I do not wish to be changed. I am not often happy, but I would prefer to be miserable as myself than cheerful as someone else. So, I have not read it, but I have struggled to understand how it is possible for a book to do what this one has done, and now that I have had it near me for a week I believe I understand: the red book is not a book at all. It is another mind. It is not another mind in the benevolent sense. It is another mind like a virus. What I mean is: if I were foolish enough to read the red book, I would become the mind within it. That is what has happened to the poor unfortunates at Transport. I know this must sound as if I had lost my bearings. It feels as if I had lost them completely, but I thank God I have finally understood the nature of the danger I'm facing: the loss of all that I've become. Someone is trying to un-Geoffrey me, to have me un-Morehoused.

Bear with me, Martha, I know this must sound peculiar, but I have proof. For the past week I have had the book on the night table beside my bed, and for a week I have had the clear sensation of sleeping with a man. (I do not mean sexually.) Though there is no weight on the mattress beside me, and no snoring, there is everything else: a vague odour of the body, a heat on the covers where he sleeps, a creaking of the frame when I am lying still. And how do I know it is a man? Well, aside from the sense I have of my co-occupant's maleness, I have lately been dreaming of a Norwegian man with an imperfect command of English. And every night it is the same: I am in a darkened room as a chandelier with wax candles gradually descends from an impossibly tall ceiling. As it descends, I see I am in a wooden room. The room smells of pine. And then, six feet in front of me, I see a thin and naked man with short, milk-white hair. Where his eyes should be, there is darkness, and his tongue has been pulled out at the root. How does he speak? He speaks with an eel he keeps in his cheek. (In other circumstances, I'm certain I would find this charming, but it is a sinister act in this context.) And how do I know he is Norwegian? His accent, the eel, which stinks of brine, and his only topic of conversation: Kierkegaard's teeth. (They're an unspeakably dull subject.) And, on each night, I have kept utterly still, in the wooden room, while the Norwegian spoke of teeth and moved his hands before him, seeking me out. And how do I know he is seeking me out? Because as he was speaking of the Philosopher's teeth, he said, "Are you there?" And as he was speaking of the Philosopher's tongue, he said, "I can feel you." For ten nights, we have been in the same room, six feet away from each other, and for ten nights he's chosen a different path through the room. He has not taken the same path twice. Sooner or later, however still I keep, and it is just as difficult to keep still in dreams as it is in life, he will find me. I have thought of moving away from him, but on the third night, when I began to lift my left foot, he heard me immediately and moved towards me. His teeth were white and the eel was in a frenzy, but I woke up as he touched me. (It was a revolting touch.) So, two things at least are clear. First, should the Norwegian find me, I'll wake up as someone else, as another of the poor souls at Transport. Second, I must do something about the book. It is a danger to me, but I can't bring myself to destroy something that belongs to Mr. Freedman. These people love their book so much, I have serious doubts about returning it unread let alone in tatters. And, as you know, I have worked at Transport since 1967, over twenty years in the same place, moving slowly but steadily up, making a living my parents would have been proud of. In a way, work has been more of a home to me than my homes have been. I can not risk offending Mr. Freedman. So, burning the book is out of the question. I have thought of reading selected passages, the title, say, and a few sentences from here or there, just to give the impression I have read the whole. But if the book's mere presence is so disturbing, what would reading it be? How do I know that knowledge of the title alone is not enough to destroy me? And if the title is dangerous, how much more so a sentence or a phrase? For all I know the typeface could kill me. So, I have had sleepless nights. Tonight, for instance, I am too tired to write, but I am writing to keep myself awake. The situation is intolerable. The more tired I am, the less I am able to perform my duties at work. (I suspect I am already drawing attention to myself on that score.) But work itself is the cause of my sleeplessness. Every time I see one of them with the tip of their tongue hanging out, it's as though I received an electric shock. I can not relax. I can not sleep, not even in the spotted cafeteria. Still, I tell myself I must be resourceful, plucky even. Perhaps all of this is not hopeless after all. I cherish the possibility that I am having a violent but temporary psychotic episode, that I am mistaken about the red book and the white Norwegian. But if this is a psychological derangement, I should seek help, but if I seek help I will have to speak of all this to a complete stranger. The thought is almost as humiliating as the Norwegian is frightening. And what have I done to deserve this? I have wanted only one thing from life:

quiet. I have wanted quiet and a place to work in quiet and a home that was quiet. No television, no swimming pool, no fancy furniture, nothing elaborate. A simple place and a quiet life. I don't deserve my predicament. Maybe it is a test. But then who is the administrator? That's the question.

I am tired. How is my Uncle's greenhouse? And what about the ants? Last night I had a vision of you and Frederick alone on Baffin Island, the world white save for the egg-yolk sun and, at your feet, a brown anthill from which the insects crawled in such number the land around you was a black circle. You see what sleeplessness will do?

Yours,

Geoffrey

6. March 7, 198-

Dear Cousin,

How are you? I am in the spotted cafeteria. It is another cold day. The city is white; the roads are dark. It's all as it should be.

I no longer remember exactly, but I suspect my last letter was alarming. Your letter in response certainly alarmed me. I felt quite guilty having upset you. It is at times like this I wish I had a telephone. (Frederick's suggestion that I use lithium was considerate, by the way, but lithium would have put me to sleep, and I didn't want to go to sleep.)

Also, I'd like to assure you that I am not at all "delusional," as you so kindly put it. There is a red book at Transport, and there is most certainly a Norwegian whose mind is the mind of the text. These things, which are really the same thing, have terrified me for months. They still frighten me. As well, it is observable that my co-workers, all except one of the janitors, who is illiterate, and Ruth

Kennedy, who is allergic to paper, all of my co-workers now share certain inexplicable ticks: the tips of their tongues protrude, they mispronounce "eye," and they use fragmentary speech. The causes of my distress were genuine, but I was too panic-stricken to deal with them. It is my panic that upset you. I'm sorry.

Still, it would be hypocritical of me to downplay my condition. (Most of the hair on my back has fallen out, for instance.) And I don't want to give the impression I am completely out of the woods. As I write you today, I am carefully eating my macaroni and cheese, and carefully looking out of the window at the city below. I am not used to eating with my tongue out, and that's only one of the problems I've encountered in the past few days.

Five days ago, I gave the book back to Mr. Freedman, unread. Since then, I have done my utmost to behave as the book's readers behave. It has been a nerve-wracking week. You can imagine the difficulties. I am involved in a tricky subterfuge, but this is the only way to avoid reading the book, to escape the Norwegian, to belong again as I used to belong.

The easiest thing is keeping my tongue out. I still have to think about it, but when I wake up in the morning I stick the tip of my tongue out. When I leave the office at four in the afternoon, I retract it. It is embarrassing to be seen with my tongue out. Two days ago, an older woman pulled on my coat sleeve and cursed me. She was so indignant. And, just yesterday morning, a young man tapped my shoulder to ask directions to Billings Bridge. As soon as he saw my tongue, he backed away and moved on. I suppose I could keep my tongue inside my mouth until I step into the Transport building, but as I sometimes meet my co-workers on the way in, I think it's safer this way. Besides, I have taken to reading the *Citizen* in the morning. I hold it close to my face as I ride the buses.

I realize it is dangerous to pull my tongue in at four o'clock, but by then I'm usually too exhausted to keep up the charade. Also, I have taken to holding a hand over my mouth until I reach Carleton Place.

The most difficult thing is to deliberately mispronounce "eye" and "I," or to avoid them altogether. It's not that I have much occasion to speak while I'm at work. I sit in my cubicle and correct the correspondence going out. Entire days sometimes pass with me at my station, head down, underlining, crossing out, checking spelling, and changing grammar. Were it not for lunch, and the little demonstrations of esprit de corps expected of you, this mispronunciation would be no problem at all. As it is, it's complicated, and it's humiliating when I'm speaking to those who don't work on the fifth floor. (I'm not convinced my accent is any more humiliating than the tip of my tongue, but still . . .) And then, as if to make matters worse, Mr. Addison on the seventh floor lost an eye while skating on the canal (hockey puck). The day I spoke to him, three days ago now, he was still wearing an eyepatch and he had with him two glass eyes of almost identical blue. He had to choose between them. Unfortunately, I was at the seventh floor photocopier with others from the fifth floor when he asked me which of the glass eyes looked most realistic. Years from now I'm certain to look back on all this with humour, but my effort to tell Addison that the robin's-egg blue was closer to his natural tint . . . it almost killed me. I manoeuvred around the various "eyes" and "I's." I was virtually incomprehensible for a full five minutes while trying to give the impression of being lucid and at ease. In the end, I think Addison thanked me. In any case, he didn't let on he noticed the slightest peculiarity. All I can remember saying is

– Addison . . . Addison's oos . . . blue . . . robin's-egg blue . . .

over and over until it seemed to me any normal human being would have had enough. And it worked. It was as if I had always spoken this way, with my tongue out. He thanked me; I'm sure of it.

It goes without saying that speaking in incoherent fragments is difficult, but, really, I am so self-conscious now, so nervous about the impression I make, I rarely make sense in the company of others.

(This too has made very little difference in my dealings with co-workers and supervisors. I'm beginning to wonder if I ever made sense at all.)

Anyway, today I've bitten my tongue only twice. It's a victory of sorts. And, in celebration, I have allowed myself to write this letter, here in the spotted cafeteria where I'm unlikely to be spotted. It feels good to write full sentences like this, as though the whole of the English language were moving beneath me like a river. It feels good.

At least there's one place the book hasn't touched.

I've just finished the last elbow of macaroni, so I'll say goodbye for now.

Yours,

Geoffrey

7. March 18, 198-

Dear Martha,

How're you? I'm using lunch hour to write. I'm in the spotted cafeteria, of all places. I hope all's well with you and Frederick. And I hope Aunt Lisa's recovered from her fall.

I have the feeling you and Frederick have found my last few letters alarming. I'm sorry. I realize I gave the impression things were dire, but everything's fine, really. And it's business as usual here at Transport. I was going through an early mid-life crisis, I think, so I think I exaggerated some of the situation here. But don't worry about me, that's the main thing.

Yes, it's a little peculiar that everyone here at Transport walks around with the tips of their tongues out. But, you know, when one of the mucky-mucks from Energy, Mines, and Resources complained about it, I've got to admit I felt pretty annoyed. After all, who is Mr. Roger Dupont to come in here and complain? It's common knowledge we're more efficient than Energy, Mines and, anyway, I feel a lot less embarrassed by the tongue matter than I used to.

I feel comfortable, now, mornings on the bus. People understand I'm from Transport Canada, I think. And I admit I feel a certain pride.

Also, believe it or not, it's easier these days to say "ooh" instead of "eye." Who says it has to be pronounced "aye" anyway? And, it being arbitrary in the first place, who is Mr. Dupont to criticize the way we speak? Is Energy, Mines, and Resources going to set the rules for inter-departmental communication? What gives them the right, if you see what I mean?

It's true all's not exactly as it should be. I still haven't read the red book. I feel as if I know something about it, though. And I feel it would be good if I could read the book. It's such a small thing that keeps me from my peers. After all, what is a book? Pieces of paper, page after page of words, strings of letters and conventional markings. Where, in all that, is a "mind" to hide?

Still, a few days ago, I had decided to glance through the book, to look through it one word at a time (at work, of course). I was clever about it, too. I cut a small rectangle in a sheet of black construction paper, so I could control exactly how much I saw, and then I borrowed Mr. Freedman's copy. Well, I couldn't get past two words of the title (I mean, of course, I only allowed myself to see two words. The words were in bold face. For all I know, they're the only words in an otherwise blank book. If it comes to that, they may even be the author's name, but I couldn't get beyond them):

NORWEGIAN ROADS

The only other thing I saw, as I closed the book, were pages filled with numbers. In the state I was in, the numbers frightened me almost as much as the words had.

I can't remember if I told you the dream I had about a naked Norwegian, but it was a nightmare, and for a moment there, wide awake at work, I was standing in a darkened room, waiting for the thin man to strangle me. After that, you can see why I won't be reading the book. Much as I'd like to.

Anyway, I'm fine and I'm doing well.

And I'm finished my macaroni and cheese.

Yours,

Geoffrey.

ALTERED STATEMENTS

M.A.C. FARRANT

M.A.C. FARRANT, ANTHROPOLOGIST OF THE ABSURD AND THE AUTHOR OF FIVE COLLECTIONS OF SHORT FICTION INCLUDING *WHAT'S TRUE, DARLING* AND *ALTERED STATEMENTS*, LIVES IN SIDNEY, BRITISH COLUMBIA, ON VANCOUVER ISLAND. HER PERVERSE POSTMODERN MELODRAMAS, TOLD FROM THE VANTAGE POINT OF THE IRONY BOARD, OFFER AN ANTI-TOXIN TO CULTURAL CONTAMINATION.

THE DEPARTMENT OF HOPE

If the public has been confused again, we're sorry. We know it happens each morning at daybreak with the unearthing of the Image Store and, like most citizens, we're concerned with the eruption of unsanctioned images which can appear at that time, particularly those images of sickness and death, and of phantom landscapes emitting a strange and haunting beauty. Our early morning radio newscasts which break into sleep have been designed to subvert these rebel images and we urge citizens to make use of them.

We at the Department understand your distress but again remind you that it is dangerous to indulge in independent dreaming and fantasizing or in exotic reading of any kind. Indeed, we actively discourage these seditious practices. Our aim at the Department is the eradication of the unknown and we're confident that the citizenry endorses this goal.

A machine which will program your imagination for you is in the developing stages. In the meantime, continue with your imagination suppressants.

ADDENDUM FROM THE DEPARTMENT OF DEPTH

We realize that the public's impatience with life is due to their lack of success during this season's egg hunt and we take full responsibility for the hunt's failure. Many citizens have complained that the eggs were not only too cleverly hidden but were disguised as well, and therefore we regret the confusion that the giant babies caused. The eggs, of course, were hidden in the babies' fists. But because the babies were hideous, deformed, and mindless, as well as giant, the public refused to approach them. We apologize for the distress and the deaths that subsequently occurred – the public wailing, the suicide epidemic. The giant babies, we believed, were a clever foil for the eggs, and we'd hoped that the public would be more enterprising in searching them out. We know that many citizens feel that something important has been left out of their lives and consequently devote much time and frenzy to the egg hunts in order to recover what they believe they have lost. It is regrettable that this season so few eggs were discovered; each egg contained a drop of wisdom in the form of a printed message imbedded in hexagonal prisms on the egg's surface. The failure of this season's egg hunt has left the public's imagination in a dangerous state of flux.

In order to calm widespread agitation, several of our staff will be on the road during the month of March. As a gesture of goodwill, the Department has initiated a replacement search, one which should not be too difficult for the public to grasp and which offers citizens an opportunity for levity.

Workers will be appearing incognito at public gatherings and the Department is pleased to issue two clues as to their identities:

Clue #1. They will be alone, aloof, and bemused, indicating by their manner an overwhelming lack of need.
Clue #2. During the course of conversation they will be imparting three new insights.

The job of each citizen is, first, to identify the field worker and then engage him or her in conversation during which time the insights will be revealed in full. The three insights are about death, bagpipe music, and balding men, and will be imparted in a lively and amusing manner. We are confident that these new insights will create in each citizen a feeling of joy.

A caution, however. The joy will be temporary, lasting only until the Department's next event, the annual giraffe sightings, when the public's mood will change to one of awe. Already several hundred giraffes are being groomed for the event, their long necks craning above their enclosures in anticipation of the sweet geranium plants which many citizens shyly place for them on their apartment balconies.

PAPER

That's right, Ma'am, we have only one piece of paper left and when we get another one we'll let you know. In the meantime you'll have to try working with empty spaces. There's much to be done with those. No, we don't know when to expect a second piece, these things aren't subject to any known predictions. Paper arrives when it will but we have our people working on it. The last paper storm was some years ago, on the Prairies, but because of the rush, much of it was ripped. And you know we can't predict the storms. As for free paper, it flutters from the heavens at odd occurrences, so there's no predicting that, either. Why don't you try sitting under an oak tree at full moon and see what happens? It could be some time before we get another piece in. Yes, we know it's difficult; our people suggest you try silence instead. Or if you're desperate, what about the margins of old books? Many have tried pasting margins together with some success although we agree it's not the same because of the flaking. Yes, we're sure you've used up your allotment of cardboard boxes but that's no reason to start crying. What about walls? Many are doing that now. The series of novel houses, each room a chapter. It's brought a revival of reader participation for those so inclined. Yes, we realize the electronic screen is useless, there's no taking it to bed and, no, you can't have this last piece of paper. Something of importance might have to be said. In the meantime, take a number and wait in line.

EXPERIMENTS

The practice of putting old people inside metal cages and placing them in schoolyards is to be discouraged. There is not one shred of evidence to support the view that this activity will retard the aging process. Our experiments with caged old people have shown that it is not possible to infuse youth; youth is not a scent that can be worn to dissolve the years. And hundreds of children swarming over such a cage, we have observed, will not result in suppleness in an old person's skin. If anything, under such conditions, old people become even more cranky than they already are; it has been reported that a number of children have been scratched by the elderly trying to grab their arms and legs through the bars. Side-effects from the caging of old people: namely, they rapidly turn a dull yellow colour – both skin and clothing – which is most unpleasant to view; they become adept at issuing profanities, delivered at the shriller end of the musical scale; and if left unattended for longer than two weeks, they turn into granite, a stone of little use to the industrial world.

Our experiments further indicate that the youth of children cannot be extracted, rubbed off, or otherwise worn with positive results by an old person. Practices such as jumping from schoolyard roofs into groups of children, smothering oneself with children at birthday parties, rolling with them under Christmas trees, or the wearing of small children on the back like a bulky shawl are of little use, as is the practice of maintaining a child-like demeanour. For these reasons, the Department of Experiments strongly suggests that old people abandon the pursuit of joy and return to their small airless rooms. We find it distressing to witness their mindless capering on the public lawns – old men riding tricycles, old women dancing with each other in wedding dresses. The public lawns should be left to the solemn pursuit of childhood play.

URGENT MISSIVE CONCERNING THE BORING WHITE WOMAN LOBBY

Even though it is the stated mandate of this Department to integrate minority groups into mainstream culture whenever and wherever possible, the Department is still not willing to entertain the demands from the Boring White Woman lobby. We are not yet convinced that they constitute a minority in the classic sense, despite their repeated attempts to convince us otherwise – the petitions, demonstrations, media events, and so forth. Events, we might add, which can only be described as exercises in pitiless whining. Furthermore, the Department rejects their claim that they constitute a minority group because they live – happily, they insist – with men. Attendance on children is also not proof of visible minority status and no amount of Mother's Day cards delivered to this office in black plastic bags will persuade us otherwise. Motherhood has been known to cross all boundaries, both of gender and colour, and is not the special domain of Boring White Women. In fact, we expect a public apology from the Boring White Woman lobby because of their challenge to our declaration that the old-style nuclear family is dead; we expect nothing less than their denouncing of this abhorrent fantasy.

The aim of this department is the disbanding of the Boring White Woman lobby into more appropriate groupings – into one of the many victim groups, perhaps, or into associations for the specifically afflicted.

Staff are again reminded that fraternizing with Boring White Women will not be tolerated, and any Department member who attends a Boring White Woman event as a guest will be immediately dismissed. (Refer to the enclosed invitation, *THE BORING WHITE WOMAN REVUE.*) Such invitations are never harmless; Boring White Women are legend for their guile and deviously feminine ways while maintaining an outer appearance of shallowness. In truth, they are extremists and their attempts to gain minority status is an infiltration tactic, a ploy to regain their formerly privileged position.

The influence of the Boring White Woman lobby must be countered at every turn; they've had enough special attention and their access to special programmes for minority groups will continue to be denied. Do not believe the Boring White Woman lobby when they claim they are lesbians, if not in body, then at least in heart.

Effective immediately there will be a ban on Boring White Woman charity events. The Department of Diversity declares that citizens will no longer be won over by the obvious sentiment of such endeavours. Diseases and the Poor will now be championed by one of the minority groups from our approved list, crushing once and for all, we believe, the irritatingly benevolent social worker image for which the Boring White Woman is renowned. As well, the following bans continue: bridge groups; committee work; self-help groups which focus on maintaining loving relationships with men;

and mindless consumerism which, we now know, is the special province of Boring White Woman.

Field workers are urged to continue in their derision of the Boring White Woman lobby, keeping in mind our recent and spectacular successes in dealing with their counterpart, The Dead White Male, now reduced to whimpering on the sidelines of history.

In closing, congratulations are due to those staff members who have successfully forayed into Boring White Woman territory – the suburbs. The Department is pleased to note that several of our favourite special interest groups are now operating within the public schools where they have wrested control of the parent-teacher agendas. It is cheering to see the Boring White Woman lobby marginalized to the status of hot dog server where they belong. May they remain there.

DISASTERS

Field report: five households surveyed.

Household #1: All the disasters were pretty good but we liked the earthquake the best because of the way the freeway bridge snapped in half like it was a pretzel. We liked seeing the survivors and rescuers tell their stories; they looked so beautiful on TV, so solemn and eloquent. Some even cried and we liked that; we appreciated the way the camera got up close to their faces, catching their tears in mid-flow.

Household #2: Watching the volcano erupt and the lava flow in its slow, deadly path towards the subdivision was pretty upsetting for everyone and we were glad there was a panel discussion after the show because our fears were erupting all over the living room and we needed reassurance. Volcano experts said eruptions only occur where there's a volcano, so we're glad we live on the flatlands; no lava's ever going to squish our house even though it looked nice in the TV picture, cracked grey and hot pink inside, quite lovely.

What we have to worry about here is snakes and poisonous spiders and you should have a disaster show about them, the way the victims die and all that.

Household #3: We hated the hurricane; it was so boring. No rooftops flying, no cars flipping over. You do see a couple of black kids crouched beneath a freeway overpass and a lot of severely blown glass but so what? The only interesting thing was the way the hurricane dwarfed ordinary ranchers but we only got to see that for a couple of seconds. On the whole don't bother with hurricanes again. Not unless we get to see some real destruction, squashed bodies and a lot of blood. We give the hurricane a 2.

Household #4: The flash flood made everyone mad. Because it served them right. There they were, a guy and a woman and her six-year-old daughter sitting on the roof of a pickup truck, stranded in the middle of a muddy, fast-flowing river. They shouldn't have been there in the first place, any idiot could see that. That guy was stupid (stupid!) to drive across the river. Several residents of the area even said as much. In future, if you're going to have a flash flood you'd better warn people not to drive through it. Watching that guy and woman and kid on top of the pickup for so long was really irritating. We could imagine the argument they were probably having because the guy figured he could make it and didn't. And not the kid's father, either, that was obvious – baseball cap, fat, and a beer drinker to boot, a low-life is what we figured. When the helicopter finally came our hearts went out to the Grandmother waiting on the shore with a blanket for the kid. Everyone here hopes she'll get custody because it's plain the mother has no sense when it comes to men; her choice nearly cost the kid her life.

Household #5: We think the Department should beef up its disaster series; this month's offerings were ordinary fare and we're getting bored with the show. The freak wave was a bust: an old woman toppled like a stick doll, a screaming ambulance, cars smashing against each other, a baby howling inside a semi-floating station wagon. Big deal. In our opinion, the Department needs to have death make an actual appearance. There needs to be bleeding bodies and hysterical, mourning mothers hurling themselves over the corpses. The closest the Department came to real-life disaster was during the earthquake: a car, a new Acura Integra, squashed under the freeway. The car was only eighteen inches high; the fireman said the car didn't have a chance. Now, that's a disaster!

Please add your suggestions to the preceding list keeping in mind that all disasters must be "natural"; i.e. not subject to political interference and not environmentally sensitive. Forthcoming disasters will focus on "killer" insects and reptiles, collapsing mountains – mudslides, avalanches, rockslides, and the like – and freak windstorms, with an emphasis on toppling powerlines and the spectacular profusion of life-threatening electrical sparks which can occur at these times.

SCAPE

WE ARE THE AMORPHOUS AUDIENCE NERVOUS FOR ANOTHER FUNFIX. WE DO NOT INTERACT, WE BEHOLD; WE VIEW, ARE TARGETED AS AUDIENCE, AS VIEWERS. WE ENGAGE AND DISENGAGE LIKE MOTORS. WE CLAP LIKE MORONS BEFORE SELECTED FUNNYMEN. THE FUNNY WOMEN ARE ALL UGLY. WE DISH IT UP; WE LIKE IT TASTELESS. WE COLOUR CO-ORDINATE OUR IDEAS TO MATCH THE PREVAILING WINDS, THIS YEAR NEON, NEXT YEAR RUST. THE ONLY RELIEF OCCURS WHEN FEAR BREAKS THROUGH THE FIFTEEN ALLOWABLE SHADES OF PLEASURE TO PANIC THE VIEWING HERDS OVER TV CLIFFS. WE'VE BECOME NO MORE THAN A CHIP OF AN HISTORICAL SOUND BYTE. NO MORE THAN EARLY BIRDS SHOPPING FOR THE ENDLESS BIRTH AND REBIRTH OF CELEBRITIES. THERE IS NO ESCAPING THE MARKET RESEARCHERS. WE ARE PIGEONS WITH A STARRING ROLE IN A VIDEO CALLED "TARGET PRACTICE." WE ARE BEING TAPED BEFORE A DEAD AUDIENCE. TOMORROW IS A POP SONG.

AN IMPORTANT NOTICE TO ALL ENFORCEMENT OFFICERS

The terrorist group SPEIV (Society to Prevent the Eradication of Inner Voices) has resurfaced. Printed messages have been appearing randomly on citizens' home entertainment screens, on several of the giant television terminals which line the major freeways, and on work screens at the Department of Silence. Public exposure has been limited because the duration of these messages has been brief and, to date, the public's distress level remains low. This, of course, could change in a matter of hours, erupting into the hysteria and gruesome public flagellations that occurred during previous SPEIV assaults. Officers should therefore be warned that a major SPEIV offensive may be in the offing. The following captured fragment may indicate the direction such an assault might take. It is reproduced and circulated under conditions of strict secrecy and will be the subject of the next departmental meeting. Department members may wish to take a reaction suppressant before reading it.

". . . the Department of Secrets says there are no secrets. But we say there are many secrets. Here are some of them:

1. *The idea of the unknown has been obliterated; what's palpable has been made unknowable enough.*
2. *Your consciousness has been willingly limited; any "other" reality is now classified as mental illness.*
3. *Your consciousness has fled; your consciousness is in hiding.*
4. *The subversive wing of* SPEIV *operates under the name "The Rules & Regulations of an Institute called Tranquillity" in celebration of our spiritual mentor, William Hone (circa 1807), the great English satirist who pioneered the role of the public informer. Who throughout his works said, "conscience makes cowards of us all." Who dared to ridicule royalty, self-serving governments, and all oppressors of vibrant, questioning thought. We are proud to call ourselves Honers, to sharpen our wit, to*

perform our random assaults in his honour. To gather together voicing our rallying cry: EVERYTHING MUST BE QUESTIONED. *We dedicate ourselves to splendour and diversity. We are the protectors of the unforeseen, the perpetuators and guardians of the novel. Join us. Imagine a strange singing, a mechanical choir erupting from the cities like the whistles and clanking of broken pipes. It is still possible for our silenced voices to be heard. . . .*

THE GREAT SALMON HUNT

VERN SMITH

VERN SMITH LIVES IN TORONTO'S KENSINGTON MARKET, WHERE HE WRITES IN A PURPLE-AND-GREEN ROOM. BORN IN WINDSOR, ONTARIO, IN 1965, HE SPENT TWO YEARS AS BASSIST WITH THE DETROIT PUNK BAND TONY AND THE TOOL BITS IN THE EARLY 1980S. HE HAS WORKED AS A PHOTOGRAPHER, DRIVER, CADDY, AND CHARTER FISHERMAN. "THE GREAT SALMON HUNT" ORIGINALLY APPEARED IN HIS BOOK *GLUE FOR BREAKFAST*. HE IS WORKING ON A FOLLOW-UP COLLECTION CALLED *COMMUNITY OF UNFIT MINDS: THE CHICKEN-BLOOD ALLEY STORIES*.

Mom still calls it my rough patch. I had cashed the last of my Unemployment Insurance cheques, my savings account had fallen into the red, and the Canada Savings Bonds Gramps bought me when I was a kid were just about spent.

It was spring. My roommate Geoff had decided to give Alaska one more chance and moved back to Anchorage. I scraped together first and last, and rented this postage-stamp bachelor in Kensington Market to cut costs. As for friends, I cut all my ties. I disappeared. I just let myself go.

By early summer, the sun had bleached my hair out. It grew long and straight. I stopped wearing socks in favour of a pair of old sandals, cutoffs, and second-hand T-shirts I found in the market. I was poor. I didn't have any friends. And I was alone.

It's amazing how little you can live on when people don't have your new address – people like collection agents. But money was still pretty tight until I fell into a summer job. I found it through some guy who worked the Seven Seas fish stand where I bought fresh pickerel each week. He put me in touch with a charter-fishing captain named Adrian Rhondo.

Adrian ran a boat called the *Rip Tide.* His previous first mate had quit without notice, so he was pretty desperate. Could be that's why he hired me on the spot, offering four to seven days a week. At seventy dollars a charter, plus tips, it was plenty to see me through the summer. Even though I wasn't much of a sailor, I was pretty comfortable guiding the *Rip Tide* through Lake Ontario after a couple of crash courses. Only when the water got gloomy and mean did Adrian take over. For the most part, he used fish-finder software to locate schools of salmon, and barked orders to me.

Adrian wasn't like most bosses. He cackled like Satan, promising to get me enough weeks to qualify for UI all over again in the fall. When business was slow, he even loaned me a bit of cash. And once I gained his confidence, Adrian started bringing me on cigarette-smuggling runs to Buffalo.

It was the week before Labour Day when the Cairns Bros. Trucking magnates climbed aboard the *Rip Tide.* Adrian, as he always did with repeat customers, warned me about Terry and Jamey Cairns. The *Toronto Star* was sponsoring this summer-long fishing derby called The Great Salmon Hunt. Writing off the $600 charter as a business expense, the Cairns Bros. were after the $100,000 prize that came with the largest catch.

Lake Ontario was a sheet of amethyst that morning. No whitecaps, no ripples, no waves. As we left the harbour, a carp broke the glassy water diving below with a tiny insect, leaving a perfect row of circles behind. Two miles later, we were drifting in a slow troll. The city core, the SkyDome, the CN Tower, and the Gardiner Expressway were enveloped in a green plume of smog, as if a lime rainbow had wrapped itself around downtown. It looked like that every day from the lake. It was almost solid waste. I never knew it was that bad, that it looked that bad, until I worked the *Rip Tide*.

From my perch up on the flying bridge, I looked down to Adrian prepping the last of the six lines we'd be trolling on. He wore a faded Daytona Beach T-shirt with a hooked marlin fighting on the front. The oversized tee was draped over cutoff army shorts and matched his black canvas sneakers. I guessed Adrian to be in his late thirties, but he never talked age, and I never asked. His scalp was nothing but stubble, forever in-between shaves. Adrian's tanned face had been etched and aged into leather by summers of sun and heavy winds. But his eyes didn't fit his surly face. They were filled with the bluest blue, seeming to wax in apology whenever he called out sharp orders. The boat was his home, and the charters were simply an inconvenience he had to deal with to keep it that way.

Adrian told me the same guys would come out every year. They thought they were getting smarter and smarter, but they just made it worse and worse. The lake was clogged with yahoos chasing that brass ring, and the Cairns Bros. were yahoos through and through.

"Keep your course till you're told otherwise, Jonzun," Adrian barked, adopting the stern tone he used on me in front of customers.

"So Adrian, you been following The Great Salmon Hunt story in the *Star*?" Terry Cairns wondered aloud, flipping open his first can of Coors Light.

"Yes, Mr. Cairns, I know all about our poor man leading the pack in Brampton. By the by, no business of mine, but it's a bit early for your grogs. You might want to be recalling that breakfast you and your brother blew all over my deck last summer."

"Not to worry, captain, we got Gravol. I'm a little groggy . . . I want to talk about going after that big fish. I was reading about that Brampton guy, too, the one who caught the thirty-nine-pounder –"

"Thirty-nine point five," Adrian corrected. "And drop that captain crap."

"Yeah, well, the thing of it is, the poor bastard caught his thirty-nine-point-five-pounder in June. The paper said he's all fucked up, waiting for the contest to end. He's sweating, hoping and praying someone doesn't bag a bigger one. Can't eat, can't sleep."

Jamey giggled. "Probably couldn't get a decent chubby under that kind of pressure."

"Yeah," Terry answered. "Probably not good for shit, and I got a feeling we're going to ruin the poor bastard's life today."

"Let's just fish, Mr. Cairns," Adrian said. "If we catch your beast, it'll be by accident."

So we fished. Occasionally, Rorschach-like smudges showed up on Adrian's fish-finder, and he would call out a change of course. By 8:30, we'd been out for more than an hour. A couple of chinook salmon had hit our blue-and-silver Nasty Boy lures, but we'd caught nothing. The Cairns Bros. were getting impatient.

"Any fish left, Rhondo, or did you round 'em all up?" Terry snapped, reaching into his cooler for another Coors Light.

"Patience," Adrian counselled. "You always catch supper with me."

"Maybe we should change lures."

"Sure, Mr. Cairns. We can do that. We can do it your way, or we can catch fish."

At quarter to nine, Terry caught the first chinook salmon, a five-pounder. By half past, the Cairns Bros. bagged two more salmon and a rainbow trout, but nothing like the beast they were after. Then Jamey lost a poorly hooked fish. Just after ten, Terry stood up to a stagger. He wasn't hammered, but the beer wasn't helping his unsure sea legs. He took two steps forward, before stumbling back. Then Adrian slid his sunglasses down his nose and winked up to me. That was his signal, his warning that someone was going to get sick.

The water was no longer still. We were drifting on a bit of a groundswell. The *Rip Tide*'s twin engines were almost idling while the thirty-two-foot Trojan gently rolled and bounced, aggravating

Terry's queasy innards. He fell to his knees, crawling to the stern to retch into the water. Jamey tried not to watch, but within a minute he was vomiting over the stern, too. I quietly snickered, seeing the brothers sprawled out on the deck, scratching at the boat's floor.

Jamey was the archetypal younger brother, softer than Terry, almost a sidekick. He only spoke after the big boy spoke, and, even then, his speech was an add-on to Terry's dialogue. So it seemed appropriate when he only started puking after seeing the belches shrieking out of his big brother's midsection. I wasn't sure whether it was beer or motion sickness. I looked down at the two men in their forties. They were a pathetic sight, hunched over, green like the smog over the SkyDome.

It was just as well that they were sick. It kept them occupied when we didn't get a hit for the next hour. The light wind and the strain on the taut fishing lines made this eerie sound, like a dozen whistles blaring in the distance, as waves slapped against the boat.

"Feeling better, Mr. and Mr. Cairns?" Adrian cracked, interrupting the silence. "I hear it helps if you watch the horizon."

"Better," Terry said. "Good enough to start drinking again."

"Yeah, gonna get another Coors Beer," Jamey chimed in.

"You're not wanting to be doing that," Adrian said, smiling at Terry. "What about that new woman you told me about? Must be planning a fish-fry, or something, tonight. You'll want to keep yourself fresh."

"Naw, spent last night with Janet," Terry said with a boastful scratch.

Jamey looked to his big brother. "Again? You're seeing a lot of her. It's none of my business, but I just don't want to see you go through all that grief again."

"Naw, no paternity worries. Janet's like fifty-one, and precisely one hundred and twenty-five pounds. Good, firm ass. She doesn't want to knock herself up and bugger up her outfits. She just wants to go out. See, she married some rich wop . . . dropped him out of sheer boredom."

"You sure she's not after your money?"

"Jamey, Janet's just into having fun and going places. We're going to some artsy-fartsy musical in North York."

"Just be careful, is all."

"Look, this chick goes Dutch on everything, and get this, her favourite song is "My Way," Sinatra's version. None of that Elvis shit. She's a woman after my own heart."

"I still prefer the interpretation of the late Sid Vicious," I added.

The Cairns Bros. gave me this strange, contorted look, not so much at what I said, but because I actually spoke to them. I looked away to the stern where a rod was craning down towards the water.

"Hey . . . hey we got . . . FISH ON . . . THREE O'CLOCK," I shouted.

The graphite trolling rod snapped back into the sun when the line slackened. Adrian ripped the rod from the holder, pulling up and rapidly reeling until the line stiffened. From the flying bridge, I watched a huge chinook salmon break the surface about a hundred feet out and pull down again, leaving the *Toronto Star* building in the background.

"Whoever's up, put on the fighting-belt," Adrian ordered.

Jolted from his post-beer breakfast throws, Jamey moved first, wrapping the adjustable plastic belt around his waist. Terry then steadied himself, grabbing Jamey's shoulder and ripping the belt from his brother's midsection.

"You got the last one," Jamey pouted.

"And you had the last hit, little brother," Terry snapped, fitting the belt to his own waist.

Adrian held the rod against his torso. "Put your sibling rivalry aside and settle this, boys, or me and Jonzun will have this one for ourselves."

Terry stumbled forward to hold the rod's shaft. The reel wailed while the fish ran with the line, knifing a transparent streak into the lake. Terry Cairns frantically cranked the reel with his right hand, but the fish kept running, taking line the reel couldn't hold.

"He's losing too much string, tighten the drag," Jamey shouted.

"Do that and your brother will lose it. That fish has enough piss and vinegar to break our line. Jonzun, keep pulling this animal and tire him out."

Terry sobered himself with thoughts of the salmon hunt. "What the hell do we have? Could this be our boy?"

"I won't say no, but land him before you put him on a scale," Adrian answered. "He's trying to make sure we get spooled right now."

"Already got your share spent on your uptown bitch, huh brother?" Jamey sniffed.

Terry scowled, reeling and pulling backwards. "My share? If this is the freak I think it is, I'm afraid it's my fish and my cash, little guy."

"Oh, nice. I thought the plan was to split it no matter who pulled it in."

Terry grunted, pulling back more line and reeling more slack. "Sit down and shut up, little lady."

Jamey fell back into the starboard chair, crossing his arms, remaining dutifully silent like the bullied child he was.

"Mr. Cairns, keep the line tight . . . and Jonzun . . . Jonzun, bring us to a drift and then an easy, tiptoe reverse," Adrian shouted, reeling in the last of the other five lines to avoid tangles. "Creep into the fish. Don't let him bugger around with the line. We don't need him taking any slack."

From the flying bridge, I could see we'd lost most of the line. There was maybe another fifty feet left. I brought the *Rip Tide* to a drift and slipped into reverse, crawling backwards. Christ, even Adrian thinks these slobs might actually land the fish they're after, I thought. I worked the boat as well as I could in reverse. Terry made up line quickly as we gained on his prize.

"Keep doing what you're doing, Jon, and a pinch starboard," Adrian barked.

As ordered, I guided the boat slightly right. The fish was tiring, ailing from the wound to its mouth, the screaming expanding in its head from the terror of running from a pull it couldn't understand.

"Turn that crank nice and steady, Mr. Cairns," Adrian smiled. "Jonzun, our fish . . . he's going to get his second wind and run like a banshee when he sees our tub. Back off the reverse and drag him again before he sprints."

Terry stood reeling effortlessly until the fish came up again. It was more than three feet of glistening silver scales tiredly twisting and weaving. Just as Adrian said, the fish got its second wind, madly churning like a broken windmill from port to starboard, and back again.

The fish was twenty feet from the boat when Adrian told Terry to step backwards. Dipping the net into the lake, he told Terry to reel steadily. The fish took a few more feet of line, but Terry kept hauling and pulling and reeling. The fish was too exhausted by then. There was a mad thrashing near the stern.

In an instant, Adrian's biceps tensed under his T-shirt. He lifted the thrashing, netted animal over the stern, and dropped it on the deck. Blood oozed from the wound the lure had carved, spearing through the top of its mouth. The fish gasped, opening and closing its mouth and huge gills, kicking out a sharp, clean sound by slapping its tail on the deck. But the beast's emotionless eyes refused to glaze over with pain, as if its pride was at stake. It was the biggest, thickest salmon I'd ever seen.

"I'm not wanting you to get too excited," Adrian said, "but I think . . . oh hell . . . this animal has to comfortably be forty-two pounds."

"I told you this was our year," Terry cried. "Jamey, get the video going."

"No muscleman poses till I clobber it and kill it, Mr. Cairns."

Adrian slipped down below to retrieve his kill club, a wooden stick that was about a foot long, wrapped in steel at the end.

Terry spat. "I want footage of him gasping and flapping around. Go with the camera, little brother."

Jamey was out of his pout, gleefully running the camera, while Terry reached into the net for his prize salmon. The barbed lure was still snarled in its jaws. Terry struggled with the salmon's gills while it bled on his sweats. He needed both hands to hold the fish out, raising it to the sky. The indignant salmon twisted in his grasp, madly gasping and flapping. I was climbing down from the flying bridge when I realized Terry had lost control.

"I told you to leave the fish alone," Adrian screamed from the hatch. "Put it on the deck and step on it till I get there. Where's my goddamn kill club, Jonzun?"

In the next moments, the great fish curled and thrashed, slipping from Terry's grip. But it didn't hit the deck with a thud. Instead, the salmon's drop to the boat's hardwood floor stopped less than halfway. The two open Nasty Boy barbs sank through Terry's NO FEAR T-shirt, ripping into his meaty stomach like the salmon had been mounted there. Terry's screaming filled the deck. His arms flailed, and his legs danced a crude jig for the video. The salmon kept savagely whipping its head and tail.

"GET THIS FUCKER OFF ME," Terry screamed. His stuttered breaths blended with the sound of the wet fish ripping and bashing about on his chest. "PUT THE GODDAMN CAMERA DOWN, AND HELP ME, JAMEY."

The *Rip Tide*'s radio blurted out a meaningless message just as Adrian emerged from the hatch and froze. Jamey and I were paralysed, too. In the mad struggle, the weight and the hook and the fight continued ripping a gash deeper into Terry's stomach. Pieces of flesh peeked through his NO FEAR T-shirt.

Seemingly dancing four feet off the ground, the fish's mouth gasped open and shut, open and shut. It writhed through an angry air-swim in the midday sun. Terry grabbed at the fish as though it was a greased pig. He tried holding it by its slippery scales, and actually had his hands around the salmon's torso at one point. But the creature slipped away. In those last wild moments of resistance, the fish rolled, snapping open its mouth and exposing rows of tiny teeth. It bit down on the Nasty Boy lure, continuing to tear its mouth and Terry's chest, both of which were shredded and mangled.

It's trying to kill Terry Cairns, I thought.

Terry slapped at the salmon, sweeping it loose with his right hand.

We stood motionless as the fish fell from Terry's midsection, bleeding from its open mouth and twisting in the air. It fell onto the fading finish of the port rail with a dull thud, bouncing once off its top fin. Flipping onto its right side, the salmon's icy eyes never changed while it tumbled downward like a bent corkscrew. Its wide, silver tail swished upwards. The great salmon was falling back into the water. There was a splash. It was gone.

The only sound for the next several seconds was Terry's hoarse gasping. All four of us remained still, smelling the mix of fresh water, fuel, salmon, and Terry's blood. Interrupting his own tortured panting, Terry grabbed the net, stabbing it into the water. He was crying and stabbing. His screaming rants were littered with loud, angry grunts.

"He's gone, Mr. Cairns," Adrian snapped. "Sit down."

Terry Cairns hunkered a step before letting his ass drop to the deck. Blood oozed through his white NO FEAR T-shirt and smeared his hands. The Nasty Boy lure was still stuck in his stomach, its barb keeping a foothold in his flesh. A garbage bird swooped and squawked, grabbing a decaying piece of something from the lake's surface.

"Somebody pull this goddamn hook out of me," Terry seethed.

"I'll do no such thing, you're liable to spring a leak, sir," Adrian said, tossing a dusty first-aid box to Jamey. "Patch up your brother, and leave that spike in him. They'll deal with it at the hospital."

Terry looked to the water with crinkled green eyes, bringing his cut forefinger to his mouth to taste his own blood. Over Terry's bitter murmurs, Adrian mumbled something about wanting these guys off the boat before one of them died. Terry's grumbling faded as I climbed to the flying bridge. My back ached when I sat down, easing the throttle forward.

I knew I had missed out on a pretty lavish tip, but I didn't care. I just didn't want Terry to have that creature stuffed and painted and nailed to his wall. I didn't want him taunting the great salmon's corpse every morning over his greasy breakfast.

When I glanced over to the *Toronto Star* building, most of the smog had lifted, but there was still a faint green ring. I heard some snarling below, and looked down to watch Terry pushing Jamey and a string of gauze away with one hand, while he held his bleeding stomach with the other. I thought about all the people I used to know, schlepping tables, working in offices, answering phones, typing for failing men like the Cairns Bros. I didn't know what I wanted to do. I wondered why everybody had to be something. I didn't know where I was going, and, for the first time, that seemed to be all right. Keep breathing, I told myself, keep sane, it's all right to stumble around and just get by.

The summer was fading, and Adrian would be laying me off in a few weeks. I didn't want to think about it. So I just let it go. Something will happen, I thought.

Maybe Mom was right. Maybe it was my rough patch. After all, I was poor. I didn't have any friends. And I was alone. But somehow, I was happy.

THE GREAT HANGOVER (MONTREAL, 1976)

DANIEL RICHLER

DANIEL RICHLER IS THE HOST OF "BIG LIFE," THE ALTERNATIVE GROOVES AND INFORMATION SHOW ON NEWSWORLD. HE'S ALSO BEEN ON "THE NEW MUSIC" AND "IMPRINT," A LITERARY SHOW HE CREATED TO GIVE EQUAL TIME TO STREET POETS, BEST-SELLING AUTHORS, AND THE MYSTERONS WHO WRITE THE INSTRUCTIONS FOR IKEA FURNITURE. THE NEW YORK TIMES BOOK REVIEW NAMED HIS 1991 NOVEL KICKING TOMORROW ONE OF THE YEAR'S BEST. HE ENJOYS SNOOKER AND TECHNO, WISHES HE HAD MADE A REAL CAREER FROM ONE OF THEM, BUT CAN'T PLAY EITHER FOR SHIT.

Following morning, after his shower, he stood in front of the mirror and swabbed a patch clear. His hair was kite string tangled in a tree. His body plump white and muscleless as a larva. He leaned close, nose to the glass, nose to nose, chin to chin. And weird, eh, how elsewhere the universe was spiralling vastly, crackling with energy, and elsewhere the planet was busting apart with political crises and uncountable emotional traumas, and here his world had shrunk down like a dwarf star collapsing in on itself, to his concern for this one little pimple. And so suicide was out of the question this week, for sure. Die young but leave a beautiful corpse, remember that.

He squeezed himself into his bell-bottoms, squirmed around, doing knee bends, tiptoeing, till his cock and balls were reunited to one side like a squashy packet of Gummi Bears. Pulled on a paisley headband, a belt buckled with a Harley-Davidson eagle, plus his authentic Canadian regiment D-Day combat jacket with the red curtain fringes sewn on the cuffs and the Ban-the-Bomb patch on the back. He selected a T-shirt that bore an image of Colin Sick of the Paisley Noses, a photo taken just minutes before he'd died of a mysterious brain hemorrhage. (Or so it was rumoured; Robbie'd heard it also said that the singer had injected himself with a horsecock-needleful of crystal meth, diluting it with water drawn up from a toilet bowl, and that he'd been careless, for apparently, Spit Swagger, the group's drummer, had just thrown up in the same toilet, and Colin had neglected to flush it before dipping the syringe in. Robbie had yet to verify the truth of either story.) The image had been printed on a film of sticky plastic and ironed on at the Prairie Buffalo T-Shirt Emporium and Head Shoppe, in the Alexis Nihon Plaza. After three washes the cheap shit was already breaking up, but Robbie preferred it like that; the chips reminded him of the way oil paintings and frescoes crack apart after a century or two, and they invested Colin's portrait with the decadence and intrigue associated with historical decline. Colin's imperially bored expression registered no surprise at his own head exploding: the Twentieth-Century Schizoid Man had kept his cool to the end. And there was a caption:

COLIN LIVES

over which Robbie had scrawled, in fat black Magic Marker,

SUCKS

“Oh. You look extremely GROOVY,” Rosie told him when she showed to pick him up. (Apparently, they’d made a plan – out on the lawn of the Church of St. Anthony – though he was fucked if he could remember what for, exactly.)

Down in the dungeon they shared a beer. “I like this place,” she said, looking around. “It’s a living *womb*.” She curled a strand of hair around her index finger, thoughtfully. “I can never trust men, I’ve decided.” Tucking the hair behind one ear.

“Yeah,” Robbie replied, good-naturedly, for he knew she couldn’t be thinking of him; he, Robbie the Gallant, exempt from the company of Men Women Don’t Trust.

“Like for instance, you should have *called* me. We had a good time last winter, *I* thought. What if I hadn’t never bumped into you yesterday?” Slipping a hand between her thighs, looking at the ceiling. “Boys smell like fast food, I think . . .” Squinting at the marijuana leaf flag. “Anyway I’ve decided I’ll give myself a gin abortion if I have to. But I have to say I would still want the baby. In *principle*.” And opening them unself-consciously wide.

“Chrissake,” Robbie said. “What happened?”

“Oh, mellow out, Bob.” Clamping them shut. “Give me my space will you? Nothing *happened*. I’m just saying *if*. I mean, every time I’m alone with my boss he’s all over me. And, ouch, he’s so ROUGH. So here I am, delicate little Rose. Five-foot-six, forlorn, circulation cut off by pantyhose invented by men.”

“Rosie, uh. Maybe the way you – maybe you, sort of, lead him on.”

“Oh yeah, typical – *see no evil*,” she snapped, clacking her gum angrily at him now. “You and he and my daddy would all get along like *houses* on fire. I don’t LEAD the guy on, Bob. He doesn’t *need* to be led on.” Then she crossed her legs with what Robbie took as an expression of finality. And uncrossed them again.

It was June 24th, she reminded him – St. Jean-Baptiste, Quebec’s Fête Nationale. So they took a Boulevard bus to Côte-des-Neiges and walked from there, high up to Beaver Lake, where Mount

Royal's southern plateau looked over the city and – on days when the wind blew the haze away – all the way to the St. Lawrence River.

Robbie, who liked to sit right in front of the amplifiers, was stunned with disappointment to see how many people had gotten there before him. He staked out a little territory, as much as Rosie's beach blanket would cover, somewhere in the centre of the anthill of humanity that bristled with flags and waving arms, and soon they were both lying beneath a big sky getting a buzz off a bottle of fizzing warm apple cider.

All over the mountain, while the music played, children tugged on kites and families perspired around barbecues; French-Canadian hippies handed out political pamphlets and flags with fleurs-de-lis on them, mimes in whiteface did their utterly compelling act of standing still or being stuck inside glass boxes. The only whiff of violence (apart from the fact that the music was so loud fish were floating up dead on the surface of the lake) was a story that circulated in the crowd about an incident involving the Montreal chapter of the Satan's Choice and their arch rivals the Dead Man's Hands, over a cocaine deal. Another story had it that several of the bikers had gang-banged a teenage girl in the bushes, on the east side of the mountain under the giant electric crucifix. But there was so much peace and love and music and political fervour in the air that no one was about to get het up over a little thing like that.

Robbie lay on his back watching smoke curl lazily upward, listening to the music performed on a stage half a mile away, and thinking about how the word *humanity* has the word *ant* in it. The earth was a vast dish tipping, revolving vertiginously in a luminous universe, the centrifuge pulling him around like a great, lethargic fair-ground ride. He could barely see the stage at all, but there was so much sweet metal music spilling out from the banks of speakers, like a drawerful of cutlery crashing to the floor, that his skull was numb, and there was still enough noise left over to smack against the rows of houses at the edges of the park and bounce right back again.

He tried to estimate how many people were there. It was certainly the biggest crowd he'd ever been in. Maybe even bigger than Woodstock!

"*A partir d'ici et pour un an!*" the immensely popular Yvon Deschamps dictated into the microphone, his arms outstretched.

"*A PARTIR D'ICI ET POUR UN AN!*" THE crowd responded as one massive, joyous voice from all over Mount Royal.

"*J'vais pas parler Anglais!*"

"*J'VAIS PAS PARLER ANGLAIS!*"

"Dey're not gonna speak Hinglish because dey don't know *ow* to speak Hinglish," Robbie chuckled to himself, splitting a match down the middle to make a flimsy roach clip.

Rosie squinted around and whistled low. "You know what, Bob? There's a *renaissance* going on here. Dig it. The best and heaviest music in North America, the best and heaviest BOOKS, the best ART, the heaviest POLITICS. It's crazy, but right now there's a genuine *revolution* happening, and no one in the outside world even knows about it."

"The best and heaviest dope," Robbie murmured.

Politics was not his strong point, but as far as he dug it, Quebec separatism went like this: the *pea-soups* had had it up to here with being bossed around by the *Anglos*, who had all the money and the culture and the smarts. It was Dad who called French-Canadians pea-soups, because that was their national dish, but to Robbie's generation they were *pepsis*. That's because, and Robbie was sure he had read this in a scientific magazine, the average Québécois drinks eighteen gallons of pop a year; that's tops in Canada and second only to certain southern U.S. states. Anyway, now the pepsis wanted a spot guaranteed on the hit parade, and in their own language; they'd tried bombings and kidnappings before, but today a whole lot of pepsis felt the only way to be was out of Canada altogether.

That was it, in a nutshell. Robbie meanwhile is preoccupied with working enough spittle up in his dried-out mouth to moisten the end of an enormous spliff before the glowing tip falls off and burns Rosie's back. And Rosie meanwhile has pulled a copy of *The Compleat Illustrated Handbook on the Psychic Sciences* from her beach bag.

She rolls over, shows him. "Palmistry, astrology, dice-divination, cartomancy, moleosophy, dream interpretation, telepathy *and* ESP, graphology, yoga, and omens."

"Moleosophy?"

"The study of moles and their meaning. I have one on the areola of my left nipple. Look, see?" Robbie looks. "It means I'm an active, energetic person. Want to meditate!?"

He shrugs. Can't hurt. Rosie whispers to him his confidential personal mantra, cupping her hand to his ear – *forrum* – and shows him the lotus position.

He has trouble concentrating. Not just because he's stoned, and not because he's at a rock concert; it's just that the benefit of repeating a Sanskrit word over and over in his head and picturing nothing but a white screen, utter nothingness, for twenty minutes, frankly eludes him. Dad would probably laugh that it shouldn't be such an impossible task for Robbie of all people, but he'd never appreciate the real problem: Robbie's Sanskrit word sounds too much like the *Montreal* Forum, and Yvan Cournoyer and the Canadiens keep skating in to push a puck around and score on the power play. In his mind Robbie calls an end to the period and brings on the Zamboni to clear the ice of tuques and ice-cream wrappers and frozen spit, in slow ovals, and fill his mind again with utter white. But it's futile. He opens his eyes a fraction and peeps over at Rosie. She's sitting with an upright back and her fingers poised, her eyes wide open, vicariously enjoying his perfect transcendence.

"Good try!" she says. "Now gimme your palm. Boy, I'm reading *everything* these days. Tea leaves, toenails, bus transfers, toast. Fate leaves fingerprints all *OVER* the place."

Everything except intelligent books, thinks Robbie the Big Reader, rolling his eyes. He knows Rosie wants his palm only to make physical contact with him, and her extreme eagerness makes him retreat farther. Though in the end his curiosity wins out.

"Ivy?" Rosie says. "Lemme see. Hmm. No, I don't think so. I don't see her in your future at all."

He pulls away, wipes the damp on his jeans.

Rosie shrugs, then crosses her arms to pull off her tank top; points her toes in the air, and slips off her tights. Then she stretches out on her belly beside him in a minuscule black bikini, closes her eyes, and demands he oil her all over.

"I'm so shortsighted I can't see the stage anyway," she says. "You can give me the play-by-play while I listen."

He examines her body, sees how her curves are traced with swirling trails of hair – not dyed black like the hair on her head, but gold as a bumblebee – on her cheeks, on her arms, down her back, too. Her shoulder blades like wings. Her wasp waist. The startling rise of her rump and the tantalizing shadow where her bikini-bottom spans the valley – her golden down disappearing there like a pollinated path.

He looks up to see a couple of guys, hairy as buffalo, ogling her, too. He gives them a defiant look, like – bug off, this is *my* queen bee. Pours a palmful of baby oil on her back and works it in. Rosie reaching back with one arm and deftly unhooking her bra. But after Robbie sees them turn away, he thumbs her flesh without enthusiasm. He's really saving himself for Ivy. Just because Rosie and he made out last winter in an episode he'd rather not dwell on right now thank you very much, doesn't mean he's *committing* himself, exactly.

Soon he's aware of her standing up. He hears her voice, up in the clouds, saying she's going in search of a Johnny-on-the-Spot. He watches her swan off as he remains cross-legged on the beach towel, his fizzing warm bottle between his thighs, all pumped up as happy and buoyant as a multicolored hot-air balloon.

With the hot bubbles of alcohol burping up the back of his nose and tickling his nostrils, the sun grips onto his shoulders for a blazing piggyback. His eyelids feel huge, lowering as slow and heavy as canvas awnings over the entire world. He swallows to pop the underwater pressure in his ears. More bomblets of cider explode in his nose like tiny depth charges. Bathysphere of booze. He's going down, safe and sound and abso-tively posi-lutely answerable to no one.

When he eventually came to, Rosie still hadn't returned. That was the first thought he had given her in an hour. Or two. Well, the crowd was humongous, she was bound to get lost for a while.

After ten more minutes, however, he grew anxious. Maybe she didn't like him anymore; maybe she had taken off. With someone else. He twisted around and craned his neck to find her, but the crowd was too immense.

Then he caught sight of her, and she was wandering off in the wrong direction. He thought of yelling, but there was no point – the music was way too loud, and he'd be risking his life to call out in English in *dis* crowd – so he just stood and waved, like a castaway on a desert island. She drifted off aimlessly, like a boat with a luffed sail. He fired a shot into his temple and rolled his eyes. Now the buffalo guys were shouting at him to sit down.

Rosie was a bobbing pinpoint on a sea of bodies, veering off again, tacking back, more or less. Now only ten or twenty paces away. She wore a worried expression, not much else. He shrugged and sat down. She was so close, surely he didn't have to call out. She stepped right by.

The buffalo guys wolf-whistled. One of them, an oily polka-dot bandana bunching up his stringy hair, stroked her hand and cooed, "*Taberouette, t'es ben cute, toi. Viens faire un tour par ici.*"

Rosie looked down at him angrily, whipping her hand away, and said, "Fuck off, you stupid boy. I can't understand a thing you're saying, but I know I don't like it. I'm trying to find my *friend*."

"Ayy baby," he said, "come ere an sit in my lap. *Quest-ce qu'y a, j'fais pas ton affaire?*"

The other one had a row of fleurs-de-lis tattooed across his shoulders. He grabbed her ankle. Rosie shrieked. "Ayy baby," the animal said. "*Chus pas assez grand pour toi? Viens donc ici* an sit on my face."

Before Robbie could decide what to do, she had wrenched herself free and, kicking the guy squarely in the chest, toppled over backward and landed with a plonk on her own towel.

"Bob!" she said with a wobbly voice, and Robbie saw in the bright sun how flecks of mascara were suspended in her tears. "Why didn't you shout where you *were*? I was *scared*. I couldn't *find* you."

"Hey," he said, irritated. He held it against her that she should allow herself to be seen crying. Ivy never would. She wouldn't allow you to have such a picture of her, like a drooling beast, in your memory. "Don't cry, k? People're looking. Really, Rosie, why don't you just wear glasses?"

She looked at him wildly. Her lip was trembling. She rolled her gum into a hard little ball and pinned it between her front teeth. "Bob, I think I hate you. I'm being hassled by a couple of goons and you're embarrassed 'cause I'm *crying*? Fuck off, you stupid jerk."

"Uh, gee, Rosie." He put his hand on her knee. "I'm sorry. You mix me up, that's all."

She brushed it away. "Yeah, isn't that typical. *I'm* being threatened with rape, and you want to talk about *your* personal crisis. Well, take off if you can only think about yourself. OK?"

She turned her head in the direction of the stage. Robbie watched her with nervous interest. She was batting her eyelashes and chewing her mouth. He knew she wasn't enjoying the concert – that more than anything she wanted to talk. And sure enough: "I mix you up, do I, you poor confused thing. Here's what you should know about me, then: I don't wear glasses so I don't have to *see* all the goons who want to hassle me. It's OK if I only have to hear them, well, it's *partly* OK, but if I look them in the face I'm DOOMED. That's all they want, and I won't give them the pleasure."

"What about working at your club, then?" Robbie said, superciliously. He'd been wanting to get around to this for a long time. "All men do there is stare, and you give them lots of pleasure."

"But standing real close and staring the customers down is, well, it's *different* – like, when they look into their drink as if they've found something floating around in it, they're just like little boys. And anyhow, the bouncers *protect* me in there. Out in the REAL world I don't *want* to see too clearly."

"But, Rosie, maybe if you didn't, uh, dress the way you do, you wouldn't attract so much, you know, attention."

Rosie punched him in the arm and gave him a resentful glare. "You sound like a politician," she said, her voice clogged. "What should I wear? Rusty spiky armour? Why should I change the way I *dress*? Sexy is fun, although the way most men behave, you'd think it was a THREAT. Why *should* I change the way I dress? Men should change their *minds*, instead, like, turn 'em in and get a new, improved model." She blew her nose on her towel. "I'm all forlorn now, Bob. I want to leave."

Robbie felt shitty. Truly he did. He held her arm, like a male nurse, guiding her through the crowd. On the bus he stared hard at anyone who might be curious as to why her eyes were wet.

The bus passed through Westmount, only one stop to the park now. He prepared to stand up, taking her hand.

"Oh no, not me," Rosie said. "I'm going all the way home. *Alone please.*"

Robbie pulled a glum face, real hangdog, like the sun and dope had softened it to Silly Putty. He slumped his head down between his shoulder blades. He held on to her hand sorrowfully, gave it an ingratiating squeeze. At last she looked at him.

"Bob!" Squinting in disbelief, shifting her weight away to get a better look. "You look so sad. Have I really upset you? Wow. Now, that – is – DYNAMITE!"

In the middle of Westmount Park was a brightly painted booth equipped with a sound system, known in the neighbourhood as the Kiosk. There was a concrete clearing around it, with blistered wooden benches provided by the municipality to keep all the trouble in one place. Across the park, past the swings and past the library on Sherbrooke Street, you could always hear the supreme heaviosity of guitar riffs, whumping out over the trees.

It was mostly Anglo-Quebeckers who gathered there. Westmount High students, famous in the city for the achievement of being perpetually stoned. (Years ago Robbie's parents had refused to send him there for fear of "bad influences," but look now, he thought, at least this school is still standing.) These cats liked to just hang out, revving their bikes, perching on the backs of the benches like patched-up parrots, smelling of patchouli and savage BO. They smoked joints and grooved, sunlight flashing off the little mirrors embroidered into their Indian-cotton frog shirts. And the main thing was that to maintain your cool, you had to act unfriendly. You had to sit there looking like a Paisley Noses album cover, just being a lizard with a sewed-up mouth, sitting in twilight, in the crack between worlds, Castaneda-wise, not releasing a drop of emotion. Now Robbie wondered why he'd come. He looked around him with a sinking heart. He'd been so *up* until he saw these long faces, these indolent bystanders, these pseudohippies gone prematurely to seed, still waiting, he observed sourly, for another generation's revolution, still playing someone else's old romantic records. The Lugs. The Head. The Yores. He knew better. The CIA had defused the sixties by bombarding the hippie community with downer drugs and chemical mindfucks. If you doubt it, just look around. Like, six blocks over and a short hike up the hill Canada's coming apart, it's having a revolution all of its own, *and none of these turkeys even knows about it.* To Robbie, the sixties was a dirty word; he'd found out what a scam it all was – just before the fire razed his school down to several rows of seared gym lockers, he'd caught a glimpse of how it all worked. He'd been backstage. Ivy had shown him.

Brat was here, wearing a Vietnam combat jacket with the sleeves pinned up to reveal his thalidomide hands – fins really, crab claws without a shell – which he was now using to pass on a roach with surprising dexterity, the strange economical speed of dwarfs. He was cool as all get out; he acknowledged Robbie and Rosie's arrival by blinking slower than normal.

Louie Louie called out heartily. "Ayy, *allô*, white man! *Taberslaque!* You can see your religion in dose pant!" Big hulking Louie Louie in army surplus shit-kickers and a brown bomber jacket as buffed and battered and caked in dirt as the hide of the old bull itself. Extending a meaty fist. Yes. Louie Louie was a pepsi, the son of the janitor at Westmount High, and once assistant janitor himself, embraced by the Westmount clique by virtue of the high-quality weed he dealt; he used to store the stuff in toilet rolls, high up on a stockroom shelf where his bent old man couldn't reach, and open shop in the cans at lunch hour. That was before Officer Gaunt made a goodwill appearance, on tour with a lecture entitled, "Pot or Not?" and brought in his dog for an inspection of the premises. The way Louie Louie talked about it now, is Papa was taken de hearly retirement, *hosti*.

Joggers and mothers passing by with carriages looked askance at the tribe, and Robbie felt pleased to be thought of as party to trouble. Louie Louie was such a gronker, closer to seven feet than to six, his hair short as a GI's, his eyebrows shaved off, eyes as dull as gunpowder, neck as thick and dirty as a tire; he now worked in a poultry factory at the eastern end of the city, where it was his job to chop the little beaks off newly hatched chicks to prevent them from pecking one another to death in the overcrowded cages where they were fattened for slaughter.

"I'm *also* reading *The Bible and Flying Saucers*," Rosie announced, pulling yet another ragged paperback from her beach bag. She held it up for Brat to see, pointing to the photographs as if teaching a baby. "It's like, when you read Psalm 104:3. 'He makes the clouds his chariot.' What do you think that *really* means, guys?"

Robbie passed buttons of mesc around, popping one right into Brat's mouth.

"No, really," Rosie said, accepting one with her tongue stuck out. "What does it mean?"

"It means you shouldn't believe everything you read," said Robbie, who was reading nothing at the time.

Time passed and people sat. It was incredible how the Anglo cats there could sit and sit and sit, saying zilch in *either* of Canada's official languages, not least Robbie himself, with his COLIN SUCKS T-shirt proclaiming the sum total of his commitment to the maintenance of intelligent life on our planet.

Half an hour later he was feeling brutally nauseated, which was a welcome change in tempo, at least. By then Rosie had turned away to read the palm of some furry freak in a crushed-velvet shirt. Robbie observed them with a seasoned stoner's intellectual disdain. These people, with their ankhs and vibes and karma and signs. This bullshit, this time wasting, this inertia, this empty decade. The only authentic thing they'd inherited from the sixties, he thought, was a terminal case of superstitious mindwarp. The vanity, he thought, to imagine you're part of some cosmic plan, that you can find a personal reference to yourself in any cheap paperback index of the zodiac. And still in his mind he was stuck on Ivy. Ivy again, who was addicted to reality (so she used to say), and the last he saw of her in the hot smoke, her glistening wrists, slipping from his grasp.

He went off to throw up in the bushes, returning, immensely relieved, to wash the mesc's soapy taste down with beer and hear himself say something, to no one in particular,

pigs, fuck,

in two voices, one for each ear, out of sync like an effect on a heavy record: the one euphoric, made light with giddy foolish amusement – the source of which he can't determine at all – the other flat and foul as death's own burp. He's frightened by the intensity, the sudden shift, and his skin crawls.

And in fact has anyone, may I ask, seen, or heard about Ivy?

"*Yow! Eek!*" These are Brat's first words. "The devil's own daughter."

Two hours now Robbie's pelvic bones have ground against the bench, and at last the lamplit world begins to bloom. The stained-glass park slips and slides all around them, peeling away like the acetate cells of an animated cartoon. The multicoloured leaves appear gloved in a malleable varnish, and each one has a distinct musical personality. The trees now chiming. Sucking up tones from Earth's core and dispersing them into the star-filled air. The chocolate-brown earth humming. And the four of them on their backs watching this verdant orchestra in its bonging bowl of midnight blue milk, speaking only in bursts.

School's fucked, he hears himself say. *Heh, I mean look at me. If this is the best they can do.*

A crescent moon flits by like a swallow, white as talc, leaving seventy-five powdery tattoos of itself across the stomach of the sky.

Uff, the gronker goes. *Uff uff.*

Robbie watches a crystal-mint leaf detach itself from a twig and tinkle down. And an epiphany, playing itself out like the tumbling flakes in a kaleidoscope: we're all rushing down the cosmic flow. Consciousness is just an illusion. We only *think* we're thinking. Thoughts are only circuits flashing, we're really juicy robots programmed into this microchip galaxy. Man, I hope I remember this later. Turning his neck and through his jellied windowpanes he sees Brat on his back with a foot propped on a knee and his head on a swollen root, still and solid, enamelled like a garden gnome with his arms chipped off.

Bob, Rosie says. *I see love colours when I'm balling. You?*

Robbie turns to her. He likes Rosie's ski-jump nose, her plummy lips, but she's too, he has to say it to himself at the end of the day, too *clingy*. She doesn't hold a candle to Ivy, who showed so little affection that when she *did* touch you, you knew she probably meant it. Frankly, he's turned off by the way Rosie likes to hug all the time in public places, pressing her nose behind his ear and making his neck wet with her breath, smelling as she does of frangipani and Bubble Yum. When she clambers onto him like she has now, squeezing his waist with her thighs, he thinks with distaste of what he's read in *Bosom Buddies* magazine about girls enjoying horses between their legs due to a phenomenon known as equus eroticus. He's embarrassed for her: he figures a person should communicate their sexual style subtly, not announce it like some three-ring circus. He makes like a lizard with a sewed-up mouth.

At midnight they move on, sluggish, smuggling a bottle of St. Antoine Abbé apple cider into the Westmount Roxy, the air musky with passionflower and hashish, and get blotto watching *Woodstock*. (It's Robbie's nineteenth time. Ivy used to work here, and in the good old days he always got in for free.) Rosie sucks his fingers and makes them sticky. He's vaguely aware of this. He concentrates hard on the movie, wishing in spite of what he said about the sixties that he'd been a part of the whole groovy business, that whole exuberant crowd. A crowd with a purpose, doing its own original thing. He rocks out, although by 3:00 a.m. he finds himself melancholy once more. Ridiculously sad in fact, *weeping* – as he discovers when his lips taste salt – to see that field of garbage during Hendrix, for it looks exactly like what he feels has been bequeathed to him as a seventies guy. He feels so ambivalent, he hardly knows himself. People were part of something back then, or so it was reported. All he senses he's a part of is some Great Hangover; he's grabbed at the end of the sixties, and like a lizard's tail it has come off in his hands.

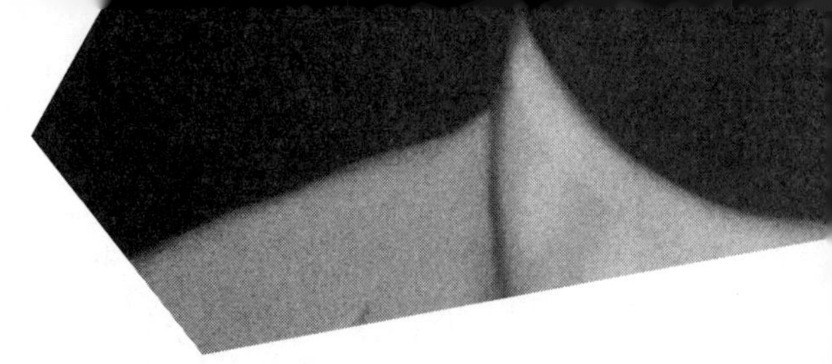

BASH

RICHARD VAN CAMP

I didn't know whose house we were going to party at. All I knew was that Juliet had invited Johnny and Johnny had invited me. I was very nervous, but being the Ambassador of Love, I figured this was my chance to be around Juliet.

I wore my newest black jeans and my whitest socks. I ironed my black Iron Maiden "Powerslave" T-shirt, the one where Eddy is on the pyramids in Egypt. I showered and I even flossed my teeth. I met Johnny outside his place. He had showered too, and the part in his hair was perfect. His feathered hair looked like the wing tips of ravens, they whispered so thinly at the ends. He wore

RICHARD VAN CAMP IS A MEMBER OF THE DOGRIB NATION OF THE NORTHWEST TERRITORIES, WHERE HE IS CURRENTLY WORKING FOR *MACLEAN'S* MAGAZINE AS A WRITER IN ELECTRONIC RESIDENCE. "BASH" IS FROM HIS FIRST NOVEL, *THE LESSER BLESSED*, PUBLISHED IN 1996. RICHARD'S NEW NOVEL, *COME A LITTLE DEATH*, WILL APPEAR IN 1998 ALONG WITH A CHILDREN'S BOOK CALLED *WHAT'S THE MOST BEAUTIFUL THING YOU KNOW ABOUT HORSES?* (WITH GEORGE LITTLECHILD). RICHARD VAN CAMP WRITES TO FEEL CLEAN.

faded Levi's and had a thick red cotton shirt. He left the top three buttons undone so you could see his chest hair. He had a little patch that he liked to show off; I guess that was one of the benefits of being Metis. He was wearing a jean jacket, and as he lit a smoke, his hair fell over his face.

"You packin' rubbers?" he asked.

"Naw," I sniffed, "don't need 'em."

"What?" His eyes went big.

"I'm so damn hot, my women buy my rubbers for me – I'm a safe sex sonovabitch!"

"Jesus," he smirked, "I thought you were serious."

"Just joshing. Coulda been, though – I'm something!"

He shook his head, smiling. "Leonard."

"Is your mom home?"

Johnny tensed up. "Yeah, why?"

"Just wonderin' if sometime I could meet her."

"Larry," he answered, "that's one woman you never want to meet."

"Wow," I said. "Shereshly?" That's Raven talk for "Seriously."

"Seriously. Let's go."

Johnny didn't know where the house was, but I did. It was by Conibear Park. It was in the Welfare Centre, a pretty rough part of town. We knocked on the door and were greeted by an older woman. She was dressed up, and I could tell she was off to the Friday night dance. Her hair was still wet and she didn't have any make-up on. I could smell her shampoo and her perfume, the combination of which smelled like rust metal roses, I could see her cleavage: Bananas!

"Hey," this perfect stranger said, looking at me, "you're Verna's boy, ain't ya? I used to live on your street."

"Yes, ma'am," I said, all flushed and hot. I didn't recognize her but was too embarrassed to say anything.

"You men here for Juliet?" she asked.

"Yeah," Johnny said, "She here?"

"Yeah," the woman said, turning around and walking into the house. "She's putting my kids to bed."

Johnny and I stood outside.

"Do we go in?" I asked stupidly.

"I guess," he shrugged. I stopped in the porch and took off my shoes.

"Pussy," Johnny scoffed, "taking off your shoes at a house party. What a putz." He dropped his jacket on the floor on top of a small shelf that held boots. I hissed and hung it up. My mom never allowed anyone in our house to drop a jacket or hat. If you do and a woman steps over your clothes, that's it. You're done for: bad luck and you'll never catch a moose. I hung it up for him and carefully hung mine up too.

Like I said, I'm Dogrib: I gotta watch it.

"Hey, man," I whispered, "I got respect for the lady and her house."

"Yeah, yeah," he said. He pushed me aside and walked into the kitchen.

The woman came out of one of the hallways, towelling her hair. "Juliet'll be out in a few minutes. Hey!" she yelled with wide eyes when she saw Johnny's runners on her kitchen floor. "Whatsa matter with you – ain't you got no respect?"

Johnny turned around and pushed past me. His face was red as he took off his shoes.

"Bitch," he whispered.

"Hey, Juliet," the lady called out. "You picked yourself a real winner."

"Oh, Auntie," Juliet said as she rounded the corner. She had a lit smoke and an ashtray in the same hand. "Relax."

"Hi, Juliet," I called softly. I couldn't look at her. I just looked down at her clothes. She had on those black jeans, the ones that I liked the best. She was also wearing a cool blue shirt. As always, her hair and her make-up were perfect.

"Hi, Larry," she said. "Come in."

I could tell she was disappointed I had come. Now I felt like a Leonard. When she saw Johnny, her eyes lit up and her smile changed; this time it reached her eyes.

Johnny and I sat on the couch. Juliet was talking to her auntie in the kitchen. I read a magazine while Johnny kept messing up my hair.

"You're not going to get any tonight, Larry-poo," he said. "You got monkey-hair."

"Maaaan," I dragged, "don't touch the hair. Besides, it doesn't look like this is a party after all."

"Yeah," Johnny said as he eyed the place, "you're right. I thought this was going to be a shaker. I wonder what they're doing tonight in Hay? Man, they sure know how to party in Hay."

The living room had a huge TV, a cheap stereo, and a black velvet Elvis singing to the guests at the Last Supper. There were hippie beads for doors in the house; they hung down like dead spaghetti. The lights were red, which was really neat. Heart was howling, "Let me go crazy crazy on youuuuuuu . . ."

"Hey, goofs," Juliet's auntie called out, "don't bust my stereo, don't wake up my kids, and leave the food in the fridge alone. There's pop and chips in the pantry."

"Okay." I jumped up. "See you! Have a good time!"

Johnny elbowed me and said, "Kiss-ass."

"Hey, man," I answered, sitting down, "I got respect."

"Ooooooooo," Johnny said, widening his eyes in mock admiration.

We sat there not knowing what to do. I kept trying to pretend I was reading something mighty interesting and Johnny turned on the TV with the remote. He kept flicking through the channels.

"So," Juliet said when she walked into the room. "What do you boys want to do tonight?" She kept looking at Johnny. Johnny stared at the TV.

"Dunno," he said. "Who's all coming over?"

"Oh," she sighed, "whoever wants to, I guess."

I kept my mouth shut. This was my first party and I didn't want to blow it. I noticed that Johnny was playing it cool, not making eye contact. Juliet kept staring at the clock.

When Juliet got tired of trying to pry answers out of Johnny, she began to talk to me. At first I just answered yes or no, but I soon found myself talking to her and loving it.

"Tsa full moon tonight," I said. "Does the full moon make you crazy?"

"No. Something else," she answered and crossed her legs.

"What?"

"Lonely," she said, sliding her hands between her thighs and looking at Johnny. "The full moon makes me lonely."

"Humph," I said, looking at the situation. If I ever swallowed the barrel, I thought, it would be under a full moon. My mouth would be full of water when I did it. Just like Shamus told me. The pressure of the water would take my head clean off . . .

"Hey, want to see some puppies? My auntie's dog just had a litter."

"I got allergies," I explained.

"Are you serious?" she asked. "They've been up here all day. We usually keep them in the basement. Shouldn't you be itching and scratching or something?"

"It's only if I see the puppies, then my eyes get all watery and I get itchy."

"Sounds like you're suppressing something," she said.

"Yeah," Johnny said, "like his little happy hard-on."

"More like my whole fuckin' life," I said.

As they laughed, the doorbell rang.

"Well, look who's here," Darcy said as he walked into the kitchen. He had a bottle of Jack Daniels in his right hand and a case of beer in his left. He had his eyes on Johnny, and the way he was gripping that bottle you could tell he was itching to scrap.

Johnny got up, his face flushed. His hands were fists and he stood his ground.

I stood up too and walked towards Darcy. Juliet was behind him, saying something I couldn't hear.

Darcy stopped when he saw me. A smile crept across his face.

"Oh yeah, the kid," he said. "How's it going, Lare?" he asked. I took the case and the bottle from him and put them on the table, then shook the beefy hand he held out. I could tell by his breath and sleepy eyes that he'd been drinking for a while.

"Not too shabby," I answered. "Scoop?"

He eyed Johnny over my shoulder. "Just looking for a shaker."

"Well, there's the dance at the hall tonight."

"Naw," he said. "Can't, got barred for being rowdy."

Juliet put her hand on Darcy's shoulder, and he limped back into the porch. His chunky ass under those sweat pants rippled. I turned and sat down. My armpits were dripping sweat and my knees were shaking. I was quite surprised I had stood up and done something.

"Man," I said. "That was close."

Johnny looked at me and said, "The hell was that all about?"

"That?" I answered. "Darcy gave me a concussion last year. I could have pressed charges but decided against it."

"Well, thanks for telling me." Johnny scoffed. "You and Thumper – bum buddies . . ."

"Johnny," I sliced, "if it wasn't for me, you two would be toe to toe right now, and I bet he'd be kicking your ass."

Johnny winced, so I continued. "You may have taken him in round one, but he's got some booze in him. Believe me, when he's drinking, he feels no pain. Right now I bet he's running on pure adrenaline. I seen him once take on two of the Mercier boys when he was loaded. He damn near kicked their heads in."

"Fuck."

"Yup," I said. "Now why do you call him Thumper?"

"That, little buddy," he said, "is something you'll hear about soon enough." Johnny messed up my hair and we watched some more TV. Juliet and Darcy talked for a long time on the porch. I was pretty scared that Darcy'd try something with Johnny, but at the same time I wanted to talk to him. I'd be a liar if I told you he didn't scare me, but something about guys like Darcy always intrigued me. I knew he had had his share of drugs, booze, and fights. He was everything I wasn't. He was bad news, but still . . .

"Yo, Lare!" Darcy called out.

I went into the kitchen. Juliet walked past me, heading for Johnny. Darcy was standing by the stove and he waved me over. I noticed right away that the stove elements were bright red. My first thought was that he was going to burn me, the next that he wanted a tattoo, and third, that he wanted to get his ear pierced.

"You know what hot-knifing is?" he asked, holding two knives in his left hand and a beer in his right.

"No, Darce, can't say that I do."

"You ever do drugs before?"

"Nope."

"You wanna?" he said, a grin widening across his face.

Every fibre in my body, every molecule, every atom was screaming no, but instead I said, "Sure."

Van Halen boomed on the stereo and a light went out in the house.

"All right!!" he said, smiling like a Buddha. He slapped me on the back and reassured me that tonight was going to be great.

"Go into the bathroom and get me a roll of toilet paper."

I did. There was one roll with hardly any paper left on it, so I took that one. Darcy, upon seeing my pick, grunted, "Sure you ain't done this before?"

"Yup," I said. I noticed he had his knives propped in between the ribs of the red-hot elements. Their tips were glowing like horseshoes before the blacksmith hammers them into shape. I noticed some tin foil flattened out on the counter with a big chunk of black Plasticine in the centre of it and a whole bunch of baby Plasticines all around.

"Okay," Darcy said, "watch this." He pulled the knives out from the ribs of the elements and with his right blade touched one of the

Plasticines. It stuck to the blade. He touched the left blade to the baby Plasticine and pressed the blades together. This hissed off a white smoke, which he puckered his lips for and inhaled.

The smell hit my nose and my eyes began to water.

Darcy held his breath and motioned for me to get the toilet paper roll.

"Okay, man," he said as he exhaled, "put your mouth over the end of the roll. Don't waste any . . . this is from Colombia, man . . . people died to get this to my main man in Hay River."

He did the same procedure with the baby Plasticines, touching the blades together at the other end of the toilet paper roll. The smoke went into my face, nose, and mouth. Darcy put the knives down and covered my mouth and nose with his hands. I just about fainted; my knees wanted to buckle and my eyes were crying. The only thing that kept me standing was Darcy and his gorilla grip.

"Fuck, man, dontwasteitdontwasteitdontwasteit . . .," he commanded.

My lungs heaved and my throat was on fire. My hands were ripping at Darcy's and my eyes were wide open, looking at the ceiling. About twenty seconds later, Darcy decided I was allowed to breathe. I coughed and ran into the bathroom. I ran the water and drank about a gallon. When I looked in the mirror, I saw Darcy laughing.

"Weez brothers now," he giggled.

I wiped my eyes with a towel and said, "Let's do some more."

I hot-knifed about three more times. Never had I smelled or tasted anything so harsh. It felt like I was swallowing fire. I think more smoke went into my hair and eyes than anything. Darcy kept me in his famous "dontwasteit" grip. I felt normal at first and I thought that I would be invisible to the smoke, but then my black-outs began.

At first, it was like somebody had turned me off. I totally blanked out. When I woke up, I found myself sitting on the couch. The TV was off and Darcy, Johnny, and Juliet were inches from my face, laughing and yelling. I could hear the Cult blaring from the stereo, "She Sells Sanctuary." I just sat there numb and happy.

"Hey, Lare," Johnny asked, "how do you feel?"

I wanted to say fine, but couldn't. All I could do was smile.

"Look," Darcy said, pointing to my smile. "He's got a permy."

They all laughed harder.

The next thing I knew, Darcy had a five-dollar bill in my face and was saying, "Goooo cliiiimb the telephoooone poooole outsi-iiide."

I noticed Johnny and Juliet's laughter coming from the kitchen.

I looked straight into Darcy's eyes, straight in. I thought of all the things he could do to me but it came out anyway: "Fuck you, moose cock."

The next thing I knew, I was on the living room floor looking up at the crystal chandelier. Steve Perry's voice wailed about a small-town girl taking the midnight train going anywhere. On the wall, Elvis was singing into his mike. All of the disciples looked towards Jesus.

For no reason whatsoever, I remembered this joke I had heard once. I couldn't remember how it went or who told it, but I stole the punch line and I started to say it. I started to moan, "Mommy, your monkey's eating Daddy's banana . . ." and then I started to wail, "Mother, your monkey's eating Daddy's banana . . ." and then I started to howl, "Mother, your monkey's eating Daddy's banana!"

After a while, I settled down and whispered, "I am my father's scream."

I guess I spooked everyone 'cause it sure got quiet. I looked out the window and I could see someone moving outside. I sat up and looked really hard into the frame. I could see a black man outside the window. He had a smile on his face from ear to ear and he was laughing at me. Shamus?

"Wait a minute," I thought, "just wait one goddamned minute."

It was the Blue Monkeys of Corruption!

"Hey!" I yelled.

"Hey what?" Johnny yelled back.

"Time is it?" I yelled.

"Quarter to nine. What's wrong?"

"Get the Blue Monkeys the hell out of here!"

"Who?"

"Blue Monkeys! You know, from India. They're missing their hands and arms. They're after the hash, man. They want the smoke!"

"Get off the dope, man!" Johnny yelled and I could hear laughing.

"No more!" I pleaded. "No more!" I was so scared that it got funny. Don't ask me why, but I laughed until I was crying and then I laughed some more.

"Hey!" I yelled.

"Hey what?" Juliet yelled back.

"Time is it?"

"Five to nine."

I thought an hour had passed. I laughed harder than the first time. The monkeys disappeared.

The next thing I knew I was sprawled out on the kitchen floor watching Johnny and Juliet kissing. AC/DC was on the system roaring on about the highway to Hell. Johnny had her on the kitchen counter. He was standing and her legs were wrapped around him. They still had their clothes on and Juliet was running her hands through Johnny's hair. I knew something magical was in the air. Johnny knew I was watching and kept winking at me. I didn't have the giggles but I just couldn't stop staring. It was like a movie, only real.

"Let's go check on the kids," Juliet said. "I gotta go check on the kids."

Then I blacked out and found myself in the bathroom. I was inches away from the mirror. I was looking into my eyes, trying to catch my pupils dilate as I turned the lights off and on, off and on. The door was closed and I was alone.

That was when I heard the water bed in the next room.

First I heard the slish slish slish and the stirring of bubbles and then I heard Juliet. Her breathing was heavy and excited.

I hopped into the bathtub and pressed my ear into the wall. I wanted to hear everything. My socks were wet and my head was ringing but I just had to hear Juliet.

The water bed became frantic. The wood frame was hitting the nearest wall and I could hear Juliet's voice, the sweetest voice I have ever heard. It was a gentle shiver, the edge of a whisper, the tender shake of a leaf, it was now, here, and she was panting, "Oh Johnny, oh Johnny, come on, come on."

She went on and on. I was so alive listening to them. My heart was pounding and my blood was pumping. *Juliet, Juliet.* I started to fill my mouth with water from the tap.

"JULIET!" a voice boomed out.

There was a thunderous pounding on the door that shook the house, shook the room, shook my little black soul. My first thought: My mother has come to castrate me. My second: Jesus has come to collect. And my third: It's the cops!

"Juliet, you're supposed to be watching the children. Get your clothes on and get out here!"

I froze. All I knew was that it was a woman's voice and that I was in the bathtub stoned and hard. My mind was going a million miles an hour. I was a rabbit, choking in a snare. I was falling through ice. I was slamming the hammer down on my father. I was –

The pounding got louder.

"Juliet – now!"

I heard the water bed sloshing and Johnny tripping.

"Shit," he whispered.

I heard the door open and Johnny step out into the hallway.

"Who the hell are you?" the voice yelled.

No answer. I heard Johnny walk down into the kitchen and into the porch.

"You stay right there, Mister! I'm going to have the cops down here in two minutes . . ."

Still no answer from Johnny. Now he started calling my name, wondering where I was.

"Larry? Lare? Larry?" I could tell he was heading outside.

"You get your ass back in here," the voice called out the door.

"Fuck you!" he called back.

I got out of the tub and stopped at the door.

"Shitshitshitshit." Panic. Total and absolute panic. My eyes bulged and my balls sucked back into my belly. I hunched and squinted, prepared for a beating. Who the hell was out there and why were they after me? What did they want with Juliet and Johnny? I just about pissed my pants. I got brave; I opened the door. There was no one there. I walked past the door to the bedroom Johnny had come out of. I looked in as I walked by.

I saw Juliet.

Juliet was sitting on the bed looking at me. Her shirt was off and I could see her breasts. I wanted to look but couldn't. I couldn't pull myself from those sad, sad eyes. It was like something was broken inside. It was like I had listened to something that wasn't supposed to happen.

I stuttered a goodbye.

She didn't answer. She just kept staring at me. She had the eyes of a fawn shot in mid-leap. The Blue Monkeys of Corruption laughed and howled, putting the rifle down. And like my mother's gaze, I realized what it meant:

Slaughter.

I was the beast.

I was close to the beast.

He was running beside me.

I could hear the hoofs scrape against the pavement before the deliverance kick to a swelling face.

And there were scorch marks on the road where we danced.

Someone was screaming at me to kick

to scrape a face raw

the skin and slaughter
to sniff again
to scrape again through the window
to hear my cousins pop and burn
shards of glass in my back
screaming glass
to see my father fuck –

"Who in the hell are you?" the voice boomed. I jumped and turned to meet it.

IT WAS JULIET'S MOM!

I froze, my eyes wide.

Mrs. Hope looked me over. She put her hand on her hip.

"You're Verna's boy, ain't ya?"

"Yes, ma'am," I said. I could hear Johnny outside still calling my name. I stammered for explanations. Everything was moving so fast. I walked past her and into the porch. The door was open and I could see Johnny. He was putting his shirt on and he had our shoes in his hands. He motioned for me to get my ass over there.

"You little bastards!" Juliet's mom called out after me. "I'm going to call the police."

"Whoopdeefuckindoo!" Johnny called back, laughing, "the cops!"

"Yeah!" I hollered. "Yeah, ya fuckinbitchcow!"

Johnny looked at me puzzled and mouthed, "Fuckin' bitch cow?"

"I'm going to have Social Services here in two minutes!" Missus Hope called from the porch.

"Hoooly fuuuck!" Johnny and I yelled together and we began to run. We ran down the paved roads in our socks. The ground was cold and I started laughing. Johnny started laughing too, and he handed me my shoes. I suppose we could have stopped to put them on, but it just seemed hilarious running down the back roads of town. We were sprinting and laughing, yelling and out of breath by the time we cut through the potato fields down by our street. We ended up by the track outside the high school. My lungs were burning and I was wide awake. My socks were still wet, caked with dirt and slush. I wasn't buzzing any more, but I sure was anxious to hear what Johnny had to say.

"That was close," he said as he put on his shoe. He was tipsy, so I let him use my arm for support. He was still giggling a bit, looking down. "Manohman, what a night. You get stoned, I get laid, we're all happy and the cops are out looking for us."

My feet were freezing. "Don't forget Social Services, too," I added, looking over my shoulder.

I didn't think Missus Hope would call the cops. But I was scared she'd call my mom. Man, I'd die if my mom found out. I'd just die.

I laced up my shoes. "What'd you guys do?"

Johnny laughed again. "Oh come on, Lare, I made her and she made me. We had sex, skronked, humped, penetrated souls. We fucked!"

"What's it like?" I asked. My mouth betrayed me. I wanted to take it back and act like I knew. But Johnny didn't seem to notice. He straightened up and took a step forward. He leaned into my face and said, "A bit too bony for me. She did this thing with her hips when she was riding me . . . man, that hurt. But other than that she was okay."

"Did you use a condom?"

"Fuck no," he said, "and if she gives me the clap, I'll kill her."

"Well, maybe you should take a shower or something," I stammered. What a fuckin' thing to say about Juliet. I remembered sex education and what the doctor had said: Fort Simmer is the STD capital of the Territories. He said that a shower would get rid of some of the bacteria.

"I got a system," Johnny whispered. "I use a toothpick."

"WHAT?!"

"I stick it in the tip of my dick and scoop out all the jupe. That way no little disease gets me. No burning sensation when I urinate, no cheezy white discharge . . . you know, no passing fire."

"Wow," I said. "That's pretty smart." (For a fuckin' asshole)

"Damn straight!" he boasted. "Invented that little technique myself."

"Right on." (Fuck off)

We paused for a moment and I think it may have registered what had happened. Somewhere in the world, we had made the nervous fingers of rain explode into the white palm of snow, but here, in Fort Simmer, I could no longer see the Jesus in Johnny. We walked. Johnny said he had to go home and get some sleep "after the toothpick did its magic." I nodded and walked home alone. I snuck into the house quietly. I didn't even take off my jacket. I went into my room, undressed, and went straight to bed.

It was about twenty minutes later when the phone rang. I snatched it up so my mom wouldn't get it. Who was it? Social Services? Juliet's mom? The cops?

"Lare!" Johnny yelled.

"What?" I whispered. He had AC/DC blasting and he yelled, "The Big Kahoona wants to know who the fuck the blue monkeys are and what the hell was that with 'Ya fuckin' bitch cow.'"

I heard him laughing before he hung up. What a guy!

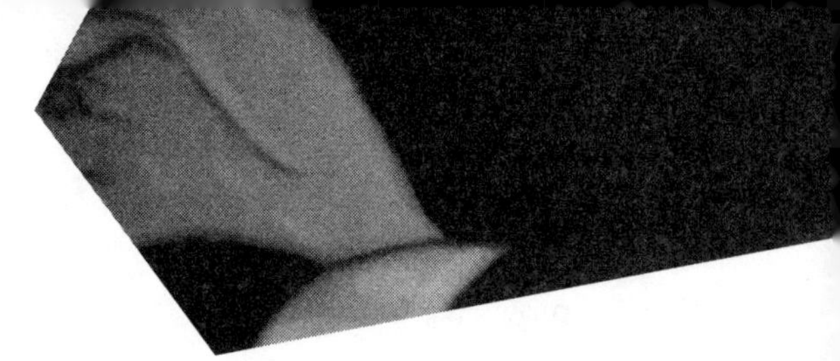

FALLING DOWN

MATTHEW FIRTH

FOR THE LAST THREE YEARS, MATTHEW FIRTH HAS WORKED NINE-TO-FIVE AS A TECHNICAL WRITER IN WINDSOR, ONTARIO. HE HAS BEEN A COOK IN A SOUP KITCHEN, A GARBAGE MAN, AND AN ASPHALT RAKER. HE'S MOVED FROM BEING EDITOR OF THE TRANSGRESSIVE LITERARY 'ZINE BLACK CAT 115 TO BEING AUTHOR OF FRESH MEAT, WHICH COMPRISES TALES OF URBAN MISERY. "IN EXCHANGE FOR A SIX-PACK OF LABATT'S 50," HE SAYS, "A GARBAGE MAN WILL TOSS ABSOLUTELY ANYTHING INTO THE TRUCK'S HOPPER. ANYTHING."

The guy making my sub has one arm. His left arm is severed just below the elbow. It hangs there like an eel, the stub pinkish and portly. His right arm works feverishly, grabbing cheese, tomatoes, lettuce, ham and then slopping goops of mayonnaise on bread with a thick butter knife.

"How long you been at this, Murphy?" I say.

"Goin' on twenty years."

Whenever I'm pissed and enamoured with his single-handed dexterity, I ask him how long he's been making submarine sandwiches. I know the answer. I've been coming into his shop for as long as it's been open.

"Pickles on the side," I slur.

"I know," he says.

Back in the booth I dig in.

"Don't ask for any," I warn Walter.

Mayonnaise drips from my knuckles.

"I won't. I don't eat that shit," Walter says.

Murphy's leaning against the sliding doors of the fridge staring at us as he smokes. He's a grizzled old fucker. Tattoos creep up his right arm like ivy and disappear beneath his white T-shirt. The stub has no tattoos. I never ask him about his arm. I jaw away at him on every possible subject except the stump. How did it happen? For all I know he leaned too close one day when he was slicing ham and shredded his appendage like so much mozzarella. I start giggling.

"What's so funny?" Walter asks. Bits of lettuce spray out of my mouth.

"Murphy," I yell. "With a name like that, you gotta have a couple of beers in that fridge somewhere."

Murphy butts out his cigarette on the linoleum.

"Finish up, boys, I've had enough for the night."

He stares at the dimly lit street like a sailor searching the skies. I fill my mouth with sub, choke it down. He shoos us away with his lone hand. Walter and I stumble to our feet, swing through the plate-glass door. Murphy dims the light of his neon sign.

We blunder up the street. I feel heavy, weighed down. When my left boot slips off the curb and I fall on my ass in the gutter, I realize just how drunk I am. I look up at Walter. He's laughing, his left arm pointing at me, his other arm wrapped around his guts like he's trying to keep his intestines from spilling out.

"You stupid fuck," he yells.

I role over, pick myself up.

I see Murphy through the street-light blur. He's standing outside his shop. He's shaking his head, wondering what ever became of the well-mannered boy who used to wander in on his way home from school for a pop and fries to ruin his dinner. I turn away, carry on to the corner. Walter trails behind, still going on about my disastrous fall.

"Listen –" I interrupt. "I'm going to Horton's for a coffee."

"Fine by me," he says. "I've had enough." He sets off down Aberdeen Avenue. I can hear him chuckling.

Two hours later I'm telling the server about my summer job in a Gravenhurst coffee shop.

"An independent shop," I spit. "Where we actually cared about the food. Not this prefab corporate bullshit."

"Keep it down," he says mildly. I realize I am yelling. Still, I'm his only customer. A while ago there were a couple of older guys sitting at opposite ends of the shop, sipping their warm drinks and gazing out at the traffic-starved streets.

I make it home. I lie on my futon and stare at the water stains on the ceiling. I can't stop thinking about one-armed Murphy dipping his fat knife into the mayonnaise jar. I get up, put a pot of coffee on, slide the door open to my fourteenth-floor balcony. I peer out. The city comes back to life, one light at a time.

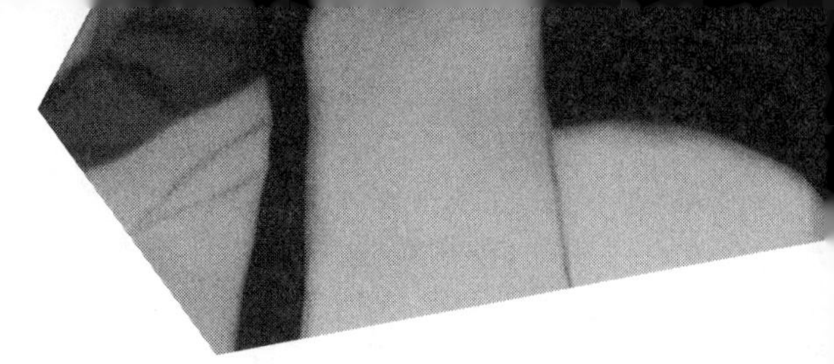

RESCUE

CORDELIA STRUBE

CORDELIA STRUBE HAS PUBLISHED FOUR NOVELS DEALING WITH DYSFUNCTIONAL RELATIONSHIPS AND URBAN CALAMITY INCLUDING MILTON'S ELEMENTS, FROM WHICH THE STORY "RESCUE" IS TAKEN. SHE LIVES IN TORONTO WITH HER FAMILY IN CONSTANT FEAR OF HER TAXES GOING UP. SHE WRITES BECAUSE, AS SHE SAYS: "I SUSPECT THAT I AM NOT ALONE IN MY PREOCCUPATION WITH WHAT I HAVEN'T ACQUIRED. AROUND ME I SEE THIS DISEASE TAKING ON EPIDEMIC PROPORTIONS. CALL IT TWENTIETH-CENTURY ANGST – THE UNFULFILLED LONGING FOR A LIFESTYLE LIKE THOSE IN THE MOVIES, ON THE BILLBOARDS."

At first Milton thinks the man wearing the baseball cap is an undercover cop about to arrest him for concealing an illegal weapon. But then he notices the camera on the shoulder of the bearded man behind him.

"We're from CKGY-TV," the man in the baseball cap explains. "We wondered if you would mind talking with us."

"About what?"

"The rescue."

Milton nods at the camera. "Is that on?"

"Does it bother you?"

He shrugs. Mandy, who has been arranging Leonard's plants around the living room, stops behind him in the doorway.

"Who are these guys, Milt?"

"TV people."

"Is this your wife?" the baseball cap asks.

"I'm his sister. Is this 'Candid Camera' or something?"

"No, ma'am," the baseball cap replies. "We just want to talk to Milton about rescuing the girl from the fire."

Milton stares hard into the black eye of the camera. "I have nothing to say."

Mandy pokes him. "Of course you do. My brother's always putting himself down. It's a family trait."

Milton feels the camera sucking up his face, his confusion. He doesn't want the whole world to see him like this. "Turn it off," he commands.

"All right." The baseball cap signals something to the bearded man. "Look, Milton, we're on your side here. You did something great, and we want you to be remembered for it." A girl, carrying a clipboard, bustles up the steps and whispers something in the baseball cap's ear. He nods then looks back at Milton. "Listen, if you want us to go, we'll go, but I think you should know that Teresa's in the car, and she wants to meet you."

"Who's Teresa?" Mandy asks.

"The girl he rescued."

"Why doesn't she come out?" Milton asks, although suddenly he's afraid to meet her, afraid she won't like him, will think he's ugly and stupid. Maybe she remembers him differently from what he is, maybe she thinks he's handsome and heroic.

"We asked her not to come out until we'd spoken to you," the baseball cap explains. "We're hoping to film your reunion."

The sun glints off the car's windows making it impossible for Milton to see inside. He wonders if Teresa is looking at him, already disappointed. "We don't even know each other," Milton says.

"That's the point," the baseball cap responds.

Mandy prods Milton's shoulder. "My brother's a very quiet person. Everybody thinks he hates them, but really he's just shy."

"Do you mind if we come in for a few minutes?" the baseball cap asks.

"Of course not." Mandy nudges Milton aside and opens the door wide. "Listen, if you want news stories this is the place for it. My brother's got AIDS, and I'm homeless."

Milton can't believe she's talking like this. He wants to shut her up but can't think how with all these people around.

"Milton has AIDS?" The baseball cap's eyebrows shoot up his forehead.

"No, my other brother. And my sister is a street prostitute."

"You don't know that," Milton argues.

"So what is she?" Mandy demands. "A nun?"

Milton has a feeling the camera is still on because the bearded man hasn't stopped aiming it at him. He turns his back to it and looks out the window at the car. He hasn't even showered or shaved. If he'd known this was going to happen he would have worn his clean jeans.

"And my son," Mandy adds, "is a victim of sexual abuse. But I can't really talk about that without his permission. All I can say is that the people you least expect turn out to be the child molesters."

Milton turns on her. "Would you shut up?" He pictures himself as he must look through the camera lens with his messy hair, his plaid shirt worn at the collar and cuffs – a loser. He doesn't know what to do with his hands; he tries pointing a finger at Mandy. "You don't even know what you're talking about." He stops pointing but leaves his hand suspended in the air. It feels weighted, clumsy; with the whole world watching.

Mare appears at the top of the stairs. "What's going on down there?"

"They want Milton to be on TV," Mandy explains.

"Who wants what?" Her eyes shift from Mandy to the baseball cap to Milton to the bearded man. "Who are you?"

"Are you Milton's mother?" the baseball cap asks.

"Who wants to know?"

"We're doing a news report about the street girl Milton rescued."

She squints. "Milton what?"

Milton's mouth twitches. He grabs the baseball cap's arm. "Just go get her," he mumbles. The baseball cap nods to the girl with the clipboard who hurries out. "Mother, go back to bed."

"I'm not going anywhere. Who are these people? All day long people come and go in this house."

Milton flops down on the couch. Leonard's ball-less cat climbs onto his lap and licks his hand. Roughly Milton pushes it off then realizes that this too will be revealed to the world. The world will think he's cruel to animals. Suddenly every move he makes feels wrong. He'd like to scratch his nose but worries that this will make him look nervous or shifty. He'd like to check to make sure his fly is up, but he doesn't want the whole world looking at his crotch.

He feels trapped inside a TV.

She doesn't look anything like Ariel, and Milton fears that they found the wrong girl, that this is an imposter, some girl who wants to be famous.

"Why don't you both sit on the couch," the baseball cap suggests.

"I don't know if this is her," Milton says.

"Ah . . . it is, Milton," the baseball cap assures him.

The girl looks at him. "You don't recognize me?" Even her voice sounds different; older. Then he notices the black high-topped sneakers.

"I guess I do," Milton concedes.

"So, Teresa," the baseball cap asks, "how do you feel now that you've met your rescuer?"

"All right."

Milton gets the impression that the baseball cap is waiting for her to say more, but she doesn't. "What about you, Milton?"

He shrugs. "The same."

"Milton," the baseball cap continues, "did you know that Teresa was trying to commit suicide?"

"Not until later."

"Did this shock you?"

"Well, yeah. I mean, she's so young."

"I tried to do it when I was nine," Teresa offers.

"Why?" Milton asks, suddenly annoyed with her.

"Because my dad kept raping me." She says this simply, without resentment, and Milton can see how being raped by your dad could make a person want to die.

"So what stopped him?"

"Nothing. I left."

"Did your mother know?" the baseball cap asks.

"Sure. She didn't mind. It kept him off her." Again she speaks without malice, as though relating someone else's story. Milton wonders if the glue has numbed her brain.

"Why did you try to kill yourself this time?" the baseball cap asks.

Her eyes drift around the room. "I get tired of finding places to sleep."

"But you'd found the house," the baseball cap points out. "Couldn't you have slept in the house?"

"Someone would've chased me out."

"You don't know that," Milton argues. "Maybe someone would have found you and given you a place to stay. You never know what can happen." Leonard's cat jumps on Teresa's lap, and she pets it. "I just don't think," Milton continues, "you should go around killing yourself just because you've got nowhere to sleep. I mean, it's not like you're going to be homeless forever."

She looks at him. "How do you know?" Her eyes are paler than Ariel's, and watery, even though she's not crying.

Then he remembers that Connie is back on the street. "I just don't think you should go around killing yourself until you're older."

"Why, Milton?" the baseball cap asks. "At what age is it all right to kill yourself?"

"When you know things are only going to get worse."

"I know that now," Teresa says.

"You can't know that now," Milton insists.

Teresa looks at him. "You think you know that."

"What?"

"That's why you came into the fire."

Avoiding her eyes he rolls up his sleeves, wondering how she knows he was trying to kill himself. He remembers a movie about a ghost inhabiting a woman's body. The woman's husband couldn't understand how all of a sudden she knew things about him he'd never told her. Milton wonders if Ariel's spirit is inhabiting Teresa's body and speaking to him.

"Is that right, Milton?" the baseball cap asks. "Were you attempting suicide yourself?"

If he lies everybody will go on thinking he's a hero. If he tells the truth they'll know he's just another doorknob trying to kill himself. Maybe Ariel's spirit is challenging him to speak the truth.

"Milton," the baseball cap persists, "were you attempting suicide when you ran into the burning house?"

Suddenly he wants the whole world to know. He's sick of trying to please everybody. Even when they think he's a hero he still feels like a loser. He wants to spit in their faces. Wants them to see that they made a hero out of a loser, see that it makes no difference who he is. They made him up and now they want him to be Bruce Willis or somebody. "Fuck 'em," he grumbles.

"Pardon," the baseball cap says.

"Yeah, I was trying to kill myself."

"Can you tell us why?"

"Because I didn't want to live."

Leonard's screams stun everyone in the room except Mandy. "Sometimes he screams when he wakes up," she explains. "He told me he dreams he's healthy then wakes up and remembers. I'll go see if he wants anything."

Mare, for no reason that Milton can understand, has been quiet for the last twenty minutes. She stands, clutching her abdomen, staring at Leonard's door. They all hear him sobbing and Mandy trying to console him.

"You all right, Mother?" Milton asks, but she doesn't respond, only shuffles down the hall to her room and closes the door.

"Is he going to be all right?" the baseball cap inquires.

"He's dying," Milton points out.

Nobody says anything. Milton looks at the girl.

He still wants to save her and tries to remember what the Vietnam vet said to the high-school-drop-out hooker that made her believe that life was worth living: something about apple pie, how if he didn't get crushed by the concrete the first thing he was going to do was have a piece of hot apple pie with ice cream. The hooker said she'd go with him. But Milton has no pie in the house and can't think what to offer the girl. She just seems like a lump to him. There's no life in her. She might as well be dead.

Like himself.

He can't stand it, can't stand being dead. "I just think," he adds, "you shouldn't go around killing yourself when you've got a whole life ahead of you." He can't understand why he wants to hit her when she's homeless, a glue addict, and a victim of sexual abuse. He should feel sorry for her. His mouth twitches again, and he covers it with his hand. He's angry with the girl for wasting her body. Ariel's spirit is flitting around without a body. Leonard's is rotting.

At least Milton and the girl still have their bodies.

He looks into her watery eyes hoping to find something to hang onto, but there's nothing there. She's already gone. When she kills her body, no one will notice. They'll step over it in the street. The other day Milton stepped over a body and only later wondered if the man had been dead. He sees bodies in the street all the time and tries not to look at them, tries to believe that they have nothing to do with him, that it's the world's fault. The world let the teenagers cut out the blind man's tongue, let Connie become a drug addict, let Teresa's father rape her. The world took away

Milton's job and his wife. He stares menacingly into the camera at the world, but all he sees is himself huddled on his couch in his plaid shirt and dirty jeans.

As the baseball cap and crew leave, Milton offers Teresa a baloney sandwich because he doesn't want her to go in case Ariel's spirit is inside her.

"Do you think they'll show us on TV?" she asks.

"I don't know. I didn't get the feeling he thought we were all that great."

"We should've cried," she says. "They always show people who cry."

"I think he expected us to be happy to see each other."

Teresa picks up a pickle and looks at it. "I never feel sorry for the people who cry. I think they cry on purpose, because they're on TV."

Milton sips his Coke then stares at the can in his hand, slowly turning it around. "So how did you know I was trying to kill myself?"

"You couldn't have known I was there."

Milton sees her point and feels stupid for even thinking about spirits. "Are you sorry I rescued you?"

She wipes mayonnaise from her mouth with her fingers. "I don't think about it."

He hands her a piece of paper towel. "Are you going to do it again?"

"I don't know." She wipes her mouth with the towel.

Milton flicks a piece of baloney rind off the table. "It just doesn't seem right that we're trying to kill ourselves when my brother's dying."

Teresa finishes her sandwich, leaving the bread crusts on her plate. Milton wonders how a homeless person can be picky about crusts.

"It just seems to me," he continues, "we should count ourselves lucky to be alive. I mean, I'm sorry about your dad, but people get over that, you know. I mean, there's people you can talk to, professional people." He thinks about the shrink with the hairy mole and wonders why he's saying these things when he doesn't believe them.

"Do you feel lucky?" she asks.

"Sure."

He knows she doesn't believe him, and he avoids her eyes by rapping his empty Coke can against the edge of the table.

"If you feel lucky, you have no right to kill yourself." She stands and pulls her fake fur jacket off the back of the chair.

"You can stay here," Milton offers.

"No thanks."

He knows that she wants to get away from him so she can sniff more glue.

She opens the back door. "Thanks for everything."

"Sure," he says, although he knows she doesn't mean it.

THE NAME EVERYBODY CALLS ME

LEO MCKAY JR.

When Frick raised his eyes again, the road appeared as a mirage, a quavering film of light. In the dark ditch ahead, he thought he saw something: a flash of white. He slowed the car a little. The rain was coming so hard he couldn't see where the road ended and the ditch began. The light from his headlamps slid across the water on the road, leaving the pavement beneath it black. Suddenly there was a flash before him. He jumped on the brake pedal. As the car slid sideways to a stop, there was a sound like a gunshot. Something white rolled across the hood.

"Blessed Jesus!" Frick cried. The engine had stalled. Rain pounded the car.

"THE NAME EVERYBODY CALLS ME" IS FROM LEO MCKAY JR.'S SHORT STORY COLLECTION, LIKE THIS. THAT BOOK WAS A FINALIST FOR THE GILLER PRIZE. LEO TEACHES HIGH SCHOOL IN TRURO, NOVA SCOTIA, AND LIVES IN THE VILLAGE OF MAITLAND WITH HIS FAMILY. HE HAS THIS TO SAY: "CONTRARY TO WHAT THE NOVA SCOTIA DEPARTMENT OF TOURISM WOULD HAVE EVERYONE BELIEVE, THIS PROVINCE IS NOT A RURAL MONOCULTURE THAT TIME OVERLOOKED. THE PREDOMINATING CULTURE, THE REAL RED BLOOD OF THIS PLACE IS, AND ALWAYS WAS, URBAN, INDUSTRIAL, AND COSMOPOLITAN."

There's something dead out there, he thought. He slumped forward, his arms arched over the steering wheel, his face on the backs of his hands. There's something dead out there, and I'm going to have to look at it. He considered restarting the car and driving off, not checking the place on the ground by his front wheel, where he knew whatever he'd hit was lying. But he couldn't leave. He'd been almost stopped when he'd struck it, whatever it was. It might still be alive. Even if it were dead, he should pull it to the side of the road, so it wouldn't present a hazard to the next driver.

He braced himself and opened the door. He felt his shoes dampen and become heavy as he stepped onto the roadway. The wind swept up from the bottom of the hill, sending the rain before it in torrents. There wasn't another car in sight.

He stepped around the open door and looked to the ground, at the uneven square of light coming from the interior lamp. Something lay on the pavement, covered with a torn, blood-stained cloth, breathing. He leaned over and touched it. In the cold rain, it felt warm.

Frick laid his foot on top of the thing and rolled it sideways. At the end next to him, an upside-down face appeared in a mat of knotted hair. The eyes blinked and lolled about in their sockets. The mouth, smeared with dirt and blood, opened and closed. "You son of a bitch!" the mouth shrieked. The voice was distorted with emotion, but was unmistakably that of a young girl. The hands shot out at Frick and raked at his face. Frick jumped back, his heart pounding.

The girl leapt to her feet and began running for the woods. Frick bolted after her, catching her at the bottom of the ditch, the two of them tumbling in weeds as the girl screamed and resisted him.

"It's okay. It's okay," Frick said. With one arm, he held the girl by the waist while he tried to keep back her flailing arms with his other hand.

"You son of a bitch!" the girl screeched as he carried her up the bank. By the time they reached the car, the girl had stopped screaming and struggling. She went limp in Frick's arms and was completely silent when he laid her on the back seat. He checked her neck for a pulse and shook her shoulders to see if she was merely asleep. She stirred and mumbled. Her eyes lolled, then she was gone again. He looked her over for signs of her impact with the car – a lump, a bruise, or an indication of a broken bone – but decided that the car must have been almost completely stopped by the time he'd struck her.

But she was a horror to look at. She must have been crawling through the thick brush for hours, perhaps days. Her body was covered with tiny abrasions. There were small, round marks on her inner thighs that looked like cigarette burns. On the backs of her thighs were dark red bruises, as though she'd been beaten with a stick. The hem at the back of her nightdress was soaked with blood. A dark raspberry abrasion marked the middle of her forehead, and one cheek was swollen so large there appeared to be a fist inside it, pushing out from beneath the skin.

There was a rattling noise, and Frick jumped back, slamming his head into the roof of the car. The girl had begun shivering violently in her sleep, her teeth chattering and the backs of her knees drumming the seat.

"Don't, don't!" Frick said stupidly. He put his hands out to steady her, but she continued trembling. He looked in the back seat for something to cover her, but there was nothing. He unbuttoned his wool cardigan, then carefully removed her tattered nightie and let it fall to the floor. There were dark bruises on her ribs on either side, and the tiny buds of her little breasts had both been burned in the same manner as her thighs. He lifted her gently and felt a row of raw, open wounds on her thin back as he pulled the wool sweater over her torso. In a moment, her shivering became less violent and settled into a mild tremor. Her teeth rattled quietly.

He turned the heater on full as he drove toward town. The rain subsided a little, and the outline of the highway became clear. As he thought about the condition the girl was in, his heartbeat rose in his ears. His hands clutched the steering wheel tightly. He found himself clenching his teeth. Tears rose and receded in his eyes.

"What time is it, mister?"

Frick jumped in his seat. He looked into the rearview mirror and saw an outline of the girl's ragged hair against the back window.

He stepped on the brake, and when the car had stopped, he turned around in his seat. The girl was sitting bolt upright and smiling at him. When he turned on the interior light, she looked larger and older than she had before.

"How do you feel?" Frick said.

"Fine," the girl said. She laughed.

He laid a hand on her shoulder. Her face twitched. She shrank from his touch.

"Maybe you should lie back down," Frick said.

"I'm not tired," the girl replied.

They were silent a moment. Rain drummed the roof.

"Who did this to you?" Frick said.

"Did what?" the girl said. She smiled at him openly, the dimples in her face bracketing the thin line of her lips. She looked alive now, healthy. So much colour had come into her skin that she appeared luminous.

"What's your name?" Frick asked.

She looked at him coyly. "You want my *real* name?" she asked.

Frick gave her a puzzled look.

"My name's Patricia," she said. "Patricia Works. But everyone calls me Trisha."

"Trisha," Frick said.

"It's nice of you to give me this lift," the girl said. "I don't know what I would have done without it. You can drop me on Orion Avenue in New Glasgow. Do you know where Orion Avenue is?"

"No. I don't," Frick said.

"You know the prefabs?"

Frick nodded.

"It's in the prefabs," she said. Frick turned around and put the car into drive.

"I think we should go to the hospital first," he said. "We can call your parents from the hospital. Is that okay?" He glanced into the mirror. The girl's head had disappeared.

"Trisha?" he said. He turned back around, and the girl was again curled like a fist on the seat, asleep. He watched for the even rise and fall of her shoulders, then continued driving.

The rain had stopped by the time he reached the hospital. The clouds in the night sky had broken. Some stars were visible overhead. He pulled the car into the temporary parking zone in front of the outpatient entrance. Through the glass doors he could see some people waiting in chairs. A large nurse crossed the floor in the direction of the emergency desk.

Frick stepped outside the car and opened the rear door. Trisha's shoulder jerked as he knelt over her. She bounced from the seat and sprang at him like a wild animal, her hands clawing him, her legs and arms flailing. "You son of a bitch!" she cried.

"Trisha. Trisha," he said. "Careful now. You're hurt." He grasped her about the waist with one hand and pushed himself out of the car with the other. He tried to move his free hand under her arms, but she was struggling and flailing too wildly. He had to use one hand to ward off her blows.

She slipped from his grasp and hit the pavement on her feet. As soon as she was free, she bolted across the parking lot, naked but for his cardigan.

He ran after her.

"Trisha! Trisha!" he called. "You're hurt!"

He'd almost caught her before she reached the main lot, but once squeezed between two cars in the first row, she ducked down and disappeared from sight. He ran from row to row and car to car, looking under and between cars as he went, but it was useless. She could hide from him all night here.

The nurse at the emergency desk had short grey-brown hair cut in bangs across the top of her face. Her breasts were the size of loaves of bread. Her white uniform bunched up a roll of fat under each arm. She sat at a desk with a microphone near her mouth. There was a thick plate of glass in front of her with a hole in the middle of it for her to speak through. At the bottom of the glass there was a space to pass papers through. She closed a big novel as Frick approached.

"There is an injured girl in the parking lot," Frick told her. The nurse shifted between the arms of her chair and pushed a button under her desk.

After a few seconds, a security guard came through a door behind her. His big belly pushed out from between a thin pair of black suspenders. He was holding a coffee cup with a Mountie's head on it. *Medicine Hat Alberta* was written under the Mountie. The guard took a drink and set the cup on the nurse's desk.

"This is Mr. Waltzberg," the nurse said. She told Waltzberg what Frick had told her.

Waltzberg spoke in a high-pitched, scratchy voice, the voice of a cartoon character, Frick thought. "Can you describe the girl?" he said.

Frick considered the girl a moment. Her most striking features were the marks and bruises on her body.

"She's small," he said. "Dark hair. She's wearing a cardigan and nothing else. She's been beaten. Tortured."

The guard nodded and walked down a long hall that led away from the emergency ward.

Frick turned away from the nurse and regarded the outpatient area. He longed to find a spot on one of the upholstered benches there and rest.

"Sir? Sir?"

He turned around. The nurse had a form on the desk before her and was holding a pen at the ready to fill it out.

"Name?" she said.

"Frick," he said. "Michael Frick."

"The *girl's* name," the nurse said.

"What's this?" Frick asked. He pointed at the paper the nurse was holding.

"Just the regular form," the nurse replied.

Frick regarded her a moment. "Trisha. Patricia Works," he said at last.

"Address?"

"New Glasgow." Frick thought a moment. "Orion Avenue," he said. "I think."

The nurse pursed her lips. "Number?"

"No idea."

She looked at him.

"Phone?"

"No idea."

The nurse winced. She put a hand on a big hip. "No idea," she said.

"None," Frick said.

"Relationship?" the nurse said.

Frick leaned into the glass that separated them. "*Relationship?*" he said.

The nurse sighed in exasperation. "What is your relationship to the girl?"

"None," Frick said.

"I see," the nurse said. She smiled, placed her pen carefully on her desk, and folded her arms on the papers in front of her. "Look," she said, "Just what is going on here?"

"I wish I knew," Frick said. "I found her on the highway on this side of Mount Thom. She's been beaten. Tortured. It's the most horrible thing I've ever seen."

"And just who are *you?*"

"I gave you my name before," Frick said. He gripped the ledge beneath the glass. He tightened his hold until his knuckles hurt. The girl was out there in the cold somewhere. Perhaps she'd passed out again.

"Do you have some ID?" the nurse said.

"ID!" Frick said. He pulled the wallet from his back pocket and slammed it on the counter before him. He fumbled through it and took out his driver's licence, thrust it through the hole in the glass.

The nurse snatched up his licence, then reached into her desk and pulled out another form. She started copying information from his licence onto the new form. When Frick craned up his neck to get a look at the form, she angled it away from him, pulling a forearm over what she was writing.

Frick shook his head and walked away from the nurse. "One . . . two . . . three . . . four . . .," he said aloud.

As he took a seat in the waiting room, the security guard, two orderlies, and a man who might have been a doctor walked past, all carrying flashlights. The sight of the four men charging across the outpatient area so purposefully struck Frick as funny. He snickered to himself, then immediately felt guilty. He thought of the wretched little girl outside and shivered with horror. What would have happened, he wondered, if she hadn't run out in front of his car like that? She might have been lost in those woods all night. She would have died of exposure.

Directly across from him sat a man with a blood-soaked towel pressed to his forearm. The man had short grey hair. He wore green work pants and a work shirt, all stained with fresh, dark blood. The woman beside the man in green wore a blue dress with an apron over it. There were no visible marks on her, but she was rocking forward and back, moaning. She sat up straight, then leaned over, put her elbows on her knees, dug her fingers into her scalp, and hissed through clenched teeth.

Misery, Frick thought. He stood up and walked down a passageway, through a glass door to a foyer. He put a loonie into a Coke machine and pressed a button for Coca-Cola Classic. Nothing happened. He slammed the button with the heel of his hand and rocked the machine with his shoulder. It did not respond. He pulled at the coin return lever and the loonie clanged into the coin return slot. He was putting the loonie back into the machine when he noticed his mistake. The price was written beside the coin return lever. One dollar and twenty-five cents.

"A buck and a quarter for a Coke!" Frick exclaimed. He looked over his shoulder for a witness to this injustice. Through the glass door and down the long hall behind him, the woman in the blue dress stood up, put her palms to her forehead, and leaned back with her mouth open, as though she were screaming. He listened a moment, but heard nothing. He dug the extra quarter from his pocket and took a can of Coke from the machine.

He drank down the contents of the can in several long drinks. The acid liquid burned at his stomach, but with some sugar and caffeine in him, he felt better.

The nurse looked directly at him when he re-entered the outpatient area, but instead of signalling to him, she pushed a button on her desk, leaned into the microphone near her, and announced to the whole room:

"*Mr. Frick, please. Mr. Frick.*"

When Frick arrived at her desk, she slid his licence through the slot in the glass.

"What did you say that girl's name was?" the nurse asked.

Frick threw up his arms. "You know what I said her name was," he said. "You wrote it down."

"Works?" the nurse asked. "W-O-R-K-S?"

"Patricia Works," Frick replied.

"And the address?" asked the nurse.

"Look," said Frick. The Coke was burning in his stomach. "What are you trying to get at?"

"Well," said the nurse. She shuffled a stack of papers on her desk. "I called a Mr. and Mrs. Jim Works on Orion Avenue in New Glasgow. Twelve Orion Avenue."

"Twelve," said Frick. "I told you I didn't know the number."

"I asked Mrs. Works if they had a daughter Patricia," the nurse continued. "She said yes. When I told her the girl was here and she was injured, the woman hung up on me. I called back and she hung up again. The third time I phoned, the woman told me her daughter was home in front of the TV."

Frick stared at the nurse. "Is there another Works on Orion Avenue?" he asked.

The nurse shook her head.

"Well, I don't know who the girl is. But she said her name was Trisha Works from Orion Avenue."

The nurse nodded and smiled. "Thank you, Mr. Frick," she said. "There's no need for you to wait here. We have your name and address, and if our people outside do find anything, the police will know where to find you for questioning."

"Listen," said Frick. "There's a little girl out there. A little girl in desperate condition." He pointed a finger at the door to the parking lot, and as he did so, the doctor and two orderlies came through, headed by Waltzberg, the security guard.

Their expressions were blank. Their long flashlights drooped toward the floor. The orderlies and the doctor kept walking through the emergency ward and into the hospital. The security guard stopped and addressed the nurse. "We can't find anything," he squeaked. "We checked the whole parking lot. Under and around every car. We checked the graveyard next door. We even went down to the riverbank. There's nothing out there."

"You're giving up already!" Frick said. "That girl's going to die of exposure." He turned to the nurse. "You'd better call the police."

The nurse frowned and chewed at her lip.

"Mr. Frick," she said. "I appreciate your worry. But we only call the police in dire circumstances."

Frick's eyes widened. "Dire circumstances!" he said.

"I'm sorry, Mr. Frick. But this is an emergency room. We deal with emergencies every day. I have very specific instructions about when I am to call the police, or else we'd have the police here every minute. Mr. Waltzberg here," she motioned at the security guard, "is a retired member of the New Glasgow police force. I'm sure if Mr. Waltzberg can't find anything, there would be nothing the police could do. We have a lot of faith in Mr. Waltzberg." She smiled at the security guard. The guard pulled shyly at his belt.

"Do you think I'm making this up?" Frick said. "Do you think I'm some sort of fruitcake?"

"Look," said the nurse. "I have my job to do. I have my instructions to follow. I am to call the police in dire circumstances. I don't see any dire circumstances. I've already upset a woman over on Orion Avenue tonight. On *your* advice," she paused significantly, looking askance at Frick. "If you want to call the police yourself, you are free to do so." She stopped talking and folded her arms across her chest.

"I will, then," Frick said. He reached through the hole in the glass for the phone. The nurse put her big hand on the receiver. "There are pay phones in the front entrance," she said.

Frick twisted his face in anger, piercing her with his stare.

He charged to the front entrance and stood before the pay phones a moment, breathing deeply to calm himself. The police number was displayed beneath a sheet of clear plastic on the front of the phone.

"New Glasgow Police Department, may I help you?" The voice on the other end was a high-pitched squeal.

"What's going on here!" Frick barked. "Is that you, Waltzberg?"

"Who the hell is this?" the voice on the other end demanded.

Frick put his hand to his forehead. He knew he was going crazy.

"Who is this?" the policeman said. "Hello! Hello!"

"Shit!" Frick said. He slammed down the receiver and pulled the phone book from the shelf under the phone. There it was: James

Works, 12 Orion Avenue, 755-9909. He dialled the number and a woman answered. "Mrs. Works?" Frick said.

"Yes," the woman said, perhaps hesitantly.

"Mrs. Jim Works?"

"Yes." Frick heard a TV in the background.

"Do you have a daughter named Trisha?" His hand tightened on the receiver.

"Is this the hospital again?" The woman's voice thinned. "My husband won't stand for this kind of harassment. Jim! Jim!" she called.

Frick hung up. He laid his forearm against the top of the phone and rested his head against it.

Then he remembered the dress! The bloody and torn nightgown the girl had been wearing when he'd found her. If he brought that to the police he wouldn't have to explain anything. He rushed out of the hospital and into the back seat of his car. He searched on the floor, under the front seats, and down the crack in the back seat, but he couldn't find it. He checked the ledge under the back window. "Damn it!" he said. He checked again in all the places he'd already looked, then checked places he knew it wasn't: the glove compartment, even the trunk. He was looking behind a rear wheel when a dark figure appeared in the corner of his eye. He looked up. It was Waltzberg. He was holding a cheap blue pen over an open notebook.

"This is a five-minute patient drop-off and pick-up only zone," Waltzberg squeaked. He pointed at a sign on a metal post. "You'll have to leave or I'll ticket you. I can do that, you know. I can ticket."

It didn't take long to locate Orion Avenue once he was in the prefabs in the North End of New Glasgow. It was a short side street that ran along the base of a steep hill. Frick drove to the end of it, stopping in front of number twelve. The house was a prefab bungalow, like all the other houses in the neighbourhood. It was white with black false shutters at either end of the two windows that faced the street. Through the picture window came the dim, shifting light of TV. The other window was dark. In the driveway, under the glow of a floodlight, stood a faded metallic-blue Chev.

He sat in his car and watched the light that flickered in the window for some sign of human movement. None came. Just the shifting and flickering of day scenes followed by night scenes followed by commercials.

He left his car and stood on the narrow sidewalk before the house. There were few streetlights nearby, and overhead, the leafless branches of trees rattled against each other in the wind. He walked across the dead grass of the lawn and stepped onto the front step. The doorbell had been painted over, and he guessed it hadn't worked in years. He bent down and tapped lightly, but audibly, at the aluminum panel below his knees. Almost immediately he heard a quick, gentle thumping of footsteps. The inside door opened. "Trisha!" Frick said. He opened the aluminum door and stepped inside. The girl moved aside to let him in, but stared up at him with a questioning look. There could be no doubt. This was the same girl. She looked healthier than she had looked in his car earlier, not so gaunt. Her cheek, once swollen like a fist, was now back to its regular size. The nightdress she wore looked like the one he'd removed from her himself when he'd given her his sweater, but it was clean and pressed and not tattered in the least. Her hair was washed and combed and had a healthy sheen. It was done up in a braid at either side. On her face and arms there did not appear a single blemish, except a slight reddish mark in the centre of her forehead, where there had been a fresh abrasion only a few hours before.

The girl looked at him blankly, and Frick looked blankly at her.

"Trisha," he said again.

"Trisha?" came a woman's voice from the hallway behind the girl. "Trisha?"

The woman looked at Frick and gasped. She put a hand on the girl's shoulder and drew her back.

"Something's going on here," Frick said.

"Jim! Jim!" the woman called. "Come quick!"

There were heavy thumps on the floor. A slim, solid-looking man appeared beside the woman.

"What's going on here?" the man asked.

"I might ask that same question," Frick said. He looked the man up and down.

"What the hell are you saying?" the man said. His voice was deep and powerful. He stepped forward and confronted Frick directly. His hair was short and neat. His face was square, handsome, though his cheeks sagged a little with the first signs of age.

"I want you to know something," Frick said. He looked the man in the face. "I want you to know that I know. No. Not that I know. But there is something," he said. "Something –"

"You son of a bitch," the man said. He grabbed Frick by the collar and pushed him out the door. His fist hit Frick's cheek like a block of stone.

Frick picked himself off the wet lawn and looked back at the man's dark silhouette in the doorway of the house. He made his way back to the car and sat for a moment, touching the side of his face where he'd been hit. He pulled down the rearview mirror and flipped on the interior light to look at his cheek. His skin was flushed with blood and had started to balloon. His lips were red with blood. He poked a finger around inside his mouth and felt the row of holes where his teeth had cut into the flesh.

In a corner of the mirror, he caught sight of something in the back seat. He turned around to find his cardigan, neatly folded. He picked up the sweater by the shoulders and examined it. It was clean and fresh and dry, as if it had just come from the cleaner's. A piece of delicate blue onionskin paper stuck out of a front pocket. He slipped the paper from the pocket. It had been folded once neatly through the middle. A faint sweet smell came from the paper as he unfolded it and held it up to the light. Written in black in a careful, childish hand was a single word: *Please.*

ACKNOWLEDGEMENTS

I am more than grateful to McClelland & Stewart for their support of this project. In particular thanks go to Ellen Seligman for taking the book on, and overseeing it with commitment through to publication. Large thanks to editorial assistant Rudy Mezzetta and copy editor Charles Stuart, who often went beyond the call of duty, and to designer Sari Ginsberg, who was right on my creative brainwave. I am unable to imagine superior circumstances in which this collection might have come to be published.

My love and thanks to Rachel Greenbaum, both for her belief in this project when it was nothing more than something I would rant about before falling into a drunken slumber, and for her prescient suggestions throughout. How she put up with it all, I do not know.

Unfortunately, this book failed to make history as the first Canadian fiction anthology to come with a soundtrack. But if it had, the following rock mavens of the hyperboreal would have been included: Smallmouth, godspeed you black emperor, Fell Gang, Braino, Rheostatics, Change of Heart, Wooden Stars, and Pest 5000. Keeping me warm at night.

Thanks as well to the Beaver Gallery in Toronto, whose independent exhibition of the work of Toronto painter Romas Astrauskas introduced me to his work and allowed me to put forward his painting *Chicago* as the cover for this book.

Finally, my thanks to the writers, whose enthusiasm, tireless effort, obstinacy, hilarity, and bravery are a constant reminder to me.

HAL NIEDZVIECKI is the editor of *Broken Pencil* magazine, the guide to alternative publishing and culture in Canada. His fiction and journalism have appeared in publications across North America including: *This Magazine, sub-TERRAIN, The New Quarterly, Adbusters, Toronto Life,* and the *Globe and Mail.* He is a correspondent on CBC Radio's *Brave New Waves,* and a columnist for *Exclaim! Smell It*, his first book of short fiction, was published in 1998. He lives in Toronto.